Carnival Glass

Carnival Glass

Bonnie Dunlop

thistledown press

Thistledown Press Ltd.
633 Main Street, Saskatoon, SK, S7H 0J8
www.thistledownpress .com

Library and Archives Canada Cataloguing in Publication
Dunlop, Bonnie, 1950-
Carnival glass / Bonnie Dunlop.
Short stories.
ISBN 978-1-897235-46-1
I. Title.
PS8607.U55C37 2008   C813.6   C2008-904517-3

Publisher Cataloging-in-Publication Data (U.S)
(Library of Congress Standards)
Dunlop, Bonnie.
Carnival glass / Bonnie Dunlop.
[272] p. : cm.
Summary: Short stories set in prairie ghost towns, dusty ranches, west coast beaches and
small prairie cities of the '60s, and contemporary Mexico that deal with the successes and
failures of human relationships.
ISBN: 978-1-897235-46-1 (pbk.)
1. Short stories, Canadian – 21st century. I. Title.
813.6 dc22 PS3604.U6CA 2008

Cover painting (detail): *Orange Number 5* by Gary Cody
Cover and book design by Jackie Forrie
Printed and bound in Canada

10 9 8 7 6 5 4 3 2 1

 Canada Council   Conseil des Arts
for the Arts   du Canada

 ARTS BOARD

 Canadian   Patrimoine
Heritage   canadien

Thistledown Press gratefully acknowledges the financial assistance of the Canada Council
for the Arts, the Saskatchewan Arts Board, and the Government of Canada through the
Book Publishing Industry Development Program for its publishing program.

Acknowledgements

I wish I could thank my Grandma Katie Lines for saving her letters, cards, receipts and bills. When my sister (also a Katie) and I stumbled across a bag of Grandma's correspondence, some dated as early as 1913, I knew I'd found our family fortune. I have used parts of Grandma Katie's letters in this manuscript.

Thank you to my cousin Ron Lines for his astute reading and for his permission to reprint portions of his letters as my own.

To the Saskatchewan Arts Board for their financial support during the writing of this manuscript and to the Saskatchewan Writer's Guild for their ongoing support of writers in this province, most especially for the writing weeks at St. Peter's Academy in Muenster, my sincere thanks.

And to Byrna Barclay, a big thank you for choosing to publish versions of the following stories in *Transition Magazine*: "A Funhouse Reflection of My Own Sad Face" (previously titled "The Legacy"), "Carnival Glass", and "In a Bright Red Chrysler by the Highway Near Town".

For the storytellers in my family, especially
Albert Lines and Milton Lines

For my husband, Art

And for my granddaughter Drew

CONTENTS

The Road to Tofino 9

Joe's Cantina 41

In a Bright Red Chrysler By the Highway Near Town 52

The Precious Pots of Mata Ortiz 79

Ham and Swiss on Rye 107

Belly Dancing 124

Jacqueline Bouvier Kennedy and Nadine Louise 133

A Fun House Reflection of My Own Sad Face 160

Ordinary Lives 178

Carnival Glass 214

A Perfect Intersection of Vectors 233

THE ROAD TO TOFINO

IT'S A LONG WAY FROM THE SUNBURNT grass of Val Marie to the patchwork of bright blossoms in downtown Victoria. Rusty slows for a red light near the Legislative buildings, marvels at the tall ships in the inner harbour. "So Dean-o," she says. "We made it. Just a few more turns and we're on our way to Tofino. Who-da-thunk-it?"

In her antique-filled room at the Gables Bed and Breakfast, Rusty had rediscovered the luxury of a full night's sleep, unbroken by disjointed dreams. In the morning, she'd lingered over her eggs Benedict, daydreaming on the warm verandah as she watched bright umbrellas bobbing in the rain.

"Safe trip," the owner had said. "Make sure you come back." As Rusty eased her burgundy flowered bags onto her shoulders, she'd noticed their shabbiness. They'd seemed just fine when she packed them in her bedroom at home. "I might be back sooner than you think," she'd said. "Especially if your directions aren't crystal clear."

"It's easy to find the highway," he'd said. "But the road to Tofino is winding and traffic can be heavy. Just don't get in a

9

hurry. Lots of idiots on the road this time of year." He'd drawn her a simple map, marked each turn either left or right.

"North and South, East and West," Rusty had told him, "mean nothing to me. I've totally lost my bearings. I'm not even sure which way is up. Besides which," she'd said, "Avis gave me a stickshift Mustang. Nothing like the Impala I asked for."

"It'll be a piece of cake," he'd assured her. "If the seniors that flock here every winter can navigate this city, a woman like you won't have any problem."

As the twin turrets of the Gables Bed and Breakfast receded in her rearview mirror, Rusty had wondered for a moment what kind of woman she might seem to be. Tall, slim, a little on the muscular side. Slinging hash in the Redwing Café had been an exercise program in itself, one she didn't have the option of dropping. And she had her garden and her yard work too, although in the last few years, drought had taken care of most of that.

She's noticed a few lines on her face, especially around her aqua eyes, which she considers her best feature. The lines are probably more a result of the moisture-sucking prairie wind than her calendar age, which is thirty-five.

Halfway to seventy, that's what Dean had said.

Rusty watches for a break in the line of traffic streaming from the harbour bridge. The pace seems quick to her, the space between bumpers dangerously tight. For a moment, Rusty thinks about the almost non-existent traffic in downtown Val Marie. Two trucks pulling up simultaneously at the four-way stop is about as busy as it gets. She blinks, erasing Saskatchewan firmly from her mind.

She is almost free of the traffic when she spots a small museum on her right, red brick smudged with green ivy.

The plaque above the ornate cedar door reads, Highcroft Museum. The entrance is well-marked and Rusty brakes smoothly, pulls into the lot as if she'd been driving a Mustang convertible her whole life.

"We'll just take a quick look," she says. "Really, there's no rush."

The receptionist glances up as Rusty steps inside. "Welcome," she says pointing to a sign that reads, Wedding Dresses Through the Years. "It's a special display," she says. "Oh, and don't forget to sign our guest book."

"I just stopped for a quick look," Rusty explains. "I'm really on my way to Tofino."

"Lucky you," the girls say, "but sign, even if you're just zipping through. Our funding depends on the number of visitors we can verify." She pushes a fall of blonde hair behind her shell-like ear. "Third year Commerce," she says. "Trust me. Funds are tight and your signature could mean my summer job."

Rusty turns to the guest book open on an oak podium. *Rusty and Dean Peterson,* she writes and then replaces the pen in the blackened groove beneath the book. Might as well get a buck for Dean too, she thinks. I'm sure he wouldn't mind.

She begins to wander through the wedding dress display, and stops in front of a cream silk dress. Soft pleats line the bodice, gather at the tiny waist. *Joseph Connely and Ragna Herman, November, 1916.* Rusty looks at the wedding picture, at the size of Joseph's hands. They must have easily encircled Ragna's tiny waist.

Hans Hughes and Ada Tucker, July 1924. Row upon row of dainty lace, thirty satin covered buttons curving down its back. To Rusty, the older the dress, the more beautiful it seems, softer, more finely crafted, perhaps like marriages back then?

Rusty thinks of her own wedding dress, wrapped in blue tissue at the bottom of her cedar chest. Her aunt Louise had sewn it, spent hours covering tiny buttons with satin, painstakingly cutting the lace of the train.

She'd tried it on again the day of their tenth anniversary, pleased that it fit. She'd actually thought of wearing it for the anniversary dinner she'd planned — Chicken Cordon Bleu, asparagus with hollandaise sauce, and baby garden potatoes.

"You're calling it dinner now," Dean had said, when she told him her plans. "Gettin' kinda' fancy, aren't you?"

She was scrubbing egg yolk from his plate. The scrubber blurred, her hand moving faster and faster. She was surprised when she felt his lips on the back of her neck.

"Could you at least leave the damn dill out of the potato pot?" he'd asked. "Last I heard, dill's for making pickles."

She'd asked him to stop at the bar, see if Al would sell him a bottle of white wine. She hadn't thought of wine the week before when she made her trip to the liquor board store in Swift Current, but she was pretty sure that Al sometimes sold a bottle or two on the side.

It was after one AM when she heard Dean stumble up the back steps, the clang of metal as he tripped over the basin of milk she'd left there for the kittens. "Christ," she heard him say. "Goddamn obstacle course. M'own fuckin' yard."

When he dropped into bed beside her, not even bothering to apologize, she'd lain like a mummy, and for the first time, she'd wished him dead.

Yellowed newspaper clippings report the progress of the war in France. *Let Me Call You Sweetheart* is playing softly.

The wedding dresses from the war years are more practical, blue crepe, grey shantung, even a sensible gabardine. How sad, Rusty thinks. She tries to imagine those hopeful young women, marrying in haste before their husbands went off to fight, with no time to really know each other.

Rusty rubs the fading white line on her left hand, wondering about her own marriage. She'd loved Dean right from day one, with no holds barred. And she thought she knew everything there was to know about the man. Goes to show you. She gives her head a shake. It just goes to show.

First of all, she'd assumed that pregnancy was inexorably linked to marriage, at least that seemed to be the way it worked in Val Marie.

Her father was a grain buyer, and she'd reluctantly followed when he'd been transferred there with the Pool. It was hard for her. The girls in her grade had been friends all their lives. At school, she felt like a kid standing outside a plate glass window, watching a party in a cozy room just out of her reach. They were surface friendly, but she knew there was a lot that tight-knit group talked about when she wasn't around.

In the two years between the time she'd moved to Val Marie and her grade twelve graduation, three of her sort-of-friends had dropped out of school to marry. Those marriages were followed quickly by motherhood, talk of midnight feedings and formula, of colic and croup.

It didn't happen that way for Dean and Rusty, although she'd assumed it would. After two long years of regular periods, Rusty began to pray. When praying didn't work, she'd looked up fertility specialists. There were two at the University Hospital in Saskatoon. She pondered how to broach such a touchy subject with Dean.

Fingers of light pushed at the bottom of the shade. Dean rolled closer, and pushed his morning hard-on tight against her back. "Wakeup call to Rusty," he whispered and his cowboy hand cupped her breast. As Rusty turned toward him, she felt a sudden hot gush. "Oh no," she said. "Damn, double-damn."

"Shoot," Dean said, grabbing his erection, waving it like a flag. "Talk about lousy timing. I guess old Tucker's going to have to surrender."

She sniffled, and grabbed a handful of Kleenex from the bedside table. "For Christ's sake woman," Dean said as he began to rub her back, "it's kinda' inconvenient, but it's nothing to cry about."

When she told him she'd been almost two weeks late and she'd been sure she was finally pregnant, he'd dropped his hand.

"You can't be," he said, "unless you been screwing around."

She whirled to face him. "What?" she said.

"The mumps? Remember, the ones that damn near killed me the year I turned thirteen? Old Tucker's shooting blanks. Everybody in the whole Christly countryside knows." Dean's face had flushed a dangerous red.

He'd obviously forgotten that when he was thirteen, she had not yet moved to this godforsaken town. And the status of a guy's semen count wasn't something that came up in regular conversation on the dusty streets. And that even after all this time, she was still on the outside, looking in.

"Everybody knows?" she said, her voice rising. "Everybody? You bastard! And you didn't bother telling me?"

1972: Lace over satin, princess line, with a train of cut lace. Dainty daisies square the neckline. The dress seems to ripple as if caught by a prairie breeze. Suddenly, Rusty is at the altar in the stifling hot Church of the Little Flower in downtown Val Marie. The temperature is eighty-eight degrees, as it has been the last three days. A July long weekend for the record books. The old brick building is a sauna, the bricks adding their accumulated heat to the strength of the harsh prairie sun.

Rusty sees her Aunt Molly wipe her brow with the sleeve of her pink Fortrel dress. She carefully pleats the wedding program, with its picture of white wedding bells and pink rosebuds, and uses it for a fan.

Rusty turns from the church uncomfortably packed with family and friends. She looks across the wide space to where Dean stands, surrounded by his three sturdy groomsmen. He catches her eye and winks. The oppressive humidity threatens a quick summer storm. A pollen-laden wind blows through the one window that will actually open, filling the tiny church with the sweet scent of purple alfalfa and yellow clover. The humid air is heavy, coiled like a mink stole across Rusty's breast.

She searches for the solid support of her father's arm, but he's already stepped away and taken his place on the left side of the church in the bride's family pew.

Rusty's eyes dart from her father to her mother, back again. She feels the start of an uncontrollable laugh, one that might turn into a high-pitched hyena sound. Then Dean steps across the chasm and slips his brawny arm around her waist. She leans on him, her breath gradually slowing.

"Dearly beloved, we are gathered here today . . . " Rusty hears the priest's voice, faint and far away.

"Honey?" Dean whispers. "You doing okay?"

"Yes," she tells him. "Yes."

"Miss?" The curator appears at Rusty's elbow. "Would you like to sit down?" She looks around, startled to find herself in a museum somewhere along the road to Tofino, and not in that little church with Dean. Till death to us part, she thinks. Who'd have thought it would be so soon.

"I'll just get you a drink of water," the kindly fellow tells her. "It's this awful heat."

When he returns, he offers lukewarm water in a green Dixie cup. Rusty tosses it back in two quick gulps.

"Thanks," she says. "I've never fainted in my entire life. But I was this close." She holds her fingers a pinch apart.

Rusty's hands tremble on the steering wheel and she cannot recall how to shift the Mustang into gear. The pavement in the Highcroft parking lot gives off a hot oil smell and Rusty feels almost sick. For a moment, she leans her forehead on the steering wheel, her pearl-pink nails grooving its caramel leather. Then she straightens, adjusts the rearview mirror, smoothes her sun-streaked hair. To be perfectly honest, the sun had gotten a bit of help from Jenny's Salon.

You're finally on your trip to Tofino, she thinks. Come on Rusty, time to get your mo-jo going.

Charlie, her boss at the Redwing Café, had stuck her with 'Rusty' after one particularly bad dye job and she'd never managed to shake the nickname, even when she switched her hair colour to brown or blonde or just that one time, raven-wing black. Salon-colouring and professional perming make a noticeable dent in a waitress' wage so she'd resorted to Clairol's Cinnibar and the atrocious home perms she got from Arlene.

Down at the Redwing, the TV blared incessantly. The picture was wavy, flickering with the strength of the prairie wind, but Charlie wouldn't get new cable. Customers were as scarce as hen's teeth and he said there wasn't much use pouring any more of his hard-earned money down a bottomless pit.

Rusty would polish the length of the long yellow counter to sensuous sitar music, watch heavily laden camels labour up the Sahara dunes, wash chipped green mugs to the cooling view of Venice canals. The Discovery Channel, her window to the wider world.

"Christ," Charlie told her one day. "If I had a woman looked as good as you, I'd take her to some of those places you're always mooning over."

"Tell that to Dean," she'd said. She'd polished a water glass, held it to the light. "He thinks this godforsaken prairie is the destination of choice for anyone with half a brain. Doesn't care to venture any further than fifty miles away."

She turns the key in her rental car, anxious for the drive to begin. She's well aware that Dean would hate every minute of being so far away from Val Marie. "I had to do this," she says, looking to the passenger seat. "I had to."

Finally, she slips Dr. Hook into the CD player, finds "Sylvia's Mother" and turns the volume high. Then she takes a deep breath, her hand on the stick. "Easy," she says. "You've run through more than a gear or two hauling barley from the Gordon place to the bins. In a two-ton truck. No difference here really, just a lot more traffic. She eases the stick forward, pulls away from the curb.

The road niggles the edge of the mountain, folds back on itself and starts again. Rusty isn't making very good time.

She'd told the people at the Wikinninish Inn that she'd be there before five.

"From Saskatchewan?" the reservations clerk had said when Rusty gave her home address. "And you want a single? I'll take your card number. Would you like to guarantee your room? You know, my dear, if you come in late, your room could be gone. Surfers from all over the world gather here, looking for the wildest waves. They come in droves and we're straining at the seams."

"Sure," Rusty told her when the woman finally stopped to draw a breath. "I'd like to guarantee that room." Slowly, she recited the long and unfamiliar numbers. She'd had to repeat them twice. "I'm sorry dear," the woman had said, "must be a bad connection."

Rusty had cleared her throat, run her fingers over the shiny silver numbers, repeating them slowly into the phone.

"In Tofino today, mayor and council were faced with a critical dilemma. A column of decay has been detected inside the trunk of the huge Eik Cedar in the centre of town. The tree has been declared by an arborist to be a hazard. The designation presents a serious liability for the town of Tofino."

Rusty scrubbed a spaghetti sauce stain from her countertop, and wondered how many miles lay between her farm outside of Val Marie and the town of Tofino, somewhere on Vancouver Island off the coast of BC. A million, she thinks. It might as well be.

"Insurers say the tree must be removed for safety reasons, but townsfolk are up in arms. The Eik Cedar is one of the last examples of the ancient old growth trees that once covered the peninsula where Tofino now sits. It's a draw for tourists and the pride of long-time citizens."

Rusty's hands were stilled, her ears straining to hear. The porch door slammed and Dean walked into the kitchen, turned the tap on full force while he rattled in the cupboard for a glass.

Rusty put her finger to her lips. "Shh. Listen to this."

"A standoff is in progress. Townspeople have gathered at the site and ringed the base of the tree. An impasse has resulted between the determined residents of Tofino and the tree removal crew."

He closed the cupboard door and filled his glass with icy water. They were lucky, finding sweet water only thirty feet down in a sand point well.

Dean liked to complain about how often she watered the grass and her flowers, but she never did run the well dry. Crazy woman, he told her, spending all that time and energy growing flowers when all you've got to do is walk through the pasture and you can find at least a dozen different blooms.

But one busy morning, on the early shift at the Redwing, she overhead Dean going on to the guys on coffee row about how his yard was turning into a goddamn park. So she knows he's proud of what she's done, and she's got a pretty good notion he's proud of her too, although you'd never catch him saying such a candy-ass thing.

He'd told her early on that he wasn't much for flowery talk or all that mushy hand holding shit. But if you're looking for steady, he said, you've got the right guy.

She heard the clink of the glass as he set it in the sink. "How about you make me some lunch and forget about those tree huggers in Tofino and their rotten old cedar?"

Sunlight streamed into her east windows. As Rusty refilled her coffee cup, and Dean's, she noted the condition of her hands. Too much time in the flowerbeds, she thought, rubbing her fingers across the translucent trails of blue. She squirted a blob of lotion from the dispenser and rubbed it slowly into her parched skin.

The TV on the kitchen counter muttered and the familiar voice of the reporter in Tofino took Rusty's attention from further inspection of her sun-damaged hands.

"Marnie Dunham reporting from Tofino. Sometime during the night, two young men climbed eighty feet off the ground to take refuge in the tree's canopy. They vow to stay there until they are given assurances that the tree will be preserved. We are in the process of setting up an interview with the tree-sitters, who say if the tree is dead at the core, and a safety hazard, as the town council claims, then they should shore it up with steel cables or come up with some other way of ensuring the safety of passers by. A half hour ago, one of the young men dropped a handwritten note in a zip-lock bag. For some unknown reason, he included two large pinecones as well. The note reads: *A tree that began to grow in the year Christopher Columbus set foot upon this land is a shrine. We must not desecrate it or a pestilence will surely fall upon the land.*

The reporter's blonde hair was almost obscured by the sou'wester she wore. Large drops of moisture beaded on the brim. A close-up of the tree in question showed only a semi-sheer curtain of rain.

The news report ended with a shot of the harbour, with more rain pelting the boats that bobbed at the end of the dock. The camera panned the street above the harbour, the old hotel sodden and grey, the little white fish shop across the street battened down for the night.

"Let's go take a look," Rusty said. "They say the beaches go forever. And the sand is almost white. It's made from all the sand dollars that get ground down by the waves. I'd like to see a real sand dollar, hold one in my hand."

Dean gestured to his collection of rocks that have claimed two shelves in Rusty's antique buffet against the east kitchen wall. The bottom shelf featured two Buick hubcaps, chock full of assorted stones that he's gathered in the pastures and gullies around Val Marie. Dean had expropriated the second shelf from the top for his favourites. A perfectly round rock, striated purple and black interlaced with sparkling silica, was steadied by a smaller, kidney shaped one, smooth, granite black. A worry rock, Rusty thought. She's tried it, holding it in her palm, rubbing its silky surface. But it only made her worry that Dean would bring home even more rocks. She has never been happy that her delicate crystal dishes have to share space with Dean's precious rocks.

"Sand dollars got nothing on Southwest Saskatchewan," he said, picking up his pride and joy, an oval rock, rust coloured and deeply ridged. "They used to wrap this groove with rawhide," Dean told Rusty. "Then they'd just haul back and let her rip. Can you imagine hitting anything with a tool that crude? If you *really* want to get your hands on something exotic, pick this baby up. Here, go ahead."

Rusty took the rock from Dean's outstretched hand, turned it over and ran her forefinger down the groove. She wondered how long it would take to make an indent in a rock, and who might have toiled over it so many years ago.

"It is kind of cool," she said. "But still, I'd like to hold something a little more delicate. Like a sand dollar. And I really want to see that Eik cedar. Touch it too." Rusty puts one hand on Dean's power-pole arm. "We could fly out to the island. Really, it wouldn't take long."

"Okay, let's go," Dean replied. "But you know, I ain't gonna fly. If God meant men to fly, He would have given us wings."

Dean hefted the rock before he put it back on the shelf, moved the little worry rock closer, for support. "You figure out all the details and then just tell me when."

He turned to crank open the window above the sink. "But I don't see why you're so struck on going out there just to see an old tree," he said. "What the hell is so newsworthy about that? There must be more important things those reporters could focus on." He leaned into the window, sniffed the fragrant air. "Alfalfa's about to bloom."

Rusty knows Dean's viewpoint about trees. They are effective windbreaks and should be planted in orderly rows at the edge of a field or yard. When she wanted to plant a curved hedge of cotoneasters across the front yard and cut flower beds to conform with the flowing lines of the hedge, he'd lost his cool entirely.

"Jesus Murphy, woman," he'd said. "What's wrong square? Do you have any idea how much longer it'll take to cut the grass if you insist on doing all that fancy shit?"

So Rusty had let the idea drop and her lawn is dead square, just like everyone else's.

She knows Dean doesn't see the beauty in a line of stately poplars, only sees them as a way to trap the snow during winter storms and preserve precious moisture for his fields.

When he bought the Nelson quarter, two miles north of their place, Dean had inherited a renegade tree, growing smack in the middle of his summer fallow field. It was huge and spreading, like the southern plantation trees she'd seen in the movies. The tree had been a landmark for years.

Drive south until you see the lone tree, Rusty would say. Turn left at the next crossroads. Six more miles, and there we are. Two-story, white farmhouse, with a wraparound verandah. Like the Waltons. That's our place. You can't miss it, really you can't. As soon as it was out of her mouth, she'd regretted her Walton's analogy. Their place wasn't anything like the Walton's. Not one sign of a child could be found in their pin-neat yard.

She liked the idea of the tree out there alone on the land, braving the elements. But Dean said it was too hard to maneuver his cultivator around that goddamn tree and that it didn't serve a lick of use. It's a scraggly old half-dead poplar, he told her. Who in their right mind would farm around that?

When she took his lunch out to the field one summer day and saw clear sky where the poplar used to be, Rusty could not believe her eyes.

On her next rotation down at the café, she served black coffee and the special of the day with her head bowed. For weeks, Rusty didn't make eye contact with anyone.

"It's not that big a deal," Charlie finally told her. Sure there was some talk about a young pup like Dean having the nerve to cut down such a big old tree. After all, it's been there a lot longer than him. But don't worry. Somebody else will screw up soon and they'll be off on a totally different tack. Only person still really fretting is you.

So Rusty already knows Dean's not interested in the Eik Cedar, despite the fact it is eighty feet tall and eight hundred years old, give or take a decade. But she hopes he'll be enticed by her description of the beach. When Rusty first met him, Dean was the best-looking hunk at the little alkali lake where they used to party. The eyes of every girl sunning on the salt-crisped sand kept returning to Dean. Since they got married, they don't spend Saturdays at the beach anymore.

She buys a little bag of fine, white sand at a Candy's Crafts and puts it on the kitchen table in a shell-shaped dish.

Rusty juggled her schedule at the café: talked Arlene into covering two of her shifts, and Charlie said not to worry about the other two. She'd even picked up some maps of BC, highlighted the road to Tofino in blue.

The thought of those young men sitting up in the giant cedar seized Rusty's imagination. She wondered how they stayed awake, what they ate, what they must smell like by now, having already sat in the tree for twenty days. She wondered if they were still enthused about their plan or if they were fed up with each other's company and just wanted it to finally end.

Rusty sat down beside Dean, picked up the remote he'd laid aside when he reached for a handful of salted cashews. The Vancouver Canucks were winning five to three and Jerome Iginla had just maneuvered around the defenseman on a clean breakaway. Dean gestured with the Pilsner can and Rusty turned up the sound.

"Maybe we can work in a hockey game somehow," she said.

Dean looked at her, frowned. "What?" he asked.

"On our trip," she replied. "I've booked the time off. Charlie said it's been so dead lately it's no problem. Might be good for his bottom line if he works short for a shift or two."

"Trip?" Dean asked.

Rusty shook her head. "Jeez, Dean, do you ever really pay attention to anything except hockey or work? Our trip to Tofino. Remember?"

"We can't leave any time soon." Dean shook his head. "The cows are due to go to the Community pasture any day. They don't just wander over there themselves, you know."

"We can do it in four days," she said. "If we drive straight through. You said — "

"I know what I said." Dean grabbed the remote, flipped away from a Coors Light commercial and picked up a replay. "But I figured you'd forget about it soon enough. For God's sake, Rusty, use a little common sense for once in your life."

The realization that he'd never intended to go to Tofino was almost more than she could bear. She felt leaden, unable to move. Dean hit the remote again and Don Cherry's irritating comments drilled Rusty's ears. She cupped them with shaking hands and stumbled from the room.

Rusty followed the Tofino story as if it were her life on the line, not the Eik Cedar's. She sent to the CBC for transcripts of interviews with the blonde reporter, studied the pictures on the front page of *The Globe and Mail*.

One of the boys had his hair tied in a stringy tail at the back of his grey turtleneck. His eyes were ringed with blue fatigue. The other guy looked strangely out of place, his black hair curling moistly over a white collar as if he'd just stepped out of the pages of a slick magazine. Rusty ran her fingers over the picture, traced the strong line of his jaw. How could anyone possibly look gorgeous after spending twenty-eight days in a tree?

She began to dream of him at night, perched high in that old cedar tree. When he beckoned, she sprouted iridescent wings, flew to the branch below him, offering egg salad sandwiches, oatmeal cookies, bottled water, herself.

For weeks, she woke to the taste of salt sudden on her tongue.

Whenever she and Dean went somewhere together, which wasn't often, their trip was a direct line from A to B. Dean wouldn't stop for anything, not even a bathroom break unless he himself needed to pee. Rusty learned to limit her coffee intake and to squeeze that one poor muscle until she could feel it scream.

Prostate problems and too much coffee caused the old geezers down at the Redwing to head for the bathroom in a continual parade. One day, Rusty asked Charlie why he didn't just install a revolving door.

"And encourage these old goats to stay any longer than they already do?" he'd replied. "The refills are going to break me. I know for sure not one of them throws their quarter in the pot like the sign says. They think they're doing me a favour, hanging around."

"It's amazing," Rusty had replied. "When they come back from the can, they pick up the thread of their conversation like they've never left. The tableau just sits frozen in time until all the players return."

Charlie dropped the dishcloth into a sink full of bleach-soaked suds. "We'll all be frozen in time if we're not careful," he said.

Charlie went on to tell her more than she ever wanted to know about prostate problems and how they raised hell with men of a certain age. She smiled a secret smile, thinking that the same thing would likely happen to Dean someday. Then when they were heading to Maple Creek for a horse sale or to Swift Current to buy baler twine, he'd damn well have to stop. She imagined complaining to him about the frequency of his urination breaks and how all his pee time was cutting into the progress of their trip. Hard to make a mile, she heard herself say, when you've got to take a pit stop every time you get going. And when you've got the big horse trailer on behind, you don't just stop on a dime.

A few years down the road, stopping for frequent pee breaks will become a requirement for almost any man, according to the old guys down at the Redwing Café. She wonders how Dean will handle that. Rusty smiles, thinking about Dean and his slowly aging prostate, sitting there like a time bomb.

"How are you doing?" she says. She reaches over and snugs the seatbelt around the genie-style urn she'd chosen. She knew Dean would hate the ornateness of it, but it was pleasing to her eye. She told the funeral director she'd take it, and hadn't even asked for a price.

"With any luck at all, maybe we can find that guy. You know. The one who stayed up in the tree for twenty-eight days."

Antique shops dot the highway and Rusty fights the urge to turn in at every one. She'd planned to take her time, enjoy the trip up-island, but she wants to get to Tofino before dark. Driving in the mountains isn't as hard as she'd imagined, but still, her night vision isn't what it used to be.

At Duncan, she sees a sign — PolkaFest July 23 at the CommuniPlex. Dancing 1:00 PM – 5:00 PM and 8:00 PM – 11:00 PM. She checks her watch. It's ten after two and she takes the Duncan exit, follows the neon porta-signs to the arena.

Bumper stickers on the RVs lining the parking lot announce, We Live to Dance.

She stands near the back, sways to the oom-pa-pa band. A tall silver-haired man wearing red suspenders twirls his partner; they dip and part. He stomps an intricate pattern and then fluidly, they come together again. The woman's red dress drifts in their wake.

The band swings into an old-time waltz. Rusty blinks hard, glad for the shadows. The floor is a sea of grey, and she estimates the age of the dancers to be a minimum of fifty-five. Most of the women are slim and Rusty wonders if it's the dancing that keeps them that way. She eyes the men, and wonders if their prostates are doing okay. Damn you Dean, she thinks, for checking out so early. You'll never have to worry about prostate problems now.

Two women rise from a table, hesitate at the edge of the floor. One holds out her arms, the other moves into the circle of those female arms and they begin. Rusty sees them stumble, start again. The sight of those elegant women dancing burns into her brain. Rusty sucks in her breath, but the air in the arena is humid and close. She finds the exit and almost runs to her Mustang. As she heads down the highway, she savours the smell of cedar, the feel of wind rushing through her hair.

She drives steadily for an hour. "Pit stop," she says, turning to Dean. "Again. Imagine that."

On the needle-padded paths beneath giant cedars, Rusty walks slowly. She can see why they call it Cathedral Grove. Silence hangs like moss.

Two little girls lean on the split-rail fence. Rusty watches as the smallest one drops a penny into the leaf-laden stream. The older girl takes the other's hand, pulls her away. "Let's go," she says. "Wishing's for babies."

When they leave, Rusty leans on the rail and drops her own penny into the murky water. As she turns, she touches the bark of a giant cedar like she was touching an artifact. She feels a tingle in her palm. Trees remember, she thinks. Maybe he was here, on the road to Tofino. Maybe he touched *this* tree.

Rusty checks the map, unsure of how far she has yet to go. She refolds it, tucks it into the cubbyhole before she pulls onto the highway. "There's a thing or two we need to get straightened out," she says. She concentrates on the curve for a moment, the sharpest one yet. She leans over, straightens his urn. "I found the letters. Love letters, for God's sake."

She was cleaning out his tack box. On the bottom, under a brand new Navajo saddle blanket. They were tied with a half-hitch of orange binder twine.

Dear One, she read. Me? Rusty wondered. Me? His handwriting slanted to the left, the letters cramped and small, but she'd managed to decipher the soft and unfamiliar words. Dear One, she thought. He never called me that.

When she found the letters, she'd taken off her wedding rings. She put them in his tack box, under the blanket, where the letters had been. The band of white skin on her ring finger has begun to take on a little colour and with each day its outline fades.

Sunlight glances off the three round diamonds of the ring she'd bought for herself. The ad had read *Your left hand purrs. You right hand pounces. Women of the world, raise your right hand.* The way she was feeling, the new ring felt right, necessary somehow.

She runs her fingers across the intricate pattern of the urn, taps its lid with the wide band of her right-hand ring. "And the insurance policy," she says. "You were even stingy with grocery money. And now I get a cool million? I'd like to know why."

The urn leans as she hugs the bottom of a sharp curve. "You don't have to be nervous," she says. "I'm a damn good driver. It wasn't me who ran my car into the abutment of a bridge."

She fumbles for a cigarette. Ironic, she thinks. Her first reaction when the cop came to her door was to take the pack of cigarettes from the man's shirt pocket and ask for a light. And she hadn't smoked for years.

She punctures the cellophane on her pack of Player's with the edge of a manicured nail, flips the pack open. She draws deeply, feels smoke tear at her lungs. Damn you, she thinks. I don't care if you knew those roads like the back of your hand, you knew better than to polish off a dozen Pilsner and then drive home. If you weren't already dead, I'd kill you myself. Rusty slows for the Wikkinninish sign, reaches for the ashtray and grinds out her fresh cigarette.

Her room has large windows facing the shore and French doors leading to the velvet grass above the famous beach. She opens the door, peers outside, but the chill of the fog creeps in. She closes the door, flips a switch and the fireplace flickers to life, the flames dancing in the gloom. Rusty hangs her blue linen dress on the hook behind the bathroom door. Maybe when I take a good long shower, some of those wrinkles will relax, she thinks.

She's seen the pictures on the website, so she knows the beach is forever — miles and miles of fine, white sand. She pulls the velvet curtains aside, sees glimpses of white and beige, shapes materializing briefly in the mist and then melting from her sight. She finds a yellow slicker in the closet, flips the hood up and wades into the fog.

Rusty doesn't know how far she's walked. She's not sure if twilight has fallen or the fog has thickened. Shadows move just beyond her vision.

"Who's there?" she says. "Who's out there?" Her heart pounds hard and she wishes for the safety of Dean's bale-tossing arms. She's poised to run when the fog suddenly lifts. Moss-draped trees weep above a small inlet near the end of the beach and Rusty looks down, sees water pooling around her rubber boots. From her vantage point, she can see a small island. A yellow light wavers from the porch of a slope-roofed cabin perched near the edge of a cliff. She wonders how it would be to live out there, cut off from everyone in the world. Maybe something like living in Val Marie, she thinks. Maybe just like that.

Rusty had scanned the brochure in the hotel, a picture of a white sand dollar on its front. Beachcombers are asked to only take pictures, to leave the precious shells on the beach. Their decomposing bodies are the elements of the white sand. If each visitor takes one sand dollar, eventually the sand will disappear.

Rusty thinks she might just take one anyway. She'd told Dean she wanted to hold one in her hand. What she hadn't told him was she wanted one on her windowsill, so she could touch it, bring back her dream.

She scours the beach, but finds only pieces of grey driftwood, yellow sea onions coiled across themselves and a rusted Pilsner cap. She picks up the cap, thinks of Dean for a moment before she backhands it into the waves. Damn, she thinks. I come all the way to Tofino and all I find is a Pilsner cap. She scans the beach again, looking for a sand dollar, pure white, its five points imprinted with fronds of pearly grey.

Nothing. She's feeling the creeping damp and is beginning to shiver.

Turn left. She thinks it's Dean's voice, but its compassionate tone is unfamiliar to her. Without conscious thought, Rusty responds. *Count fourteen paces.* One, two, three. Rusty begins, her long legs stretching the fourteen paces to their maximum length. At fourteen, she stops. *Turn toward the beach. Now walk.* She walks. *Stop.* She looks down, sees a rim of white nearly obscured by wet sand. She bends, brushes the sand away. A perfect sand dollar gleams in the leaking silver light. She picks it up, holds it in her hand for a long time before she raises it to her lips.

To her left, a man hunches on a rotting log. He's been walking too. She's seen his khaki jacket appear and disappear in the thickening fog. He pushes his hands on his thighs, raises his eyes. Rusty is not sure if he's been crying or if the fog has beaded on his handlebar moustache, and his thick black lashes.

"Please," he says. "Don't take it. Leave it there."

Rusty turns the sand dollar over in her palm, holds it to her cheek for a long moment before she places it back on the endless beach and covers it with a brush of wet sand.

"Sorry," she says. "I wanted to hold one, for a moment at least."

The damp air seeps into Rusty's bones and her runners sluice with moisture, sucking at her heels. Time to go. Get into a nice, hot bath.

The Wikkininish Inn is one of the top ten tourist destinations in North America. Rusty took a virtual tour when she did an internet search looking for a place to stay, but the pictures have done nothing to prepare her for the majesty of the dining room. She smoothes her baby blue linen shift with her hands, wonders if a long gown would have been more suitable. She didn't wear pantyhose, hates the itch on her legs, but suddenly, she feels naked beneath her dress.

"A table for one?" the maître de asks and Rusty nods. He leads her to a table at the back of the restaurant, to the left of the kitchen door.

"When I made the reservation," Rusty says, "I asked for an ocean view."

"My mistake," he murmurs. "Usually, women alone prefer this private corner."

He leads Rusty to a table at the point where the massive windows meet. It seems to Rusty that she's sitting at the bow of a boat, suspended in space. The music of the waves, piped in from the black rocks below, rises and falls, reaches a crashing crescendo.

A waiter's reflection wavers in the windows and she turns back to the cozy yellow light.

"My name is Florenzo," he says. "I'll be your waiter this evening." Florenzo is slight, startlingly handsome, and Rusty tries to imagine him behind the counter at the Redwing Café.

"Would you like a wine list?" he asks.

"Please," she says. Then she touches his arm. "On second thought, just bring me a bottle of your best."

"My pleasure," Florenzo says. "Perhaps you'd like a paper? Something to read if you're dining alone? We've got a scrapbook. News items from the area. Seems to be a hit with our guests."

"Yes," she says. "The scrapbook, please."

The book is full of articles and pictures. Rusty finds a clear head shot of the tree-sitters and she studies their faces.

"Strange fellows," the waiter says as he shakes the napkin, lays it on her lap.

"My husband called them tree-hugging weirdos. Said what they should do if they really wanted to save the world, was get a real job."

It seemed so useless now, but she'd argued with Dean about the men in Tofino, told him that not everyone in the world was like him. "Some people have a wider view," she had said. "Maybe you would, too, if you'd pry yourself away from the pastures of Val Marie."

"I wish I could have met them," she says.

"The dark-haired one ate here," the waiter says, "with the reporter, after he finally came down. Seemed kind of ordinary. Poor tipper, that's about all I can remember." He whisks away a small crumb with a white linen napkin.

"Did you get his autograph?" she asks.

"What for?" Florenzo says. "He was just a local kid who ended up with more than his fifteen minutes of fame. Happened to be in the right place at the right time." Florenzo fills Rusty's wineglass and waits as she takes her first satisfying sip.

"I hear he's gone to the city," Florenzo says. "Pretty hard to be content changing tires at Cal's Tire Shop when you've been on TV for twenty-eight days straight. With a pretty reporter hanging on your every word."

"Oh no," Rusty says. "I was hoping to meet him. Find out more about the vigil. You know, more about what he was thinking, how he felt. I can hardly believe he'd want to live somewhere far away from the tree."

Florenzo opened the leather menu, laid it by her hand. "There's lots of trees in the cities, too. He probably hasn't given that old Eik a single thought."

Rusty picked up the menu, surprised to see the writing waver and blur.

Oysters Rockefeller, steak Dianne and, before that, she'd nibbled almost a half basket of freshly baked rolls. Rusty leaves most of her meal on the plate. The wine, however, she has no intention of leaving behind. At a hundred and thirty dollars a bottle, she feels perfectly entitled to take it to her room.

"The bill, please," she says to Florenzo and he glides away. Quickly, she slips the bottle into her purse.

"Your bill, Madame." The waiter slides a black folder onto the table. She flips it open, adds a fifty-dollar tip and signs her name. *Ms. Rusty Peterson.* She runs her fingers across her spidery signature, surprised at the shakiness of her hand.

Her bag clinks as she stands. When Rusty leans against the massive restaurant door, Florenzo appears, holds the door open for her as she steps into the night.

"It's been a pleasure," he says. "And I hope you enjoy the rest of the wine. Maybe in the hot tub?"

"Maybe," Rusty replies and they exchange a smile.

The fog has cleared and a million silver pinpricks pierce the denim sky. Rusty sees the outline of a man slouched on a cedar bench above the beach, his head in his hands. As he lifts his face to the moon, she sees the handlebar moustache, shimmering with dew. Rusty wonders if he'd unearthed the sand dollar she'd left behind on the beach and maybe taken it back to show his wife.

She shivers, folds her fringed shawl across her breasts.

He coughs twice; ragged, painful sounds. Rusty walks toward him. She fumbles in her bag, finds the half empty bottle of wine.

"Take a sip," she says and she sits beside him on the bench, holds out the blue bottle. "It might help."

He reaches for it, pulls the cork with his perfect teeth. He gulps the wine, glugs again before he hands the bottle back. Rusty puts her icy lips to the bottle. When it's empty, she lays it on the grass beneath the bench.

But it hasn't done the trick and his shoulders shake with a sudden cough.

"When you go back to the room, get your wife to make you a hot toddy. Might take care of that cough."

She smiles, thinking of all the times she mixed dark rum and brown sugar, butter and boiling water. An evening drink to quiet Dean's persistent cough. Sometimes, she was almost sure that he could dredge up a coughing fit whenever he felt the need. But it made her feel good, looking after him that way.

"My wife," the man says. "I took her out to the point. Our special place."

"That's nice," Rusty says.

"Took her favourite brand of red out there too," he says. "And two crystal glasses. Exquisite, I think the pattern is called. Hell, I can't be sure." He looks at his hands, turns the palms up. "She wanted me to go with her to register at all those fussy little shops," he said, "so we'd get the wedding gifts we wanted. But I told her I didn't care, whatever she picked would be fine with me." He wipes his cheek with the hem of his sweater. "God, I wish I'd gone. Acted like it mattered."

His shoulders hunch and he clears his throat. "I drank the whole damn bottle myself. Had to, to get my courage up."

Rusty hears his teeth begin to chatter so she sits beside him on the bench. She opens her shawl and folds it across his quivering back. His shivering subsides, like the waves on the beach. Impulsively, she touches his face.

"I threw her ashes into the waves, like she asked me to." The cry of a seagull rises and falls. "But I kept some," he says. She draws a sharp breath, and cannot really believe what he's just said. She wonders at the two of them, ending up on this bench, in this wildly beautiful place. Impulsively, Rusty runs her fingers down his stubbled cheek.

"I swished them into the last of the wine," he says, his eyes lit by the waxing moon. "I held her on my tongue, and tasted her one last time." He drops his head. "Do you think that's sick?"

"It's lovely," Rusty says.

"The wine glasses are still out there. Tucked under the lip of a bluff. I crossed their stems, pulled the grass down so no one would see. Crazy, eh?"

"No," Rusty says. "That was good. That was really good."

A wave crashes higher than any she's seen before, and the spray turns effervescent green.

"Here," Rusty says, rising and offering her arm and, together, they stumble across uneven ground. The lights of her room seem far away, like squares of yellow kitchen light viewed from across the pasture on a cold Saskatchewan night.

"Need a little help," he mumbles and Rusty guides him home.

Noonday sun floods through the French doors and she hears the gentle lap of waves. Rusty's mouth is full of grey cotton and her head aches. She reaches across the bed and her fingers brush soft ocean air. She can taste salt sudden on her tongue.

The streets of Tofino seem familiar to her and Rusty drives straight to the Co-op, where she picks out a pair of red rubber boots and a bright yellow slicker.

"We're almost sold out of the red ones," the girl at the till says as she scans the barcode. "I guess when you have to wear boots almost the entire year, it's nice to have a choice, even if the red ones are ten bucks more."

Rusty smiles, thinking that, in Val Marie, you'd be lucky to even find one pair of rubber boots in Hank's Hardware. It rains there so seldom your rubber boots might rot in the closet and they would be utilitarian black, certainly not candy-apple red.

She finds a bench near the front door and slips off her soggy runners. She is about to pull on the crimson rubber boots when she remembers a ritual left over from her high school days. She carefully folds down the top of the rubber boots, first the right, then the left. She lines them up on the bench to make sure the folds are exactly the same. Then she pulls a pen from her handbag, writes DEAN on the khaki of the folded right boot, RUSTY on the left. She pats Dean's name and finally pulls on the boots. The street is deserted so she steps off the curb and stomps in the puddles pooling on the pavement. Water splashes the backs of her jeans and drips from the hem of her slicker. A green Volkswagon careens around the corner, honks at Rusty, and she hops to the safety of the sidewalk.

"Sorry," she mouths to the driver, who glares at her. No peace brother there, she thinks, as she waves her two fingers formed to a vee.

Coffee, she thinks. And maybe some lunch. That's what I need.

The air inside the Blue Nose Bistro is warm, and steamy from the patron's wet woolens hanging on chairs near the fireplace. The special is clam chowder, and Rusty orders a bowl, sipping an espresso as she waits. She takes out a blue-lined notebook, opens the cover. *Memories from Tofino.* She'd written and underlined the heading before she left home, sure that when she returned to Val Marie, the little book would be full. But her pen only hovers above the paper like a whirlybird, stirring up the air. Finally, she closes her notebook and tucks it away.

When she's finished her big bowl of chowder and the heat from the fireplace has seeped into her bones, she knows it's time to go. She counts out seven-fifty for her lunch, adds a ten for the skinny waitress, whose feet, Rusty knows, are no doubt killing her.

She drives to the Eik Cedar in the centre of Tofino and parks across the street. The metal cage supporting its trunk has weathered from the sea air and taken on the colour of the tree trunk itself. If Rusty hadn't read the scrapbook, she wouldn't have noticed the bracing at all.

She cradles Dean's urn as she picks her way across the glistening grass. At the base of the ancient tree, she lowers herself to the ground, rests her arm on the urn. She memorizes the crooked little streets, the shops full of pottery and artwork, the shabby tourist traps stuffed with mementos made in Taiwan. She can feel the icy water of the marina, the bobbing motion of the fishing boats as they ride the waves. Her cheeks are raw, and saltwater stings her eyes.

She rubs her bloodless hand across the lid's bas-relief, toys with the brass ring in its centre. Finally, she lifts the lid and pulls out a zip-lock bag, the bundle of letters inside still held snugly by orange binder twine. She fumbles with the slipknot, chooses a single sheet from the middle of the pile. She smooths the creases and wonders if the strange warmth she feels is from her own hands or from the paper itself.

Dear One, she begins.

A hawk lands on a rope-laden post, fixes her with his fierce unblinking stare. She holds his gaze for one long moment. *Dear One*, she begins again, but she cannot carry on. She drops her head into her freezing hands and then, again, she hears his husky voice.

Now why in hell do you suppose I'm driven to write these crazy-ass letters full of words I've never said. No way she'll ever see them. But I guess I'll just write them and stash them away. For some other time.

JOE'S CANTINA

A RAIL-THIN, DOWNTOWN DOG LEADS ME TO Joe's. Dogs are everywhere — resting in the doorways of restaurants, sleeping in hotel lobbies, lolling at the entrance of upscale art galleries, roaming free on the streets. When I detour around a pile of steaming dog shit on the cobblestone street, I am amazed that the poor dog had enough in his belly to drop such a substantial load.

I notice an alcove where bright yellow stairs rise rickety to the roof. Red block letters read, Joe's Cantina, and I hear a really good imitation of Jimmy Buffet, so I follow the sound. The twilight is fading and so are my chances for a memorable time. What I am really looking for is a kick-ass time, but cursing is not yet second nature to me. Although I'm doing my darndest to lighten up.

I've saved for three years for this Mexican vacation and it's now or never for me. Although the people I've met at the all-inclusive are fun and I've never sat through a fiesta alone, they are all paired, and I feel like the unicorn must have on Noah's ark.

My new friends have warned me against wandering downtown alone, so I've arranged for a cab. I am tired of the same friendly people at the same blue pool, the endless buffets, the drinks that arrive like clockwork from noon until night. I came here for an adventure, one I can relive and marvel over, one that will warm me to the core on minus thirty nights. And so far, I've had not a one. When I asked the concierge where I might find some local colour and perhaps a great restaurant, he showed me a map of the downtown area and cautioned me to stay on the busy streets. It is mostly safe, he told me. Just please, *Señorita*, please, no going to parties with people you have just met. Bad things can happen.

Me, going to a party with people I've just met? I surely don't look the type. I am five foot one, my light brown hair curved in a neat bob that ends two inches above my shoulders. My figure is average, my eyes a washed-out blue. I do have a great voice, husky and low. After a day introducing six year olds to the wonders of learning, I don't have one ounce of energy to spare. Barely enough to mow my own lawn and tidy my snug little wartime home before I cook my vegan supper and call it a night. My social life is nil. I am someone you'd pass on the street without a second glance, unless, of course, you notice my hand. Being asked to parties by complete strangers is not a hazard. Not for someone like me.

A yellow cab screeches into the portico and Martine opens the passenger door and hands me a business card. "See the sights. When you are ready to return, call and ask for me. I will send you a cab. Enjoy our beautiful city. Really enjoy."

The bar I find at the top of the stairs is a tiny square of terracotta, open to the stars. Waiters hustle drinks as wood smoke from the barbeque drifts lazily in the still night air. There's a bandstand in the corner, the band a ragtag collection of five who all look as if they're stuck in the sixties, and happy to be there. Bubba and the Bottom Feeders is stenciled in black across the front of the biggest drum and I wonder what they were smoking when they chose such a name.

Directly behind the balding bass player, a blue-green parrot in a bamboo cage cocks his head, seeming to study the man's ponytail. The music begins again and the bird tucks his head into his wing, as if the tunes are bringing back memories he can't easily bear.

The bar is long, fronted by polished mahogany, reflecting red and yellow and blue from a string of patio lanterns strung across a rough, brick wall.

A guy perched on the edge of a wrought iron stool, his red arm resting on the mosaic surface of the bar, lets loose a belly laugh. I wonder what he finds so funny and, for one sickening moment, I'm sure that it's me. And then I remember. I blend in and disappear, like the iguanas that everyone strains to see. Even here, in this strange country, in this hole-in-the-wall kind of bar, I will be safe.

The man's touristy Señor Frog's shirt is stretched tight across his belly and the fourth button down has popped, exposing a hairy roll of sunburnt flesh. He's already had one too many by the looks of his eyes. Or too much sun. Either way, I don't like his speculative look, how his eyes examine every woman who walks in. Every one, that is, but me.

"*Señorita* is meeting someone?" A waiter in a dazzling white shirt tucked into khaki shorts takes my elbow and guides me inside.

The walls are rough plaster, in shades of orange and ocher, glowing in the last rays of sun deflected from the low-lying smog. I count thirteen tables in Joe's, all occupied except for one, situated far too close to the bathroom doors.

At least half the people in the bar are on the dance floor. So it seems to be a game of rotating chairs, like the one we used to play as children in school. When the music stops, everyone scrambles. The difference here is they don't take away a chair each time, but more and more people are coming in, so the effect is the same.

The waiter gestures toward the little table. "By the *banyos* is okay? I am sorry."

A crush of pink-tinged tourists joust with their elbows for standing room at the bar, and that won't work for me so I nod my head yes.

I have always been able to camouflage my hand, partly because I'm petite. Sleeves on suit jackets and blouses are always too long, which is good. Sweaters can be stretched a bit. When I was little, my parents discouraged my hiding and told me that I had nothing to be ashamed of, that nothing could hold me back other than myself. Of course, they had no idea what it was like for me, looking as they did. Cheerful clones of Barbie and Ken. They must have assumed their child would be perfectly beautiful too. At least I'm sure that's what they'd planned.

So it's no wonder I love the gauzy dresses you can custom order in the little shops downtown. Marie made mine soft and feminine, beautiful, with full bell sleeves. When I told her I was afraid that the cotton was too delicate, that, in a certain light, you might be able to see right through, she shook her shining head. *Señorita*, she said, this sometimes, is good. I smile when I think of her saying such a thing, and maybe believing it too. But she did agree to sew me a strappy camisole, and I can feel it soft against my skin and I can feel the handmade lace that edges the sleeves of my dress. Sleeves

44

that fall well past my fingertips — I feel almost like an angel when I'm wearing this dress.

The flash of teeth catches my eye, and a strip of bronzed skin is revealed when he bends to fish cold Corona from a tub full of ice near the end of the bar. I step around him to get to my table.

"Excuse me," I say.

"Of course. And don't worry, we'll move you away from those bathrooms first chance we get," he says, with an accent vaguely American, overlaid with Mexico. "Glad you found us tonight. Name's Joe."

The owner, I wonder? Doing grunt work in his own bar? When labour is so plentiful and cheap?

"Brenda," I say.

"Would you prefer a larger table? Perhaps you're meeting someone?"

"No," I tell him. "This is just fine. It looks like I'm lucky to have found a table at all."

His shirt is worn denim and so are his eyes. Deep crevices line his cheeks, giving him a weather-beaten cowboy kind of look, like he's spent years riding horses in the noonday sun. Draft dodger, I wonder? Too deeply rooted in this scrubby red soil to ever go home, even now, when he finally can?

"Yeah." He gestures to waiters hustling through the crowd, balancing full trays of beer through the crush. "Business has really picked up since I rounded up the band. A bunch of old hippies hooked on Jimmy Buffet. They've got groupies that would follow them anywhere so I'm lucky to have 'em here. For as long as it lasts. They're already complaining about the crowds in Puerto Vallarta, how nothing's the same any more."

One of the girls behind the bar taps him on the back and he turns to the tub, fishes out six ice-cold beer. The tub is half empty already and when he walks to the Pacifico boxes stacked in a hallway off the bar, I notice that he doesn't really walk, he sort of rolls, as if maybe part of his foot has been blown away, and I rethink my draft-dodger guess.

The music ebbs and flows, and so do the dancers. Someone bumps my chair as the couple at the next table get up and thread their way to the dance floor. He's about five foot nine, slightly balding and she's maybe five foot three, with sun-streaked hair. They're both a little on the chunky side and they're probably sliding down the hill from fifty. Not a pair you'd notice in a crowd. But when they start to dance, their footsteps flow like water across the uneven floor and every eye in the place is watching, at least for a minute or two. I would so love to dance like that, have someone hold me so easy and sure, as if he'd been doing it for years and years.

A disheveled woman bangs the bathroom door open directly to my left, vainly tugging at her dress and wiping her hands on its flowered front. She peers into a cracked mirror set into the stucco wall between the two *banyos*. She lifts her hair to catch the night breeze on her neck, and then lets it fall, a rippling river of gold. She rubs her finger over her lips, and then applies a thick scarlet layer from a silver tube.

Light spills from the open door. The man I've dubbed Señor Frog stands behind the woman and watches as she smacks her caked lips, his hand on the bathroom door. I reposition my chair so it faces away. At the age of thirty-three, I have yet to see a man's penis, and I don't want it to happen by chance on a rooftop bar in Mexico.

A small bedroom, with rough-hewn plaster walls. The bed is not large, just wide enough for my body and one other, slimmer than my own. My hair is fanned across a sun fresh pillowcase, gleaming in dim light diffused from a four-paned window high on the wall. His hand strays to my gauzy dress, and its row of tiny pearl buttons yield easily beneath his hands.

"Beautiful." He lifts the lacy gown from my bronzed shoulders and peels the delicate sleeves down my forearms, past my elbow.

I wake up sweating and ready to scream.

My Pacifico is empty. Joe appears behind me like smoke. "Pacifico?" he asks and when I nod, he turns and fishes out another dripping bottle. He wipes it dry with a yellow towel and hands it to me with a flourish.

"On the house," he says, and whisks my empty away. The yellow bottle cap is left behind, lying like a lone checker on the blue and yellow squared tablecloth. I push it from a blue square to a yellow, and back again.

I squeeze a fresh lime before I take the first cold sip and raise my face to the multitude of stars. I'm about as close to heaven as I'm going to get in this life. I love this country, I love this city, and I love this bar. And in this star-filled moment, I almost love my thalidomide arm.

The band has been on a ten-minute break, Mexican time, so after at least a half an hour, they finally reassemble. They joke with each other, shove and push a little like overgrown boys until they get back in formation and start sound checking their guitars. They love it up there, in the spotlight. You can just tell. The guy with the ponytail eventually gets them in synch and they start into "Far Side of the Moon". He sings like a bird and so does his old lady; that's what he calls her when he introduces her and mumbles the title of their next duet. Mellow notes from his guitar suddenly shift into the opening bars of "Margaritaville", and the keyboard and bass players follow his lead. The surging beat sucks spectators from their chairs and from the amoebic blob of people near the bar.

Through the crush of bodies, I see Señor Frog turn to the woman beside him, take her hand as they sidle their way to the middle of the crowded floor. You can tell she was beautiful once, but she's thickened now, her long hair losing its black, shot with strands of grey. Her face has marked the passing years but, still, she moves like a woman accustomed to admiring eyes. I wonder how that feels, to have been beautiful once. I wonder how it feels not to be, anymore.

I'm surprised to see how well he dances and she fluidly follows his every move. There are a lot of single women on vacation in Puerto Vallarta, no doubt disappointed when they realize this city is a haven for gays. Señor Frog could be dancing all night if he really wanted to. I am glad he has chosen this woman as his partner, this woman who has probably *never* sat on the sidelines at her high school dances with hopeful eyes, praying some guy, any guy, might finally ask her to dance. I don't wish that gut-wrenching feeling on anyone, not matter what their age.

The tempo of the music is getting wilder but tucked into my table near the *banyos*, I feel almost invisible and infinitely safe.

Señor Frog is dancing so hard rivulets of sweat run down the red of his face and he mops his chin with the tail of his cotton shirt without missing a beat. When the music stops, he escorts his partner back to her stool. She tries to back onto the stool, but when she lifts her butt and slides, the wrought iron stool skids backward on the terracotta tile and she lands hard on the floor. Señor Frog picks her up by the elbows and plunks her on the stool, her sandaled feet swinging free in the air.

"There you go, honey," he bellows above the noise of crowd. "Anytime a gal like you needs help with a mount, just give old Harley a call." The woman flushes, turns quickly away. Harley seems disappointed, or maybe a little sad.

The music is still frantic, but four Pacifico have put me into a languid, mellow mood. The couple next to me desert their frosty beers, drawn once again to the dance floor. They begin to jive, their moves so synchronized I know they've been dancing together for years. Her dress is embroidered turquoise, its cotton skirt tiered and when he twirls her, the skirt seems to take on a life of its own. A circle clears on the floor around them, and when the music finally fades, the spectators clap. The man pirouettes and gives a little bow, but his partner blushes and pulls him from the floor.

"Wanna cut a rug?" Señor Frog is beside me, leaning on my table with his large, meaty hands. "No reason for a pretty woman like you to be sittin' here all night like a bump on a log."

The first bars of "Changes in Attitudes" swing from the small stage in the corner where the band sweats into their headbands and shoot bright smiles at each other, as if maybe they're having more fun then anyone else.

"No thanks," I say and I begin to explain that I don't dance much.

"No lame excuses," he bellows and he grabs my hand, pulls me onto the floor. For some strange reason, maybe the beers or maybe this beautiful country, tonight I feel the beat in every bone of my body. I try to keep my rhythm damped down a bit but for the first time in my life, I feel wild and crazy and totally free. I twist and dip and twirl without a single thought to my lovely lacy sleeves, to the act of camouflage that's always been second nature to me. I look at the sky, and feel suddenly perfect under the stars.

"Right on, baby," Señor Frog hollers. "Nothing this old dude likes better than a pretty woman with a smile on her face."

As suddenly as a summer storm can roll across the prairie sky, the music slides into a sensual waltz. "Come on, let's have one more," Señor Frog says, and reaches for my hand. "Slow ones are better." His raspy laugh rises above the noise of the crowd. As he grabs my hand, I feel the roughness of his palm. I see his smile fade and something else flick across the canvas of his face.

"Jesus H. Christ," he hollers. And he raises my hand, its poor cloven fingers curling into themselves like fronds about to die. "What the hell is this? Why didn't ya' tell me I gonna be dancing with a goddamn fish?"

There's a gap in the music and the crowd is suddenly silent. Before I can move, the woman in the turquoise skirt grabs my good hand and pulls me from the floor, shielding me with her body. Pinwheels of black burst behind my eyes. The last sound I hear is Señor Frog's raspy voice, hollering that he paid eight hundred dollars for an airline ticket to find a little romance down in old Mexico and, just his luck, he ends up holding hands with a goddamn fish. Then mercifully, I am gone.

A small bedroom with rough-hewn plaster walls. The bed is not large, just wide enough for my body and maybe one other, slimmer than my own. My hair is fanned across a snow-white pillowcase, gleaming golden in the dim light diffused from a four-pane window high on the wall.

A snifter of sweet liquid moistens my lips.

"Shh." A deep voice, but soft. "Just a little sip."

Moonlight is lost in crevices that line his face. I take one sweet sip, then one more. As I drift in and out, I feel the indent of the bed when he sits beside me. I dream the butterfly wings of a kiss on my cheek.

His fingers stray to my gauzy dress.

"So hot," he murmurs, his flop of hair falling so that I can't see the look in his denim eyes. He slides his arm behind me. Tears pool in the corners of my eyes as he peels the sleeve down my upper arm, past my elbow. When he reaches my shrunken forearm and bares my cloven hand, I am suddenly sweaty, ready to scream.

He strokes my shrunken arm, lifts my thalidomide hand and raises it to his lips.

"An angel's wing," he whispers. "The tip of an angel's wing."

I trail slowly down the rickety stairs, deserted at this time of morning. Above me, the Mexican sky is filled with pinpricks of fading light, light that left the home star eons ago and is only now reaching my eyes.

In a Bright Red Chrysler
By the Highway Near Town

STARLA'S BLACK HAIR SHINES BLUE LIGHT, HAYWIRE curls tamed by an oval turquoise clip. She must have washed it this morning, Carl thinks, that's a good sign. He glances at his watch. Ten o'clock. Early for Starla to be up and around. She fills her yellow mug, glides toward the table like the dancer she used to be.

Starla's racoon eyes look a little better today, and Carl wonders if she's used some concealer or if maybe, just please God, maybe, she actually slept last night for an hour or two. She used to snuggle into the curve of his back, be out for the night almost as soon as he clicked off his reading light. But now she tosses and turns until the early hours, and finally, when she's worn herself out, and sometimes, him as well, she will drift off to sleep just as daylight begins to seep beneath the window shades. No wonder she's got circles under those sleepless eyes. But it could be just the lousy light, the sun obscured by towering thunderheads.

"Carl," she says. Her green eyes widen. "I thought you'd be out feeding the calves."

"I was," he says, as he pulls out her chair. "But I came in to check on you. Thought I'd have to pull you out of bed. Or maybe crawl back in. It's cold out today, blustery too."

The wind whips across the yard, twisting an elm branch against the kitchen window, as if to validate his weather report. The sound sends a shiver up his spine, and he snugs his faded flannel shirt closer to his back, presses his arms tight to his sides.

"How's Larry going to manage if the weather stays cold like this?" Starla says, her eyes on the darkening sky. Carl's hand begins to shake, and he sloshes his coffee onto his grandparents' oak table. It's been a while since anyone's given the thirsty wood a coat of oil. Idly, he wonders if the coffee will make a stain. His grandma, he knows, would never have approved of such sloth. Nor would Starla, in her better days.

"Let me get that," Starla says and she goes into the kitchen, returns with a red and white checked dishcloth. She moves Carl's Massey-Harris mug and wipes the spill. She steps back, squints at the spot marring the oiled oak. She wipes it again and again. Finally, Carl stops her frantic hands. "It's okay," he says. "This old table's survived a lot more than spilled coffee." Shit, Carl thinks, what did I have to say that? I've got to be more careful. Think before I speak.

A line of crushed and broken cars edges the highway, east side of town. Carl has always wondered why Sammy's Salvage hasn't had the decency to at least build a fence, and hide those savaged bits of metal from the traffic flowing by. Every time he drives by Carl's eyes are assaulted by the sight of Larry's red Chrysler. He cannot keep his eyes away. He wishes for a pair of blinders, the kind his father used on horses he trained to team.

Carl had seen the Chrysler up close when Sammy's winched it from the flattened bushes at the bottom of Rowan's Ravine, drawn to the accident scene as if he was just one more morbid bystander. He knows how it is in a small town. Lots of guys go out to the scene and take a good long look, as if by seeing the skid marks or the studying the slope of the road, they can make sense of what happened. Hell, he'd done it himself when old Joe Barber bought the farm on the curve north of town, although he has no idea why.

He'd touched the twisted metal of Larry's car, crunched shards of shattered glass across the palm of his hand. He'd even leaned inside, run his fingers across the red velvet with its blotchy brown stains.

The road through Rowan's Ravine is perfectly capped, the gravel evenly spread and a respectable depth. Right after the accident, when he was still trying to make sense of things, Carl used to park his Ford at the top of the hill, walk the road down the hill and across the fertile flat. He had paced the curve a hundred times, climbed the hill to the lookout point on the other side. He got no sense of Larry there, felt nothing in the still and silent air. Carl had tried to drive Rowan Road, but his truck slewed and slid as if driven by an unseen hand and his mind went places he could not bear to be.

At the culvert, okay, he was alive right here. The dip before the bridge, he was still in the world. But when he starts into the curve, Carl's hands convulse on the wheel. *Right here? Did his soul leave his body? Here? A few more yards, almost through? Just past the barrier? Here? Maybe here?*

Carl would pull over, his body trembling like the white aspens on the brow of the hill. It would be a long time before he felt safe enough to put his truck into gear.

Sometimes, when the kids from town showed up at the compound to gawk at Larry's smashed-up car, Carl would be there, leaning on the fender of his Ford. The boys would stand around, leather-clad backs humped against the cool wind, puffs of smoke rising like secret signals from their midst. Carl wanted to tell them to go home, but the only thing he did was give them a half-hearted wave. Sometimes, he moved in close enough to hear their words. A couple of the braver ones came over, told Carl they were sorry, how their whole school seemed numbed by the news. Something in the tone of their soft young voices soothed Carl's ragged soul.

When the insurance adjusters were finally finished and Sammy's hauled the Chrysler from the SGI compound to the line of ruined cars at the edge of town, Carl missed those flocks of black-clad boys.

"More coffee?" Starla pulls her hands from his, and lifts her yellow cup. Carl shakes his head. He watches Starla puttering in the kitchen, thinks of all the times he'd watched her and Larry from the shadows of his shed. Starla digging in her flowerbeds full of roses and Larry, rag in hand, polishing his beloved red Chrysler angled on the curve of their drive.

"Lunchtime, guys," he'd hear Starla call. Carl would lay down his crescent wrench, glad for a chance to straighten his back. As he walked across the scrubby lawn, he could smell strong coffee wafting in the air.

"Look at that crazy kid," Starla would say. "If he polishes that dash much longer, he's going to wear the thing right through. I told him if he doesn't leave those dials alone he's going to rub the face right off the clock."

One time, he watched as she gathered three sandwiches, wrapped them in waxed paper. "Be right back," she said and then spent the rest of the lunch break sitting with Larry. Carl could see her twiddling with the radio dial, winding the window up and down and running her fingers across the back of the seat, her eyes bathing Larry with her pure white love.

Larry ate quickly, kissed Starla's cheek, and handed her the waxed paper. "Thanks Mom, not many guys lucky enough to get lunch delivered right to their car. Except at the A&W. Ever thought of applying for a job? You could probably be the manager. Shape the place up."

Starla beamed when she carried the wrinkled waxed paper back to the deck. She sat beside him, smoothing the paper with her hands. "I don't think that kid would remember to eat if I didn't take lunch out to him," she said. "Imagine, being so struck on a car."

The wheat fields were full of gold, and Larry still hadn't lent Carl a single hour of his precious teenage time. Today's going to be different, Carl thought as he rinsed the drying yellow yolk from his breakfast plate. Today he's going to get something other than a ten-dollar chamois in his hand. Carl heard a rumble and raised his eyes from the melmac dish. He saw Larry unfold himself from behind the wheel of his Chrysler and carefully pick his way toward the porch. Carl was suddenly awed by Larry's beauty. Strange word to describe a boy, Carl thought, but he is beautiful, just like Starla has always said.

Carl rubbed his damp hands on his bib overalls, felt the aching muscles of his legs, the tug of his jeans at his slightly thickened waist. Carl's hair is sandy brown, Starla's black, yet somehow they'd produced a Viking, with a smile so white you could see it from across the yard. His face had the chiselled look of a statue, his features honed until they were perfection, even to Carl's untrained eye.

The oil-hungry hinges on the porch door screamed and Carl ambled into the breezeway. "Welcome home," he said, and Larry raised red-rimmed eyes. "It's about goddamn time."

"Jeez, Dad," Larry said. "I'm sorry. I was watching a movie with John. Went to sleep on the couch."

"Yeah," Carl said, "I imagine you did. But we've got bins to fix. The barley's ready to go."

"Can I sleep for an hour or two first?" Larry asked, flashing Carl his brightest smile. "I'll be a better hand with an hour or two under my belt. Wake me up at noon and I'll work like a dog. I promise"

"Okay," Carl said, his determination dissipating like rain drops on parched prairie soil. "Grab a zee or two, but I still expect a good day's work out of you, even if it doesn't start till the day's half done."

He could smell chili, with the welcome aroma of fresh-baked buns close on its heels. "You've been busy," he said to Starla as he lathered his hands at the kitchen tap. "Too bad Larry doesn't take a leaf out of your book. Or mine. Get his butt out of bed when there's work to be done."

"He's just a kid," Starla said, lifting the lid and adding a scant teaspoon of brown sugar, the secret ingredient, to her famous chili. "Just because your dad almost worked you to death before you turned eighteen is no reason to take it out on Larry." She plunked the lid back onto the pot and pirouetted back to the kitchen sink, her feet barely touching the floor. When Carl saw vestiges of a dancer in Starla, he sometimes wondered if his dogged determination to make her his wife was the best of choices, for either of them. He'd been so sure. He'd even thought she'd be relieved, eventually, not to be teaching little gap-toothed girls to plié. Carl only tolerates cities, does his essential business there, all the while straining at the bit like an ill-mannered horse in his haste to leave. When Starla mooned around about being lonely and how the silence was driving her mad, he didn't pay her any mind. He figured she'd adjust soon enough and come to love the place like he did. And, after Larry was born, she stopped talking about her city friends, how the ballet school was doing, or what was showing at the Mendel Art Gallery.

But Carl wondered, sometimes, how often she stared out the window and saw, not the infinitely beautiful sky, but a single city street choked with vehicles and people and noise.

"Carl, are you listening? He adjusted the brim of his sweat-stained cap and pushed his troubling thoughts away.

"He left me a note. Said he fell asleep on the couch at John's. In the middle of the third movie. So he's probably really tired."

"Too bad," Carl said. "I'm getting him up. He's supposed to be helping me today."

"Let him sleep," she said. "If you need some help out there, I know how to do a thing or two."

"That's not the point," Carl replied, but he sat down at the table, and hurried to finish his chili, not wanting to start the same old argument with Starla. They'd been having it since Larry was old enough to walk.

"I don't know why you expect so much," Starla said.

"How 'bout those Blue Jays?" Carl said, as he rose from the table and grabbed his cap. Starla turned her back, clanked dishes onto the top rack of the dishwasher.

"Send Sir Larry out if he decides to surface today," he said. As he walked past the shining red Chrysler parked on the driveway, he wondered if buying a car for Larry's sixteenth birthday had been such a good idea. Seemed to Carl that since he'd gotten the car, Larry had become less responsible, not more. He ran his hand down its shiny side, touched the taillight as he walked away.

Before he took Starla to the hospital, she'd almost convinced him that Larry was alive, living out in that goddamn junkyard in his smashed-up car. That's what sealed it, the day he found himself straining to believe.

"He's there," she'd insisted. "I see his face pressed against the window every time I drive to town. Look here," she said, green eyes shining, her lovely red lips curved in a secret smile. "I take little lunches out there. But he hides when he sees me coming." She'd unfolded a brown paper bag, turned it upside down so he could see there was nothing inside.

"I heard you two fighting the night Larry left. Maybe I should have stopped you." She set the crinkled bag aside, and picked up her polish rag, damp with Silver Sparkle Cream. Her shiny spoons were aligned in perfect symmetry on the table by her left-hand side. She picked up one and folded it into the purple polish cloth. "Still, it's no reason for Larry to hold a grudge and hide himself from me."

The cloth moved faster and faster, up and down the stem of the spoon. Finally, Starla held the spoon aloft, turned it so it caught the light and flashed in the sun. Then she laid it parallel to the others, picked up another perfectly shiny spoon and rubbed it hard.

"As if I'd ever be crazy enough to get between the two of you," she said. "But you don't have to worry. He's okay, really he is. Go check for yourself. You'll see. There's nothing left of those lunches. Not one little crumb. If that's not proof, I don't know what is."

She dropped the spoon onto the table where it landed with a silvery tinkle. Carl reached for Starla's busy hands, held them so she'd stop ceaselessly twisting and turning the blackened cloth.

"It's okay, Starla," he kept saying. "It's going to be okay."

He wished for the power to believe his own lies. If only, he thought, if only. If only I'd gone along with Starla when she'd come up with her cockeyed plan, then Larry would be safe and so, of course, would she. She had actually talked to a realtor about buying a condo in Saskatoon and moving there with Larry for ten months of every year. He'll have a ton of opportunities in the city, she'd told him. And it'll be better for him when he starts university. He'll already be acclimatized. Living in the city is *nothing* like living out here. And we'll visit every weekend, promise we will. Bullshit, Carl had said. So the discussion was over before it really began. Carl sighed. Regrets don't get the chores done. Hard work does. He rose and kissed Starla before he went outside.

Light was pinking the edges of the sky and Carl was ready to spray peas on the north quarter before the wind came up. It gave him immense satisfaction, standing at his kitchen window, seeing the land change from bare and brown to hazy green, and finally to gold. But chickpeas wouldn't mature on their own, and had to be sprayed with an expensive mix of chemical and water to help them reach their peak. Too bad, Carl thought, they don't develop something to spray on kids when they turn sixteen.

Harsh sun was baking the soil by the time his sprayer ran dry. When Carl stopped to refill from the water tank, the wind blew a line of shining silver straight from the hose. Tomorrow, he thought. Maybe tomorrow the wind won't blow.

He found Starla kneeling on the living room floor, a stack of ham and cheese sandwiches close to her side. She motioned to them, her face flushed. "I know, I know," she said. "Me preaching to him all these years about how white bread kills rats. And here I am taking white bread for his lunch. Crazy, isn't it?" she asked.

Then she bent to the log cabin quilt, warm and wide, open on the hardwood of their living room floor. Starla's grandmother had made the quilt from bits and pieces of Starla's discarded dance costumes and her outgrown childhood clothes. Her memory quilt, Starla called it. She folded the quilt once, turned it, folded it again. She smoothed it slowly, pushing down firmly with her fine little hands.

She began to sing a low, whispered tune. From the doorway where he was leaning, Carl strained to hear. *If the days turn dark and cold, Momma's gonna bring you a quilt to hold.*

Carl shuddered, drew a deep breath before he called her name. "Starla?" The quilt sponged from her hands. "Damn," she whispered, "damn, damn, damn. It has to be a real small package. Larry won't even look at stuff unless it's really, really small. There's not much room when you live in a car." She dropped her head and Carl saw tears darken the fabric of her shirt. "But it's getting cold," she said. "It's getting so goddamn cold."

He thought of making her face the truth flat out. Thought of saying 'he's dead you know.' But he couldn't do it, not when she looked so frail. His job was to protect her, keep her safe and, so far, he'd done a decent job. Losing Larry was a huge bump in the road. But he was sure that, with a little more time, he could figure out a way they could both get over it, or maybe just around.

Most Friday nights, there's a line of cars all angle-parked outside the Honker Hilton. Carl shakes his head as he walks by a beat-up Bronco, rust bleeding from its front left fender, dents pocked all down the driver's side door. He wonders if Sammy's Salvage is ever tempted to hook on, and haul one or two of the worst ones away.

The air is blue, the jukebox playing Merle Haggard at full volume and Carl has to holler at the bartender when he orders his Blue. "Two?" Skinny says, his eyes popping wide.

"No," Carl says, "I asked for a Blue." Skinny cups his hand behind his ear, cocks his head at Carl. The music surges, The Kentucky Headhunters louder and more frantic than laid-back old Merle. Carl holds up his index finger and Skinny ambles to the cooler, comes back with a Blue.

"Tip yourself a loonie," Carl says and waits while Skinny fumbles for the change. Sweat beads on his beer bottle and it almost slips from his hand. Skinny palms a toonie and hands Carl his change. Crazy like a fox, that Skinny, Carl thinks. And he can hear as good as anyone when he damn well pleases.

He sees an empty stool beside Rod, a big-time farmer from west of town. "How's it going, Carl?" Rod says, as he lifts his mug of draft. When he motions to the empty stool, Carl is grateful. Since Larry died, too many guys have avoided his glance and Carl has drunk more than one beer alone. Carl has wondered if he should be the one to bring up the subject of Larry right off, so they can get it out of the way. Get on with talk of the crops and how much rain was in the gauge.

Carl slides behind the table. "Fine," he says. "It's going just fine."

"Nice to see a little rain," Rod says. "Gives us a chance to rest for a day or two. Lots of time to finish harvest yet."

Carl nods, starts to pick at the label on his bottle, worrying pieces of blue until the bottle looks like a badly decorated Christmas tree. The thought of Christmas depresses Carl and he checks the *Playboy* calendar behind the bar. He's relieved to see Miss September spilling out of her tattered leather vest, one long, brown leg thrown across a split-rail fence, and her cute little butt pushed right up in the air. Carl's had a bit of trouble keeping track of dates lately, and time flies away like fallen leaves in a gale-force wind. But when his third Blue comes up empty, he knows full well it's time to go home.

Starla smiles as she slides lacy oatmeal cookies from the darkened pan and onto the cooling rack. The bottoms are lightly browned, just like the ones in *Best of Bridge*'s glossy pages. She bites into a warm, crisp cookie and closes her eyes. Starla knows her domestic skills have been in limbo for at least two years. She thinks the smell of her perfectly baked cookies will be more alluring to Carl than the smell of Chanel Number Five.

One morning, in a sudden cleaning frenzy, she'd gone downstairs, something she'd avoided since Larry left. She couldn't bear to see his bedroom, neat as a pin.

She'd stepped into the bathroom, looked blankly at the towels, folded perfectly straight and hanging on the rack. "The toilet," she'd murmured. "Maybe I'll just start with that." She'd lifted the harvest gold lid to drop in a blue hockey-puck deodorizer. When she saw the Crown Royal bottle wavering at the bottom of the ice-cold tank, she'd felt suddenly dizzy, and sank to her knees. "Please, not you too," she murmured. "You *know* I am far too busy with Larry these days." She'd stayed there for what seemed like hours, until the cold seeped from the tile and settled in her bones. She'd thought of Carl, cleaning corrals and knew he'd be coming in soon, asking for coffee or a cookie, any excuse to check on her. She'd grabbed the edge of the toilet, and pulled herself erect.

On the lid of the tank, she'd placed a thick green hand-towel, folded like a fan.

Starla takes another quick nibble from the edge of her cookie and begins to hum a little tune. She looks down the lane, listening for the rumble of Carl's blue Ford.

"She's extremely fragile," the shrink tells Carl when he insists that it's time Starla came home. Carl has always known this about Starla.

He sometimes wonders if she'd have been totally stable if she'd stayed in the city, if she somehow drew strength from its busyness, just as he draws his from the sweep of the land. He could have married Glenys. He'd known her all his life. God knows, she was willing enough, and she would have understood his drive to spend every single hour improving his farm, instead of complaining about his ridiculously long hours, the way Starla often did. She seemed to think his love for the place took something away from her and Larry.

But he doesn't regret marrying Starla. In fact, he feels privileged by her love, as if it were a gift he can't possibly repay.

Dr. Gordon pushes at his glasses, shifts from one foot to the other, and holds his clipboard closer to his chest. "We've made some progress," he tells Carl. "But we have a long way to go. Her grasp on reality isn't very strong."

Carl feels the muscles in his belly tighten, his asshole clench. Starla may be off in la-la land right now, but he's sure he can bring her back. All it'll take is some time. And careful tending. Christ, he's been a farmer his entire life. Tending is something he knows how to do.

"Here's a prescription," the doctor says, and tears off a little piece of paper covered with squiggles that drop off the right-hand side. "Get it filled right away, and make sure she takes them. It's important she sticks to the schedule, even when she's feeling just fine." He pushes his round wire glasses up the bridge of his nose and, surprisingly, touches Carl's arm. "Especially when she's feeling just fine."

"Starla," Carls says, his fingers curling. "Starla is her name."

The pills hadn't made any difference as far as Carl could tell and, more and more often, he saw the spaced out look in Starla's eyes. When the doctor had suggested a thorough assessment in the North Battleford facility, he thought it might just help her take that first step back. Now Carl wonders if taking Starla to the nuthouse had been a good idea. He is almost certain he could have taken better care of her himself. But her mother insisted, said that Carl had too much to bear, losing Larry, and then, in a different way, losing Starla too.

"And you've got all the farm work now," she'd added. "More than one man should be handling on his own."

On one of his visits, which weren't often enough because the drive cost him a whole day's work, he found Starla curled on her rumpled bed, the shades drawn, her meal tray untouched. "Come," he said, taking her white and boneless hand, "let's walk down to the solarium, smell a few roses, get you some sun."

He led her like a zombie through the dim hallways and down the wide stairs, folded her compliant body onto a cedar bench.

"Haying's pretty well finished," he told her. "Just a few sloughs left. And I can't cut them till it dries a bit." He stroked her hand. "You should see the peonies. They're almost ready to flower. The ants are hanging around, just waiting for the day." He waited for her to tell him to get some ant bait, get rid of the pests before they found trails into her house and made homes beneath the kitchen sink, but she turned her head away.

Carl rose, wandered around the atrium. He found a small rose bush in the southwest corner, pinched a blossom into his palm. The rose released its nectar and he blessed the sweet perfume. He hated the smell of the hospital, how it clung to the inside of his nostrils, how he could smell it long after he left Starla sitting quietly in her room.

"Smell this," he said, offering Starla the purloined pink rose, its outer petals trembling in his hand.

"Why would flowers want to bloom," she asked, "when Larry refuses to come home?"

He thought, for a moment, of telling her that Larry would never be coming home. Instead, he put his arms around her thin shoulders and held her bony body close to his own. Held her and held her, until the sun settled in the west and he heard the rattle of the eight o'clock trays.

As he turned up the lane, Carl saw a light in the window, although he knew for sure there was no one at home. As he got closer, he saw a shadow move across the kitchen, a fluff of yellow hair. He blinked, blinked again.

Darlene met him in the porch, her arms full of freshly laundered sheets. "I hope you don't mind," she said. Carl noticed Starla's lavender housecoat splayed across the top of the pile. "I thought you might need a hand."

Carl was pulling his boots off, the left one resisting the pull of the bootjack. He yanked, felt his ankle stretch and the boot finally slide. "Of course I don't mind," he said. "You and Don have been a godsend." He lined his boots up near the door.

"I wish we could do more," Darlene said. "A little cleaning and cooking doesn't seem like near enough. I'm just going to make up your bed and I'll be off." She hesitated at the hallway, looked into his eyes. "How is she?"

"Better," Carl said. "She's getting better each time I go." He turned to look inside the fridge, away from Darlene's eyes.

He washes up after the eleven o'clock news, his movements heavy and slow. When he sees Starla's robe hanging on the back of the bathroom door, he leans into it, buries his head in the soft chenille. But the scent of Starla is gone.

Lakeside Memorials is nowhere near a lake, and Carl pulls into the lot, almost running his pickup over the curb. He opens the door, levers himself to the ground. The running board seems miles away, his legs feel like they belong to someone else, someone really old.

"Can I help you?" the salesman behind the counter asks as Carl pushes through the iron-heavy door. "I need to choose a headstone," Carl says. "For my boy." The man shakes his head, pulls out a folder and hands it to Carl. "Tough job," he says. "Some really nice ideas in our brochure. Holler when you're ready. I'm just printing out some invoices, need to get 'em in the mail." He scratches the side of his spaghetti-thin neck. "Gas bills for this building are higher than you can imagine. Good thing business has picked up a bit."

When he hears what he's said, the man flushes scarlet. "Take the brochure home if you want," he says. "Awful hard to make decisions like this one on your own."

"Thanks," Carl says, and sits down heavily in a brown tweed chair. His eyes blur as he turns the pages, the different colours of marble melding into black. Flat stones, oval stones, stones chiselled into the shape of a cross. An amazing array of fonts are available for the inscription, charged by the letter and also by the size. Carl rubs his eyes, rises as he slips the brochure into his breast pocket, thinking that he'll pour a good stiff whiskey first and then try to make sense of the words and figures inside. His head aches and his eyes feel like they just might explode.

When he gets into his Ford, he feels the brochure, heavy in his pocket, so he fumbles it free and throws it face down on the dash. He is surprised to hear the squeal of spinning tires, see a spray of gravel fly though the air. He checks the rear-view mirror and sees a trail of billowing dust. He wonders if driving like a maniac is genetic. If Larry drove like that once he was out of the yard and gone from their sight.

Slow down man, he thinks, slow goddamn down. Take a page out of Darlene's book. He wonders if she might be there when he gets home, her denim skirt dark with water spots, her hands warm with billowing suds. Carl has noticed the width of her hips, the solidity of her arms. Darlene's work is meticulous and measured, so unlike Starla's shotgun approach. Starla's habit of starting a slew of projects and flitting from one to the other, creating chaos everywhere, has been a trial to Carl sometimes.

Carl rolls down his window and reaches for his cigarettes. He inhales deeply, hears the delicate notes of a meadowlark drift from a field of wheat alongside the road. The field is shimmering gold, like Darlene's hair.

Suddenly Carl slams his fist into the dash of his truck, hard enough to make his knuckles bleed. Jeez, he thinks, what *is* wrong with me?

The jarring dislodges the sales brochure. It lands on the mat near the run-down heel of Carl's right boot. He glances down and the letterhead of Lakeside Memorials wavers and blurs, like it was at rest on the bottom of a shallow pond.

Carl is well aware of the high divorce rates among couples who lose a child, and he wonders if he and Starla might be heading there. He thinks of her final unravelling in the days before he took her to the hospital and how he failed to really understand. If the timing had been different, if he hadn't been so busy, he could probably have headed the whole thing off. All Starla really needs, he thinks, it to sit with me in our cozy kitchen, drinking coffee and talking. Then she'll tell me what's really going on in that pretty head of hers.

The smell of rich beef pervades the porch. Carl lines his rubber boots up on the boot tray, quickly washes his cow-stinking hands. "Starla?" he says as he steps through the kitchen door.

The slow cooker burbles on the counter and fresh buns nestle beneath a red-checked cloth. "Starla?" he says again. Carl takes a blue bowl from the cupboard left of the fridge, lifts the lid on the Crock-Pot and ladles thick, rich stew. He pushes a pile of magazines and flyers aside, makes room on the table for his bowl and his elbows. *O, The Oprah Magazine*,

October 2000 slides from the stack and uncovers a short letter in Starla's spidery hand.

Dear Larry — I don't care what kind of argument you had with your dad. You just quit being silly and get your stubborn butt back to the farm. You might think it's funny, living in that Chrysler. But it's just crazy. It really is, and besides, I cannot get through another Christmas without you. Neither can your dad. We miss you, Larry. It's time you came home. Love Mom

Oh sweet Jesus. Carl is suddenly sickened by the smell of the simmering stew.

Carl is deep in the *Western Producer* when Starla finally gets back from town, her arms piled high with packages. He hears a soft thud as she drops two of the parcels on the counter.

"Corning Ware casseroles," she explains. "Single size, with covers for leftovers. I had the girl in Stedman's wrap them in these towels." She picks up one of the bundles, holds it out to Carl. "I don't know what Larry's got for cooking stuff. Not much, I'd think. You know, I'm positive I saw him and Karen yesterday, on the corner by the post office. But by the time I pulled over, they were already gone."

Carl drags himself from his easy chair, goes to the bathroom and spills her pills into his palm. He counts them, one, two, three, four, five, tries to figure out how many she's missed. Finally, he takes two and goes to the kitchen. He turns on the tap, runs the water until it feels ice cold, same as his hands. "Here," he says to Starla. "Two quick swallows and we'll both be fine."

She looks at him with blanked out eyes, like a movie screen before the credits roll. "Swallow," he says. Her throat rolls, and rolls again. Carl shuts his eyes.

When he sees Darlene's white Toyota parked in his drive, Carl's sweet tooth, dormant for months, urges him to the house. He savours every bite of her homemade apple pies, their sugary tops perfectly bronzed. He wonders if Starla might like the recipe. Starla is a damn fine cook, when she's in the mood.

"Do you share recipes?" he asks Darlene one day, around a mouthful of pie. "Or is it secret?" Darlene smiles, pours more coffee into his cooling cup.

"Not exactly secret," she says. "But I don't share with just anyone." She smiles, touches his shoulder as she reaches to pour hot coffee into her own blue cup. "But I guess I could give it to you."

He finds Starla's battered recipe box, and digs for a blank card. He pulls one from the front. Red cherries and apples dance across the top. *Made with love,* the script says, *from the Kitchen of Starla.* The card is splattered with grease spots and chocolate smudges. He sets it aside. He pulls out another card. This one, in Starla's hand, is the beginning of a 'to do' list. *Slices for Larry's wedding dance,* it says. *Minimum of twenty. Real cream for the coffee. Tea essence? — check with Karen's mom.*

He closes the lid on the yellowed tin box, reaches for the cupboard above the fridge. When Starla's recipe box is safely stowed away, Carl brushes minute flakes of yellow from his palm.

Carl constantly rewinds the fight. He hears the car squeal as Larry lays a line of rubber on their drive.

"I don't give a damn about accessorizing that christly car," Carl had said at lunch, when Larry brought in the package and showed him the new lights. "We've got haying to do. You work on that car today and you'll be staying home tonight. Your choice."

Carl had slammed the dishwasher closed and reached for his battered cowboy hat. He sat in his truck for ten minutes, his hand beating a staccato tattoo on the steering wheel. Then he saw Larry saunter from the house, lights in hand and Starla close beside him. Larry leaned on the fender of his car as Starla slid into the driver's seat and popped the hood. Larry's golden head disappeared into the bowels of his car. Carl put his truck in gear and with infinite care, drove slowly to the field.

When he came in late from the field, Carl tried the lights himself. Turned on the key and sat bathed in baby blue. He had to admit they added a damn nice touch. Imagine taut golden skin, he thought, the indent of a bellybutton shadowed in blue light. That boy's got things to look forward to, he thought. But I'm afraid it's not gonna be tonight.

"Hi, Dad," Larry said, when he emerged from the bathroom with his hair slicked back, smelling vaguely like spice. "I'm sorry I didn't get out there today. I thought those lights would be a snap to install. Goes to show you what I know." He loped from the kitchen, reached for the keys he always left hanging on the brass rack near the back door.

"Has anyone seen my keys?" he said.

"I told you," Carl said, Larry's lime-green key ring dangling from his fingers. "If you didn't help me hay, you weren't going anywhere tonight. Pretty simple, really," he said.

"I *had* to get those lights in today," Larry said. "Come on, Dad, don't be so stubborn. I'll help you tomorrow. Work twice as hard."

"Nope," Carl said. "A deal's a deal."

"It was *your* deal, Dad," Larry replied, leaning on the counter. "Come on, give me my keys."

The movie speeds up for Carl at this point and he cannot remember what happened, how the final scene came to end with Larry squealing from the yard, the smell of burning rubber heavy in the air. Crown Royal is the only thing that stops the show. Carl realizes it takes way more than an ounce or two. Still, he's surprised to find two mickeys in his toolbox, one in the top drawer beside his screwdrivers, and another nestled beside his carefully arranged row of wrenches in the third. He takes a final sip, carries the empty bottles to the garbage barrel and tucks them beneath three oily rags.

Carl is half way dozing in the warmth of his truck. It's been months since the last quota and every farmer around is strapped for cash. The line ahead of Carl is four trucks long.

"How long do you think this is gonna take?"

"Jesus!" Carl jumps. "Must have dozed off there for a minute. Good to feel the sun."

Ken leans on the fender, fumbles for a match. Carl reaches into his coveralls for his pack of Player's. He opens the door to step outside and a mickey of Crown Royal rolls, lands in the dust near his feet.

Ken looks at the nearly empty flask. "Bastard," he grins at Carl. "You could have passed that down the line."

Carl picks up the bottle, stuffs it back under the seat. Shame sears his cheeks. He cups his hand, scratches a match with his thumbnail, and lights his cigarette. Ken leans in, puffs until he gets a light and they both draw deep.

"Next time," Carl says. "Damned inconsiderate. You got me on that."

Smoke wisps away, borne by the rising wind.

One wet morning, when Carl pulls on his right rubber boot, his toes are stopped by the round, ridged edge of the Crown Royal bottle he finds stuffed inside. The bottles seem to be multiplying, as though the goddamn things are having sex when his back is turned. He stuffs the bottle onto the top shelf of the back closet, makes sure it's covered by ball caps and woollen mitts.

He'd stopped to root out the crab grass that was taking hold on Larry's grave, ashamed that the headstone was not yet chosen, let alone placed. He'd gone back to Lakeside Memorials a time or two, but he couldn't make himself stay there, or make any kind of decision on his own.

Maybe when Starla gets a little stronger, he thought. Maybe then. She's going to, he told himself. It'll just take time.

His father's headstone was to the east of Larry, and Carl knelt beside it, rested his cold hand on the black granite, warm from the sun.

He remembered his dad's excitement when they'd announced that Starla was pregnant. The only reason I ever had kids, he had said, was so I could have a grandchild or two. They say grandparents get all the fun and none of the worry. Besides, I've been building this farm for a reason. Hard to pass it on when there's no kids. It's about damn time, is all I can say.

Starla had always been slight, fragile and, although her pregnancy was easy, birthing Larry had been hard. Watching her struggle had been hell for Carl. When years went by without another pregnancy, he'd been secretly glad.

"I'm sorry, Dad," he whispered. "I never once imagined everything would end with Larry."

When he found his way back to the truck, he fumbled for the bottle, drank and drank again. Finally, the whiskey took effect, warming and steadying his hands. He set them on the wheel and turned the key.

"I have something really important to say," Starla tells him, not noticing that he's buried in the hockey game. The players blur, the announcer's voice rising with the pace of the game. A player passes to the point, and the D-man slaps it to the net. The goalie sees the puck coming, flicks his stick and deflects it to the side. Big Number Ten grabs the rebound and slides it to the left of the goalie's thick pad. The red light flashes. Sirens blare as the goalie hangs his head.

"Just a minute," Carl says, and thinks of his hockey pool and how that stupid goddamn goalie has let Keith tie him for first and the race is really tight. He picks up the phone, dials Keith's number and listens to the first shrill ring.

"Carl," Starla says and when he sees the blankness in her eyes, Carl drops the phone.

"They're getting married," Starla says. "And Karen is pregnant. You have to convince Larry to move. He simply cannot have a family living in that Chrysler. They won't have the room."

"We'll see," Carl says. "We'll just have to see."

He runs a tub full of hot water. "A nice long soak might be just the ticket for you tonight," he says, and adds some Avon Skin-So-Soft, swirls the water with his hand. His wedding ring is loose, and Carl curls his finger to keep it from slipping into the oiled water. When he takes Starla's thin arm and helps her into the tub, he wishes she'd shake his hand away and tell him to quit treating her as if she's made of glass, but she is off in space somewhere and she doesn't say a word. Carl squeezes rivulets of water across Starla's back, the thick terry washcloth heavy in his hand. He bends to kiss the hollow above her collarbone, but then thinks of Larry, and his lips go slack.

As soon as Starla is dried and he has tucked her into bed, Carl hauls his body to the kitchen, reaches for the phone. "Is Dr. Gordon in?" he asks and is surprised to feel the measured thudding of his heart. He'd taken her to her initial appointment and listened to all that was said. The way he had figured it, if she just stayed on the meds, everything would be okay. And he'd been so sure he could handle Starla's problems all on his own.

The last time Carl drove to town, he saw the ghostly line of cars and his eyes were raked by phantom shards of shattered glass. Today, Carl sees a big expanse of light-green nothing. The grass that had browned and curled beneath the wrecks is starting to revive, pale green-yellow tendrils reaching for the sun. Two days, Carl thinks, and the goddamn place will look like a park. Larry's Chrysler is gone and so are all the other haunted wrecks that sat in rusted rows along Highway 5. Carl breathes a sigh of relief, blesses Sammy's Salvage. He wonders if the clean up is the result of some new environmental law.

A shrill ringing pulled him from a deep well of sleep and he fumbled the receiver, surprised to hear Starla's thready voice.

"Do you think it's okay?" she asked. "I know I'm better. And I want to come home."

"Yesterday," he told her, "isn't soon enough for me."

Carl fired up the Ford in a rush, almost pulled out of the yard with only a quarter tank of gas. So he made himself slow down, take things easy and slow.

He meets with the doctor before he takes Starla home. Doctor Gordon tells him that Starla has shown no signs yet, of facing the reality of Larry's death, and Carl sees defeat in his gaze. "When she starts in with her delusions about Larry living in the car, don't go along with her. State things as they are.

Carl shakes his head. "I can't. Not just yet. But I'll know when she's ready to handle things again."

The doctor looks at Carl from behind the expanse of his solid oak desk. "Going home right now is not the best option. But if she insists on checking herself out, I have no recourse." With a sigh of resignation, he flips Starla's thick blue chart closed, and picks up his business card from a shiny brass holder right beside his phone and offers it to Carl.

"I don't think I'll be needing that." Carl keeps his hands in his pockets until the doctor finally drops the card. "She'll be better off at home and I'll be spending all my time with her. Even got myself a hired hand." Carl glances up, but Doctor Gordon doesn't seem suitably impressed.

As they pass Rowan's corner, twilight intensifies the lights of town, pinpoints of yellow that blink at the edge of the sky. Starla shudders and Carl tucks the flannel throw around her shoulders, turns up the heat.

"Warm enough?" he asks.

"Perfect," Starla says. "It's nice of you to come and take me for a drive." She's languid against the leather of his pickup, warm like pull toffee, smooth to his touch. He runs his bitten fingertips through the feathers of her blue-black hair. Almost home, he thinks, almost there.

The lights at the junction of Highway 5 are landing strip bright. They etch deep lines down Starla's thin cheeks, lines that Carl has never noticed before. He eases his foot onto the brake, rolls to a stop. He checks for traffic from the east and from the west.

Suddenly, Starla gasps, throws her thin body forward. Carl sees her knuckles whiten on the blue of his dash. The cords on her neck are braided silver by the light.

"Where is it?" she says, her voice pitched high and Carl thinks of his banjo when the strings are wound too tight. Her left hand, surprisingly strong, clamps Carl's arm like a vice. "Larry's red Chrysler. Where did it go?"

Carl remembers Doctor Gordon's advice, how it's up to him to help her finally see. He opens his mouth to begin, but the unbearable truth is caught in the sudden dry dust of his throat. Instead, he takes Starla's thin hand, and rubs his thumb across her translucent skin. "They had to clean the place up," he tells her. "Some new regulations, so Sammy says."

Starla's mouth is open wide, like a guppy laid on a counter while it's five-year-old owner changes murky water in the bowl.

"When the regulations came down," Carl tells her, "Larry had to move. Him and Karen, they said to make sure to tell you goodbye."

Carl hears her start to breathe again, feels her delicate body melt into his.

"They'll drop us a line when they get settled," he says. "Might be awhile."

The Precious Pots of Mata Ortiz

MARIA QUEZADA IS SMALL FOR HER AGE, too thin, solitary in her ways. She wanders the mountainside around the dry and dusty pueblo of Mata Ortiz, searching for bits of wood to feed her family's meagre fires. Her village squats in the purple shadows of the crag-faced El Indio mountains in an area of ancient Paquime, within the fertile plateau which had been a cradle of culture ages ago. But Maria knows nothing of history, she lives her life entirely in the daily struggle of here and now.

As she walks in the twilight, Maria darts quick looks over her shoulder, as if expecting to see someone on the narrow path behind her, perhaps an ancient spirit searching for home. Curiously, she does not feel afraid. She is often drawn to the high meadows, meandering through scrub grasses, picking wildflowers, or stopping to watch a fluttering moth settle in the centre of a creamy Yucca flower. She wonders at the bravery of those little grey moths, laying their eggs in the middle of a flower so beautiful people call it the Lamp of God, the *Lampara de Dios*, but she supposes that God doesn't really mind. Perhaps He planned it that way. She dreams too much, and comes home with her shawl filled only with the pottery shards she's stumbled upon. You must remember to gather the wood, her father tells her, his lined face grim. He beats her sometimes, but only half-heartedly, as if his staff is stayed by an unseen hand.

But still, she forgets, she always forgets, to gather the precious wood.

In her small cot, cloaked by warm darkness, Maria runs her fingers over her pottery bits, and counts them like beads on a rosary. She fills them with her prayers. The moon above her is a cup, pouring streams of stars.

It is the same moon that once shone upon me as I slept, dreaming the shape of ollas, *the unique and beautiful pots fired in Mata Ortiz. The* ollas, *rubbed paper thin by my careful fingers long before the firing, remained amazingly strong. They were my canvases and I painted upon them the remnants of my dreams. Much has changed since I left the world, but here in this tiny village that time has forgotten, much remains the same.*

A rooster crows and chickens scratch for grubs in the hardpan yard. Maria is tired of sweeping and she lays her corn-husk broom aside, squats in the dappled shade. She lifts her shawl from beneath a dusty bush and unloads her precious cargo. Again and again, she rearranges the shards. A pattern begins to emerge, geometric yet delicate in design.

It is not the same pattern as I saw it years ago, but still, some shadow remains. Sometimes, I fold my hands over hers, gently. "Like this," I whisper. "Like this." Her delicate fingers begin to tingle as her body remembers the shape of a pot that I once held in my own two hands.

I did not feel the chasm that opened deep inside Mother Earth, causing her to tremble. Soundly, I slept through the rumblings as the mountain reared and straightened and tried to save herself. Great chunks of gold-flecked granite broke free, careened down the steep rock face toward my town. Still I slumbered, unaware. My beloved pots trembled and fell from the shelf, their death cries calling my wandering spirit back from the land of dreams. With my slender body, I fell upon my precious ollas, desperate to shield them. I had no time to whisper to the Blessed Virgin. No time for prayer. Thusly, I died. My spirit drifted from my body, higher and higher, until the lights of my little town became pinpricks in the multi-coloured quilt of the land. Please, I whispered. I am not yet done. Someone heard my prayer, and so I hover here, above my pottery pieces lying lost among the ruins.

The people of Mata Ortiz cross themselves as they hurry past my broken pueblo. "Artista," they whisper, "loca," as if that explains everything. Stories are told of how I bravely used my body as a shield and how I refused to run. And that I did not, in the end, save my precious pots. Or my precious self.

Maria is the only one who dares wander among those ruins. "Here," I whisper in her ear, "stop here, poke with your stick." Piece by piece, she unearths the shards, and the precious pots of Mata Ortiz are rediscovered by a small girl who cannot remember to pick only firewood, who comes home with her shawl tucked around jagged pieces of long-ago dreams.

Today is a sparkling Mexican morning. Eucalyptus leaves, hanging limp in the blessed stillness, filter sunlight onto the sand. Boys are sweeping up the blossoms blown down in last night's storm, and gather broken branches from the fine, white sand. Across the bay, the Paquime Mountains rise solid in the sun.

Barry's shoulders slice white foam as he curves like a dolphin into a dive. Then his silver head reappears, and I see the flash of pale underarm as he strokes closer to shore. He rides a wave, struggles through the breakers to the thin strip of beach where he's staked his claim with towels, a beach blanket, and two red canvas chairs. A cooler of *cerveza* is tucked under the shade of the palms.

He trowels the sand with the edge of his hand, makes a hollow for his butt, and a little pillow for his head. Then he lifts his face to the sun, his sightline on taut twenty-year-old flesh. When a bikini-clad girl leans down to lather a leg with oil, her breasts bulging above her skimpy top, his busy eyes dart like a starving bumblebee in a field of buttercups. A bee flaps its wings one hundred and sixty beats per second. Barry's eyes dart from cup to cup much faster than that. From the safety of our balcony, I watch him watching.

The crash of my pottery mug on terracotta tile makes me jump. I grab a striped beach towel, use it to staunch the spreading pool of black. After I sweep up the shattered pieces, I stare into the dustpan, as if I could read some meaning from those shards, discern a pattern there. But I see nothing, so I throw the pieces away.

"Hi." My shadow falls across Barry's tanned chest, sprinkled with wiry hairs of iron grey.

"Thought you'd never get down here." He shades his eyes. "You've already missed the best part of the day." He moves over, leaving half the blanket for me. "I made you a pillow."

I settle beside him, plump my pillow of sand and open my Danielle Steele. Before long, I feel licks of orange sun rasp my winter-white skin.

"Can you help me with this?" I hand Barry the turtle lotion. I am not sure how many endangered sea turtles had to die to produce one bottle of this creamy lotion and I was surprised when Barry decided to buy just one small bottle.

"It's supposed to be amazing stuff," he'd told me. A shadow of shame reddened his cheeks as he tucked the bottle into the complicated backpack he carries when we go downtown.

He flips the top, squeezes cool lotion across my shoulders and down the curve of my back. His fingers are efficient. There is no feathering down the length of my spine, no lingering on the inside of my thigh. The only illicit part of this act is the fact that turtle lotion is illegal almost everywhere. "Thanks." I sit up and take the lotion from his hand. "Do you want me to do you?"

"Nope," Barry replies.

The warmth of the sun soon makes me dreamy. I mean to thank him for booking us into this little piece of paradise but, instead, I drift off to sleep.

Snowflakes edged the grass in a lacy shawl, and my masses of purple petunias hung heavy-headed beneath the snow. Barry refilled his mug and gave me a peck on the cheek as he snugged up his tie. "That settles it," he said. "Snow in September, for God's sake."

He opened his briefcase, dropped three leaflets on the table. "Take a look," he said. "I've been checking out some destinations. We can celebrate twenty-five years of wedded bliss on a beach somewhere."

Cold air huffed inside as he opened the door. "I was going to surprise you," he said, "but since 9-11, travel's gotten more complicated. We'll need passports. And I think we should get Hep A shots too, just in case."

I tucked my icy feet under pink chenille. "Wow," I said, pulling my robe closer. I picked up a brochure, studied the white sand beach. After Barry left, I dream-walked to our bedroom, stood in front of our full-length mirror and stripped the robe. I tried to imagine my body, brown and lithe and tan, displayed on a sugar-white beach. And I tried to imagine why Barry was already planning our anniversary celebration. Something he has never attempted before.

In Barry's tower of steel and glass downtown, Caroline, with her ruthless efficiency, keeps our anniversary reminder in the abeyance file. The actual date is still three months away. Two weeks before December 10th, she will put a note on Barry's desk and will follow it up with a sticky the day before, just in case.

I know this because last December, I found her note in the wash. *Anniversary reminder #2,* it said. *Do you want me to pick up roses, maybe a box of Godiva's? Or did you already handle? Just trying to make sure all is well on the home front too — Caroline*

Marla and I have lunch every third Saturday in Bella's Bistro. If we break bread together for the next hundred years, my daughter and I may find some common ground. For now, she is low-fat granola and I am Crepes Suzette.

"We're already planning your anniversary party," she says. "Derrick's reserved the Shriner's Hall."

"Surprise," I say. "You don't have to do a thing. Your dad and I are going to Mexico."

Her eyes grow wide. "Mexico? Just the two of you?"

The soft jazz Bella plays over the lunch hour has changed to golden oldies, and I want to hum along. Amazingly, I still remember most of the lyrics from those long-gone 60's songs. Instead, I reach into my purse and pull out the brochure, lay it next to Marla's blunt hand. "I'm pretty sure the Shriner's will give you the deposit back."

"It's not very thoughtful of you guys," she says, folding and refolding the blue cloth napkin on her lap. "Derrick and I've been looking forward to this. I've already been working on centrepieces. I thought turkeys would be appropriate, considering the time of year." She forms her hands into a loose circle. "I started with these stubby brown candles and hot-glued maple leaves for wings and tails." Her eyes are earnest grey, magnified by round granny glasses. "The hardest part was figuring out how to attach the heads. I ended up braiding sturdy turkey necks from wire."

The image of a turkey neck is unsettling to me, and I lengthen my spine, lift my chin. On a beach, everything is on display. Marla taps the brochure with a ragged nail. "But the final result really does look like a turkey, if I say so myself. I was going to have the boys cut Kraft paper and scrunch it up so it would look like straw. We were going to make a whole bunch for the head table."

Marla is an earth mother and everything she does is crafted, baked from scratch, recycled or homemade. She refuses to have a television in the house. Barry considers the TV ban a major crime, and I know he feels sorry for Derrick, stuck without access to the NFL. What in the world do they do, he asked me, once the kids are fed and put to bed?

Maybe they talk to each other, I wanted to say.

I hope those boys don't end up being artsy-farsty faggots, is what Barry says, working on crafts with their mother all the time. Let's hope they start playing football or hockey one of these days. Although if they can't watch the games on TV, how will they ever get interested in sports?

I tell him he has nothing to worry about, although I'm no expert. Marla has been my only mothering experience and I'm still learning, one Saturday at a time.

"Derrick scanned some of your wedding pictures," Marla continues. "He's designed three different invitations. One of them is really cool."

"I'm sorry." I turn the brochure over, the beauty of Banderas Bay indecent in the face of Marla's disapproval. "But everything's booked."

She sips the last of her herbal tea. "Do you have any idea the mess you've got in your picture boxes? Really Mother, it doesn't take a lot of time to organize them. Or I could scrapbook them if you'd like."

When I told Barry how much planning Marla and Derrick had already done for our anniversary, he said he'd be damned if he'd sit in a stuffy hall and sip lukewarm tea while our old aunts and uncles and a few friends who couldn't come up with credible excuses for their absences gorged themselves on sandwiches and cake and speculated about how we've managed to stay together all these years. And the last thing we need, he'd said, is a bunch of silver trays and picture frames. If you really want silver, he told me, I'll buy you some on the beach in Mexico.

Bella's is busy, the low hum of conversation advancing and receding in waves, like the ones in the brochure of Banderas

Bay. "Can I get more hot water?" I ask and the waitress quickly refills my little blue teapot. I love strong coffee, but if I order espresso, Marla looks at me like I've just committed a crime. Bad for the blood pressure is what she says. So I sip my green tea, and watch as Marla dissects her muffin.

"They've only got four berries in a muffin this size?" she asks, eyeing the crumbs incredulously. "I should have brought my own. And these things are full of cholesterol and sugar, too."

I'd like to drop a pound or two before I expose my midriff on a busy beach and I think of asking Marla for a few of her low-fat, high fibre recipes. Marla is far too thin and bluish-pale. She swears by her diet of bran and high-fibre foods, by raw veggies and broiled chicken breasts. You should try it, she's told me. It'll add years to your life.

"Our passports came yesterday," I say.

A line deepens between Marla's brows. I am not sure if her disapproval stems from the distinct lack of berries in her blueberry bran or from our anniversary plans.

"So," she says, pinching bran crumbs into a ball, "you're really going."

"Yes," I say. "We are."

Sometimes I stay close to my own blue mountains, close to Paquime, and sometimes, when I'm feeling restless, I venture further afield. Tonight, I am drawn to the lights of Banderas Bay, to the bustle of busy lives that permeates the polluted air. I can see clearly as two people alight from the taxi. The man is excited, his hands flying quickly like the amazing scarlet macaw birds that deserted our pueblos long ago. His busy eyes dart around the cobbled drive, into the leafy lobby, resting for a moment on the cleavage of a young woman who steps past him and disappears into the elevator. The woman walks slowly around the cab, waits as the driver unloads a large grey suitcase. She smiles as she pulls the suitcase up the ramp and into the lobby. The man's eyes are still fixed on the elevator doors when she touches his arm and says something I cannot hear. Finally, he turns, takes the suitcase from her hand and parks it near the front desk. He returns to the cab, helps unload two more suitcases and a grocery bag full of freshly baked bread and cubes of various cheeses, bottles of Chilean wine. She takes the bag from his hand, straightens the French bread and the bottles of wine.

"Look at the sky," the man says. "Full of stars. Just like at home."

When she starts to say she thinks the sky looks different here and maybe it's because the stars shine from different angles in the Mexican sky, he has already turned away to pick up a smaller suitcase. My heart aches for the woman and I do not yet know why.

Barry booked this place sight unseen. I was hoping for the Hilton, but here we are, ensconced in a second-rate Mexican hotel, with mildew multiplying in the shower and along the wall behind the toilet. The only saving grace is the panoramic view of Bandaras Bay, and the sunsets that drop in the blink of an eye.

"Come out here, quick," Barry calls me from our postage stamp balcony. "Sun's about to set." He puts his arm around my waist, pulls me close. His fingers linger on the roll of flesh that has lodged itself above my waistband, pinches it as if measuring the marble on a prize beef. I squirm away, raise my glass.

"Here's to us," I say. "Imagine. After all these years."

When we got married, we dreamed of Mexico. The honeymoon we could *afford* was two nights at the Bessborough, special weekend rate.

A double-decker boat, packed with booze-cruise tourists, chugs past as the orange sun drops. Mexican blue and lime-green fireworks burst from her deck and we hear the muffled *boom, boom, boom.* Barry clinks his glass against mine, touches it to his full, red lips.

"Great sunset."

Prairie sunsets paint the sky glorious shades of red and orange and pink and, mostly, we take them for granted. Rarely do we comment on their breathtaking beauty or stop to admire. But, here, the downtown plaza is full of tourists every night, cameras poised, and everyone raves about the fabulous Mexican sunsets. Perhaps, I think, we should watch from the plaza some night. Sometimes things look different if you change your point of view.

Barry is talking to a blonde in a bikini. He picks up her folding chair and plants it in the sand near the edge of our blanket. She reaches into a striped beach bag, holds out a Corona and he motions for another. He uses one beer to lever open the other. Barry's been opening beer that way for years. In Saskatchewan, mastering this technique is a rite of male passage. Really, it's no big deal. But the woman is looking at him as if he's just performed a bona fide miracle.

She beckons another bikini over, gets Barry to crack another beer. She touches his shoulder, slides a slim brown hand down his forearm. Then she throws back her long hair and takes a thirsty drink. When she offers the bottle to Barry, he smiles, puts the bottle to his lips.

My husband is ordinary looking, average height, average build. He's still got most of his hair and it's slowly going grey, but not in that glowing silver way that makes you stop and take a second look. But he's interested in everyone and he strikes up conversations with strangers all the time. Maybe those babes on the beach can feel his puppy-dog vibes.

Barry and the blonde sit down on our beach blanket. She reclines, tugs at her halter top so her breasts spill out even more. Barry leans across her golden body, finds a water bottle in our cooler and takes a long, thirsty pull.

A peddler squats beside them, a suitcase glinting silver balanced on his knees. Barry picks up something, puts it back. Points. The peddler picks out a wide bracelet from the jumble of silver, begins to work at it with a greyed cloth. Sweat breaks on my forehead and beads between my breasts. I wonder if he's buying the bracelet for me.

When I can't stand to watch for one more minute, I flee to the shower. The ever-expanding amoebic shadow behind the tile seems darker today. Black mould has leeched through the grout, tracing a jagged line from the showerhead to the edge of the chipped pink tub. When I'm done showering, I can smell mould, on my skin and in my hair. Bleach, I think, there must be bleach here somewhere. I yank the vanity door open, move three rolls of toilet paper and a box of Tide. I touch a pile of sodden magazines and the January *Penthouse* disintegrates in my hands.

I lean on the vanity, and swipe the crackled mirror. My body is insubstantial in the billowing steam, its imperfections blurred, airbrushed like the woman in the centrefold. Quickly, I close the warped little door, and wrap myself in a thirsty blue towel.

Gone to the market, I write on a scorecard torn from an unused bridge pad. *Getting veggies for supper and some bleach for the bathroom. It's a disaster in there. Back soon. Luv Charlene.*

I grab my purse, make sure I have enough money for the veggies and perhaps a piece of pork tenderloin for the barbeque. I've seen rib-racked cows meandering barren pastures on the outskirts, so I cannot bear to buy the beef. Imagine, I think. Me. Shopping alone in a foreign city that's creeping up on three hundred thousand. Marla would most certainly disapprove.

Barry spends at least six hours of every day scanning the beach from behind the pages of his book. In an entire week, he's only progressed as far as page thirty-seven of John Grisham's *Painted House*. He's complained that he's having trouble getting into the story. I didn't let myself tell him it was because of his wandering eyes. I will likely return before he even notices I'm gone, but I leave the note, just in case.

As I step outside, I see the blue and green stripes on the back of the bus disappear in a haze of grey. Diesel duels with the sweet smell of bougainvillea. Damn, I think. It will be twenty minutes, give or take a few, until the next bus comes along. I find a patch of shade, examine the gravelled gum stuck to the sole of my sandal. With a dusty twig, I pry it free and toss it into the pile of broken glass and tiles behind me in the ditch. Mexicans create artworks from stones and bits of tile and glass. Mosaics are everywhere. Maybe I can learn this, I think, and make beauty from the broken. I work my way down the steep slope, unearth three small pottery shards and tuck them in my bag.

I watch as Maria Quezada gathers the bits of pottery, folds them into her shawl. Sometimes, she lays them on the sun-soaked ground, arranges and rearranges the pieces until a pleasing pattern appears. She imagines the completed pots, longs to make some of her own. She begins to experiment with the hillside clay, mixes it with fine volcanic ash until the consistency feels right in her hands. When she is ready, she bows her head as if in prayer, breathes deeply and begins. My heart aches when I think of my unfinished life, how I held the secret of my perfect pots in my solitary hands.

The pottery I see in the market is practical, brightly coloured, but it does not have the delicacy and strength of my pots. If Maria had been my apprentice, I would have shown her my secrets, whispered the recipes and ratios of my unique glazes in her ear. Sometimes, with great effort, much like an old woman levering herself down to a low-slung chair, I am able to enter the physical world as I knew it, and then I fold my hands over Maria's, guide so gently even she cannot feel my touch. When we form a pot pleasing to her eye, she sets it aside to dry in the merciless sun. She rises, snakes her arms above her head and begins dancing to music only she can hear. Artista, the town folk say, as if that explains everything.

In the sparse shade dappling the bus stop, I open my handbag and recount my pesos. A few tourists have discovered this cheap way of getting around, but the majority of people riding the buses are dark-eyed, dark-haired Mexicans, heading to ill-paid jobs at the big hotels and restaurants in town. I feel guilty if I delay them, even for the minute it takes the driver to count out my change. The little roadside shrine to the Blessed Virgin is filled with fresh flowers today, pink bougainvillea, creamy calla lilies, and huge purple blossoms I don't recognize. Pesos are piled high at the Blessed Mother's feet. Each day, the money columns grow. Mora, our doorman, tells me that once a week, someone from the church comes to collect the pesos. The money is used for the poor. Who decides, I wondered, in this country of abject poverty, who is truly poor? As I add to the pile of pesos close to Mary's small feet, I quickly make the sign of the cross.

The bus gears down, careens around the curve, and jolts to a sudden stop and an elderly couple step from the shadows. The man leans on an ornate cane with a silver head, but still, he falters on the uneven ground. His wife takes his elbow, helps him with that first, long step up and into the bus where he counts out the pesos, four for him, four for her. He recounts, finally drops his coins in the patient brown hand. His wife takes his arm again, helps him down the narrow aisle. I wonder if someday, that will be Barry and me.

I do a quick scan of the battered bus and spot a single seat beside a woman rocking a chubby child. When I hesitate, she slides over to make room for me. "*Hola*," I say. I take a stick of Juicy Fruit from my purse, offer it to the child. He looks at his mother and, when she nods, he takes the gum from my hand.

"*Gracias*," he whispers and he buries his dark head in his mother's breast.

The mother's ponytail gleams black, like her eyes. She's slender and, when she smiles, her teeth flash white. But it's her smooth brown skin I covet. I look at my sun-spotted hands, feel the shrivel of my prairie-dry skin.

Ten minutes later, we make an impossible corner and pull into a space only six inches longer than the bus. I marvel at the skill of the driver, threading his way through swerving taxis and battered trucks piled dangerously high with produce to safely guide us to the curb. He smiles and offers his hand as I step into the narrow street. *Gracias*, I say. I turn left at the corner, and walk the cobbled street seeking patches of shade. I have given up on becoming lustrous brown and my only quest now is to evade a burn. I've seen some nasty ones on the beach, even heard Barry offer to spread my expensive aloe vera lotion across some skinny girl's sunburnt belly.

A wolf whistle rips. I look up, see a man smile from the balustrade of a building where workmen are stacking armloads of brick. He cups his hands around his red mouth.

"*Señorita* comes alone?"

I shake my head, no, and he shrugs, goes back to his pile of bricks. His palette knife flashes and he flips a dollop of cement onto the centre of a brick.

Señorita, I think. Me?

When Barry and I arrived in Puerto Vallarta, we took a taxi from the airport straight to the gigantic new Wal-Mart on the edge of town. While I was trying to decide between blue beach chairs or red, a dark-eyed man caught my eye. His shirt was crisp white, with Wal-Mart stitched in red above the breast pocket.

"*Señora*," he said. "Welcome to us. Are you married?" I looked around for Barry but he was nowhere to be seen. "I have a big husband," I lied.

"*Lo siento mucho*," he said, shaking his head as he turned away. I knew he was disappointed, somehow, and, strangely, so was I. You'd never be asked a question like that in the Wal-Mart store in Saskatoon. But I had not been in Mexico long enough to know what is strange and what is not.

The bricklayer above turns to me again, his brown eyes moving slowly up and down my body. I flush, run my fingers down my sides and press my hands to my thighs.

When Marla was a little girl, I bought her a magic paint pad. She would dip her brush into clear water, brush the crisp paper over and over, and gradually, a figure would appear. I pose as the man on the rooftop paints me with his eyes. I feel the graze of his thick lashes as I begin to materialize, fingertips, forearm, elbow, shoulder, breast. When he turns again to his pile of bricks, I take a deep breath, wave my firm, pink arm, and walk away on muscled legs.

Salsa music calls from the cool white façade of the Costa Del Sol. The foyer is lush with foliage, shadowed and cool. I sit at a wrought iron table in the flowered courtyard. Its surface is mosaic tile and I feather my fingertips across the pieces, studying the pattern with touch. A frosted margarita in a blue, bubbled glass appears at my elbow. When I open my purse, the waitress motions, no, indicates a man sitting in shade so deep I can hardly see him.

As I savour the first tart sip, he walks to my table. "*Hola*," he says, "my name is Julio." He offers his hand. He's slim and beautiful, his hair neatly combed, the creases in his white trousers razor sharp.

"Charlene," I say. "*Gracias* for the margarita." I have already braced myself for the timeshare pitch I am sure will follow.

Julio slides into the chair opposite me. "Happy on you," he says. He lines up the salt and pepper, looks into my eyes. "*Señorita* is alone?"

"Sort of," I say. Julio's brown face breaks into a smile. "Okey-dokey," he says, "*Por favor*. We can dance?" And he leads me down wide marble steps and through a haze of greenery to the centre courtyard. Pots billowing bright pink flowers line the steps of the bandstand, their scent spun sugar floating in the air. Julio bows, folds my papery fingers into his warm, brown hand. As the music dips and swells, he places his palm against the small of my back, guides me across the gleaming marble. At first I am hesitant, stumbling, but soon the music penetrates my bones. The intricate steps make perfect sense, silhouettes moving in the window of my mind. I drift away from Julio, dip and twist to the sensual sounds. When I falter, it seems as if a soft voice whispers in my ear.

Like this, see? Like this. The pattern is already there. The body will remember.

I snake my arms above my head, salsa back to Julio's arms.

The final firing is done. When the pots have completely cooled, Maria chooses one, holds it in her hands like a mother holds a newborn child. With delicate fingertips, she checks for perfection. They are amazingly thin, yet incredibly strong. Some are tinted burnt umber and raw sienna, but burnished copper is her favourite colour, and the hardest to perfect. When she finds a flawed pot, she breaks it, the pieces hazed by the sheen of her tears.

I want to reach out, wipe her face, but I dare not, so I watch as she ties the broken ones in a bundle and tucks them away, as I once did. Like me, she believes that the broken ones are precious too.

Maria's father no longer beats her. Every week, he carries her perfect pots to market, wrapped in discarded newspapers carefully smoothed. Come, he cajoles the passing crowds, see the delicate beauty my Maria has wrought. The precious pots of Mata Ortiz. When market is over, he gathers the remaining pieces, walks home, his fingers jingling a pocketful of coins.

The music stops and Julio folds my hand under his arm, leads me to the edge of the floor. "Mucho happy feet, *señorita*."

We lean in dappled shade, cool ourselves with icy margaritas. The bass player begins to work his way through the courtyard, offers his open guitar case. A few people toss pesos as he passes. When the band begins to pack their drums and brass, I dig in my purse and tip the trombone player five American dollars.

"One more song," I say. "*Por favor*."

As the music starts again, I move into Julio's sinewed arms and follow his lead as if we've been partners for years. We float on soft waves of music, languid and serene. When the final note wavers and fades, he guides me back to our table, his hand warm on my spine. I notice sweat on his brow so I touch a blue napkin to his forehead.

"*Cerveza* for my friend," I say, and the waitress brings two Pacifico in a tin bucket full of half-melted ice.

"*Gracias*." He takes a long thirsty pull on the beer. "*Gracias, señorita*."

"It's nothing." I touch his hand, think of Barry, rubbing turtle lotion across a stranger's back, aloe vera on a sunburned belly. I wonder what the Mexican sun has done to him, to me.

Julio stands, places his open palms on the cool tile of the table. "*Gracias* for the dancing. Step by careful on your way."

A sip of cold beer clears the sudden thickening of my throat. Julio is leaving and I am surprised at how much I want him to stay.

"Dollars for Julio? American, please."

The sudden freeze of the icy beer numbs my brain. For a moment, I don't understand.

"Two hours," Julio explains. "Mucho dancing."

I open my purse, fumble for the twenty I know I have. Julio plucks the bill from my fingers, kisses my palm.

"*Gracias*," he says. "*Muchas gracias.*" And he moves like water across the polished floor.

My face is hot, and I'm breathing dust. I push the beer aside, order a margarita.

"*Grande,*" I tell the waitress. "*Grande, por favor.*" When it arrives, I drink half of it in one long gulp, push on my temples to contain the sudden stab of pain.

A bleach-bottle blonde, her hair pasted in lacquered curls, slides from a barstool. "Do you mind?" she asks. She pulls out a chair, offers me a Camel from her pack. Her face is leather, her upper lip grooved from being wrapped around too many cigarettes.

"Surprised you, huh?" She leans into the glow of her match, sucking greedily on her cigarette.

A red tide rises on my cheeks.

"Don't let it get to you," she says. "At least he's got standards. Doesn't dance with just anyone, you know."

I run my fingers up and down the sweaty stem of my margarita glass, pick up a napkin and sop the pool of water from its base. "I feel like a fool."

"So big deal," she says. "It cost you a buck or two. I think you got your money's worth. Maybe a little more." An ebony bird with yellow-tipped wings swoops through the foliage, flutters away.

"Just look around." She sucks the cigarette. "No shortage of beautiful *señoritas* here." She blows a smoke ring, and puffs a smaller ring that hovers inside. "So if I were you, I'd peel my lip off the table and be grateful for the ride."

She offers her hand. "Sue," she says. "Originally from Anchorage, Alaska. A town full of miners with pocketsful of money and no place to go. It was gambling or grub. And we served a mean T-bone at Angie's, I gotta say." She reaches for the ashtray, oblivious to the unsettling rattle of her smoke-thickened throat. "Took my stash of tips and came down here. The last ten years, I've lived like a queen."

Sue pulls a Pacifico from the bucket, squeezes some lime. "I hear prices have gone through the roof back home. Probably couldn't afford to go back." She throws back her chin, drains her beer. "Not that I want to."

I sip my margarita, savour its tartness.

"Julio used to dance with me," she says, tapping another cigarette against her pack. "But not anymore." Her eyes droop at the corners, is if dragged down by the weight of unshed tears. "So dance while you can. Because one of these goddamn days, you'll just disappear." She snaps her fingers, the staccato sound rapping across the tiles. "Pouf. Just like that."

"I know what you mean," I say. I think of Barry's big Christmas party, hosted by his firm in the Legion Hall downtown. A catered supper fit for a king and, always, a real live band, which is a treat these days.

Abeyance file Caroline loves to dance. I hope you don't mind, she'll say, if I borrow your husband for a while. The young guys just don't have the moves. So after our first obligatory dance, I'll sit and watch as my husband twirls a succession of pretty young women across the waxy floor. But I know that sooner or later, he'll get tired of catching fumbles and he'll come back to me and we'll cut into a quick jive or slip into the rhythm of an old time waltz. All eyes will be upon us as we float across the floor. When it comes to dancing, Barry and I are a perfect match.

I touch her hand. "Trust me, I know." I order another margarita and two Pacifico for my new friend.

Two men in cut-off jeans and startlingly white shirts amble in, and sit down at the table next to ours. What product could they possibly be using to get those shirts so white? Lye soap maybe? Do they still make it here? I shake my head, dismayed. Today, I have navigated the confusing streets, struck up a conversation with a rough-looking woman who might even be a hooker for all I know, found my way to a downtown bar, and what am I doing? Thinking of effective laundry products. I need help. Really, I do.

The tallest man, with ocean-blue eyes and extremely short shorts, leans over, taps my shoulder. "Do you have the time?" he says, flipping the blond lock that has fallen across his smooth forehead. "I was wondering if it's Happy Hour yet."

"It's Happy Hour all the time around here." Sue blows another double smoke ring before she stubs her cigarette. She rises, saunters over to the black baby grande. She pulls the stool closer, flexes her fingers. Suddenly, "North to Alaska", sounding strangely out of place in Mexico, floods the room. She bangs out two more honky-tonk tunes, finishes with a flourish and a bow to the crowd.

"I've still got a little get-up-and-go," she says as she rejoins me and pulls another Pacifico from the pail. "On the days it hasn't got up and went." She rasps a smoke-filled laugh.

"That was great," one of the men at the adjacent table says. "Just great. Do you know any nice, slow waltzes? Maybe your friend and I could dance."

"Maybe you could kiss my ass." Sue plunks down an empty Pacifico, turns to me. "Do you see any flaws? Something I could repair?" She rakes her blue-knuckled hands through her hair. "I might as well be a piece of the friggin' furniture. Come on, let's walk."

Sue and I wander aimlessly, stopping to gaze in the dusty windows of little shops that line the narrow streets. Come inside, the shopkeepers say, more to see. Good prices today, better than Wal-Mart, almost free. But we shake our heads, sauntering slowly in the moisture-laden air. I love the feel of it on my skin, the fact that my wrinkles have almost disappeared. The magic of Mexico, I wonder?

Baubles in the window of a small corner shop catch my eye and I duck inside. A small brown woman waits patiently on a stool as I try first one necklace, then another. A silver chain with an amber pendant catches my eye. I try it on, then lay it aside. "Special buy for you," she says and she begins to wrap it carefully in crumpled paper that looks as if it's been ironed and reused. "Only two hundred pesos today."

I begin to shake my head, no, and then I see my reflection in her sad brown eyes. "Yes," I say. "Two hundred is fine." In the dimness of the shop, I count out my pesos. The little woman closes her eyes, makes the sign of the cross and her paper lips move as if in silent prayer. I am sure she has just made her first sale of the day and I want to cry.

Sue is leaning in the doorway. "Time to go," she says. "You've done your share for the local economy. Can't support them all. Come on, let's walk."

Drawn by the blare of brass, we come to a plaza, where dancers pick their way across uneven ground. A pigeon lands on the grass near my feet, pecks at a crumb. He looks at me with unblinking eyes as I fasten the silver necklace on not yet fully tanned skin and then slowly raise my arms.

Like this, I whisper and I wonder if she can hear. Like this. See?
The pattern is already there. I smile when she throws back her
head, the sway of her hips crocheting an edge of sensual salsa
around the crowd.

"*Que pasa?*" Sue grabs me by the arm. "Have you lost your
mind?" She pulls me from the crowd, muttering to herself.
"Looks like that bastard Julio really started something with
this one."

Maria Quezada mixes volcanic ash and clay, forms a flat tortilla
base. She rubs a sausage coil of clay, drops it onto the base.
She shapes the pot with her delicate hands until she's satisfied
with the symmetry of its shape, then sets it aside to dry.

She searches the steep mountain trails for firewood, but always,
she dreams of pots. I guide her footsteps to the bones of a deer,
bleached by the sun and she tucks them into her shawl. In the
dusky light of her adobe, she lifts a fragile pot from the shelf,
sands it with the sun-smoothed bone.
    Her paintbrush is the tip of her heavy black braid. She
brushes the dye carefully, paints the pots again and again until
the colours are deep and true. Her hand is patient, her touch
light and sure. Her fire is fuelled with sticks and heaps of dried
cow dung. She forgets to cook, uses the fire only for her pots. As
the glowing embers lose their heat and her pottery strengthens
and cools, Maria rises, dances a sensual salsa to music only she
can hear.

Sue pulls me along the boardwalk. Artists are everywhere. Sculptors have carved mounds of hardened sand, revealing longhaired mermaids with pyramid breasts, pirate ships in full sail, crying Madonnas with roses at their feet. They stand beside their creations, tip pots nearby. Little cardboard signs lean against old tin cans. *Tipas, por favor. Tips, please.* I stop to marvel, to toss a peso in each of the cans.

Painters hawk watercolours of pastel sunsets and crumbling arches inhabited by scrawny black cats. There are rows and rows of paintings, and rows and rows of browsers. Come on, I think. Get off your wallets, buy a thing or two.

Acrobats clad in baggy trousers and brightly coloured, tight-fitting shirts twist and twirl, and toss a beautiful sequined girl high into the air. The lights flashing on the sequins are little bursts of fireworks. The acrobats are quick and sure and, unfailingly, they catch the flying girl.

Little ill-fed mongrels, smirking chihuahuas and poodles yap incessantly, weave in and out of the milling crowd. Babies are crying and fireworks pop. The street is choked with people, young, old, and in-between. Some barely move as they drink in the sights and the sounds, and others hurry along, heads down, as if they are on an important mission and they are about to fail.

"Come." At the breakwater, Sue and I watch the sinking of the round, red sun. A sudden blaze of green slips beneath the horizon and the crowd claps and cheers. I check my watch, amazed that I've entirely lost track of time. "It's been great," I tell her. "And thanks. Thanks for everything."

"My pleasure." Dusk throws deep shadows on the lines of Sue's weathered face.

"Gotta go," I say, touching her warm arm. "My husband might be getting worried."

"If he ain't," she says, "you might wonder why. Goddamn fool, letting you wander down here alone."

"But *you* do."

And suddenly I feel thick lashes brush my body softly, again and again. I thrust my right hip forward, raise my arm to hail a yellow cab. My colours deepen, become vibrant and strong. As I bend to the cab, I offer a glimpse of cleavage, the silk of my inner thigh.

"Yeah, but you ain't invisible yet." Sue coughs, takes another drag on her glowing cigarette.

"Laguna Del Mar," I say and wave to Sue as the cabbie pulls away, aiming his little yellow car south. Bars and hotels whiz by in a blur of white light. He's taking the curves on the low side, like an Indy driver. I lean forward, tap his shoulder.

"*Por favor,*" I say. "*Non de prisa.*" I think I'm telling him there's no hurry, but I am not entirely sure. Pinpricks of while light sparkle like crystals in a necklace strung around Banderas Bay. Moisture rolls in the open windows, smooths the lines etched on my prairie face. When we pull into the cobblestone drive of our little hotel, Mora hurries from the marble foyer.

"Did you have a good day, *señora?*" he asks as he opens my door. "Packages?" Traffic zooms by on the highway, horns are honking. A bus pulls into the bus stop across the road, snorting diesel and clanking gears. He leans closer, cups his ear, his warm breath caressing the curve of my cheek. "No packages," I tell him. "And yes. I had a very good day."

My fingers graze the shards of pottery tucked in my bag. I count them, once, twice, three times. Like rosary beads. The moon above me is a cup, pouring streams of stars. "Anybody home?" I ask. Candles flicker in the mirrors of our tiny suite, and Jimmy Buffet sings softly.

"I was starting to worry." Barry turns from the view, takes a tall glass from the freezer. He kisses me, hands me the frosted glass. On the coffee table, I see a small package, topped by a silver bow.

"Good thing I put in lots of vodka or this damn drink would be frozen solid by now."

I take one small sip of my icy chi-chi, its flavour heavy and far too sweet after the pucker of a margarita. "Thank you."

Barry drapes his arm across my back, pulls me close. He is shorter than Julio and my head doesn't fit quite so snugly into the curve of his shoulder.

"Come on," he says. "The fireworks are about to start."

"I know." I hand him my sweat-slicked glass, step out of my shoes. I snake my hands above my head, swivel my luscious hips. When I close my eyes, Jimmy Buffet fades and sensual salsa music fills my head.

Like this, a soft voice whispers in my ear. *Like this. The pattern is already there.*

Wonder dawns in her husband's eyes. He hesitates before asking permission to join her solitary dance. Yes, you may, she finally says.

I rise higher, the white lights of Banderas Bay receding from my view. Higher and wider, until once again, my eyes rest on the ruins of my beloved Mata Ortiz. Dear little Maria squats beside a dying fire, contentedly polishing a perfect olla *with a curved antler. Her hands are swift and sure. Their delicate bones have memorized my secrets, the patterns of my perfect pots.*

A surge of pure white joy fills my chest, lifts me higher still. The moon below me is a cup, pouring streams of stars.

HAM AND SWISS ON RYE

THERE IS NO GOOD MOMENT TO TELL your wife that you've met someone, so I chose Friday, June twenty-first. A time when the earth is perfectly balanced on its axis and everything is poised for change. I'm sure Sadie will cry a bit, but if she's true to form, there'll be no big scene. Quiet and questions is more Sadie's way. She'll want to know the reason; she always does. It's not enough for her to have learned from her mother that the garden should be planted by the phases of the moon, melons and vines when the moon is waning, potatoes and tomatoes when the waxing begins. She wants to know the logic behind every little thing.

She'll grill me until I tell her that my new lover is thin and beautiful, the mother of two sturdy little boys. That's the kind of detail that will cut Sadie to the bone. I don't look forward to hurting her like that. It's nothing I ever planned to do.

I've tried to imagine Sadie's reaction a million times. I'll feel better if she rails at me with curses and screams. Can you feel her hip bones when you're lying on her, Sadie might demand, her voice pitched so low I'll have to lean in to hear. I know it will kill her to hear that the woman I'm leaving her for is not some innocent young thing with stars in her eyes, but a mother, and a diligent one at that.

Does she have stretch marks from birthing those boys? Have you touched that silvered skin with your fingers? With your forked goddamned tongue? And why, she'll no doubt demand, why, David why? When she calls me David I know we've got big trouble. And believe me, right now, we truly do. So how will I answer her? I am not even sure of the reasons myself. I feel off balance, like a domino that has fallen sideways when all of the others have fallen straight ahead. I am stunned that this has happened to me. To Sadie. To our predictable yet not unlovely lives.

There's no working up to it because I'm pretty sure Sadie doesn't have a clue. I thought that after we'd barbequed the burgers and drank our customary two glasses of red, I'd just out with it. I'd tell her how I'd met Adrienne while waiting in line for a foot-long ham and Swiss, on the long weekend in May, while Sadie was planting an extra row of beans.

With just the two of us, one row of heavy bush Harmon's is more than enough. But Sadie's got this farmer mentality that won't let her ignore a spot of freshly turned earth, so she picked up the rake and began to smooth the black soil. "Why don't you run to Subway," she'd said, "get us a foot-long? When I'm done here, I'll stir up some lemonade. Lunch on the deck."

With those simple words, Sadie set in motion the entire chain of events.

"Sounds good to me." I'd checked the hip pocket of my jeans to make sure I had my keys.

The line-up in the main street Subway was long, but the woman in front of me was so breathtakingly beautiful I didn't mind the wait. Two small boys shoved and poked and whined, twining themselves around her long, shapely legs. Her black hair gleamed in the unnatural fluorescent light. One of the boys suddenly became quiet, and I felt his measured gaze, the weighing in those dark brown eyes. I reached into my pocket, pulled out a dollar bill. I keep two American dollars in my billfold at all times so I'll have the basics for my only party trick, although I have to admit, parties in my life right now are few and far between. Slowly I folded it, folded it and folded it again, seemingly intent on my task, but really, all the while, watching him watch.

"Ta-*da*," I said and held up an origami ring. He watched, unblinking, as I slipped the paper ring onto the little finger of my left hand. I held my hand level so he could see the crest on the ring, Ben Franklin's face.

"Cool," he said. I thanked him and told him making paper rings wasn't very hard; he could learn how to do it himself some day.

"I got no dollarses," he said and for a quick moment, a cloud obscured those shining eyes. "But guess what? It's a special day and Mom's buying us a picnic, to take to the park."

"That's nice," I told him. "I'm buying lunch to take home to my house."

His wide eyes appraised me, took in my short blond hair, the stubble on my chin, the faded red plaid of my Saturday shirt.

"You can come with us," he said. "If you put your hand on the blue palm tree, you can make it rain. Water sprays out everywhere."

The woman turned and ruffled his hair. "It's family day," she told him. "That's you and me and Jacob now."

She flashed me a smile, as apology for her son. "He talks to everyone these days," she said. "Especially tall blond men."

"My name's Dave," I told her and I offered my hand. "And if I didn't have work waiting at home, I just might take a lesson in making palm trees rain. Sounds intriguing."

"Adrienne," she said, her thin, cool hand in mine for only a moment.

"Foot-long with meatballs, and a smoked turkey." The kid behind the counter slipped the sandwiches into a bag, which he dropped onto the counter, before wiping his hands on the front of his apron.

"That's us," she said, and dropped my hand. She fumbled for the correct change, handed it to the kid, and hustled her boys outside.

"Sir? Your order?"

"Oh," I said. "I'll have the ham and Swiss on rye." I was eyeing up the Buffalo Chicken but Sadie would no doubt have a fit if I decided to bring something different home, especially a red-hot choice like that.

"Right sir, the usual."

"Yeah," I replied, digging for my wallet. I don't need to wait for the total, I already know what it is.

I decided to wait until Sadie and I had cleared the table and straightened up the deck, maybe even until we went inside. I didn't really want an audience and, out on the deck, there's always George. We are not the kind of neighbours who spend our evenings together, but we're amicable, George and I, often talking over the fence. I don't think he'd come to my retirement dinner, but I'm pretty sure he'd show up at my funeral. At least I hope he would.

Sadie is a beautiful woman, ripe and lush, like a pear. Childbearing hips, my father whispered the first time he met her, but it hasn't turned out that way for Sadie and me. As she brought the crystal glass to her full red lips and sipped the last of her wine, I picked up the Mouton Cadet and reached across to pour the final inch.

When Sadie spoke, I noticed, for the first time in a long time, the sweet rasp of her husky voice.

"We've got a party to go to," she said. "Con and Wendy's. Tomorrow at six."

"A party?" I'd been thinking of how long it would take me to pack, what things I might take, and what would have to stay. When you've been married as long as Sadie and me, your things meld together, so that you're not really sure what's yours and what's hers, and it seems a lot of the stuff actually belongs to the house itself.

I was hoping Sadie would let me take the big leather recliner, with its side pockets full of yesterday's newspapers and an occasional unbelievable golf scorecard that I'd been planning to plasticize and stick on the fridge so I'd have some proof for George.

Whenever I see a thin trail of smoke rising from the deck next door, I know George is about to amble over, strike up a conversation and ask about my latest game of golf. He listens perfunctorily before he launches into an epic replay of his own. It took me a while to figure out he's not too interested in how *I'm* playing. So far, George's game has been about three strokes better than mine, but I'm nipping at his heels and he knows it.

One of these days, he's going to get some news he probably isn't ready to hear. And not my stellar golf score either. Maybe

I'll let loose and tell George how my life has split into two perfect halves and how I have no idea what I should do.

George and I lean against our mutual fence, tell each other what club we used when approaching the pond on 9, how we hacked our way up 17 — that straight and easy fairway that somehow causes us both an incredible amount of grief. Our wives aren't interested in the retelling, so we pick each other's brains, try to figure out a way to beat that damn course we both know so well. We spend untold hours at the club, playing or practicing, and as long as I don't expect her to take up the game, Sadie doesn't even notice that I'm gone.

When I decided to leave Sadie, I didn't stop to think that I'd be leaving George too. I love this place and I love the peaceful evenings out in my yard. I can't imagine not ever talking to George again. Can't even really imagine not seeing Sadie every single day. Shopping on Saturdays. Sunday at the club. All the homely unremarkable things I've taken for granted. And sometimes, despised.

Two blue puffs of smoke rise above the fence that separates our yards. A train wails and a sprinkler skitters in the dusk.

"Can we get out of it?" I ask.

Sadie tells me that the party is a surprise for Wendy's fortieth birthday and that there's no way she can phone Con with our regrets. Besides, she's offered to bring two flats of her famous homemade buns.

So I decide not to tell her. At least not tonight.

Later, when she rolls over in sleep and folds her arm around my slightly thickened middle, I stiffen for a moment, thinking of Adrienne and her two little boys. I wonder if being a father is instinctive or if it's something you can learn. I move away from Sadie, my eyes wide in the blackness of our room. A cloud dissolves and blue moonlight paints faint new lines on Sadie's sleeping face. Surprised by a sudden urge to smooth her hair, I quickly turn my back. When she reaches out in slumber and begins the gentle stroking she's always done, I can't help but relax. Her fingers are footprints, dancing down my spine.

There must have been a reason I ran into Adrienne, some cosmic plan, because I couldn't get the chance encounter out of my mind. And I didn't really go looking for her and the boys, not consciously at least. I just widened my biking circle until it encompassed all three of the spray pools in our wanna-be-a-city town.

The first time I found them, I leaned my bike against a massive boulevard elm, watching as she showed them how to take half-full pails of water to the sandbox, and wet the fine sand so they could mold it into castles with turrets and bridges. As I rolled away on whisper-quiet wheels, I heard their high-pitched laughter.

Tyler spotted me one day. I was surprised the little bugger remembered me, from that one time in the Subway. Smart kid, I thought. And here I am, not smart enough to stay deep in the protective cover of the poplar shade.

"Hey," he hollered. "I know you. You're the dollar guy."

I waved to him, and nodded my head, yes. He tugged his mother's gauzy skirt and she bent her head to his for a moment before he made a beeline for me.

"Remember me?" he said. "Tyler. Come on, Jacob and me will show you how the palm tree works."

So in my perfectly pressed chinos, I followed Tyler across the sun-baked ground, almost grateful when he pushed his small hand on the molded hand print halfway up the base of a blue metal tree, making the leaves of the palm spout water, soaking my chinos and my beige silk shirt. I wiped water from my eyes and while I was doing it, Jacob stepped up and slapped the hand print, hard.

"Tag, you're it," he said as the water sprayed again and he made a dash for the jungle gym. I hesitated for only a moment before I took off after him, tackled him down in the sun-warm sand.

Sadie can never do enough to help her friends, so at the last minute, she decides to bring an ambrosia salad for Wendy's birthday, as if Con couldn't possibly have arranged an adequate amount of food for the crowd.

She gathers crisp lettuce from the row she's planted at the north end of our garden, next to the path, so she can pick without muddying her shoes. She sorts through ruffled leaves, looking for slugs and the odd piece of chickweed that's evaded the wrath of her hoe. Ten minutes for the lettuce in tepid salt water before she drains it. Sadie collects helpful hints, knowing for sure that tepid water is best for washing lettuce. She says the leaves rehydrate in warm water and that cold water shocks them and makes them go limp. *Whir-whir-whir* tells me she's at the spinning stage.

I found the salad spinner in the gourmet shop downtown when I was looking for a set of decent knives. It's poppy red and, strangely enough, the damn thing actually works. Etcetera is overflowing with gifts and gadgets and, best of all for guys like me, they help you choose something suitable and throw in gift-wrapping for free. I thought the salad spinner was enough, but when the salesgirl found out it was my wife's forty-third birthday, she talked me into a pair of really nice crystal candlesticks as well. And all I had to do was pick the card — no easy task when you're having an affair and you're no longer sure if you love your wife, if you ever really did. It took me a very long time.

Sadie liked the candlesticks but, strangely, it was the salad spinner that really pleased her.

"I love this thing," Sadie says. "I can't believe I spent years trying to dry lettuce leaves with paper towel. All that wasted time."

"Well, it's gone," I say. "And you can't get it back."

I chop the pecans and soak raisins in hot water to plump them up. I measure the oil, add vinegar and a tablespoon of Sadie's secret herbs, shake the bottle wildly until the oil and vinegar combine. Our choreographed cooking is an old familiar dance, so ingrained we could do it in our sleep.

When I burp the lid on the Tupperware container full of orange sections for the top of Sadie's salad, I feel the swoosh of air. Kind of like my life right now. I grasp the counter and slowly shake my head.

"Ready?" I ask. "It's time we hit the road."

The view from Con and Wendy's deck is crazy-quilt prairie: blue fescue grass and yellow mustard, patches of purple interspersed with rich brown summer fallow. Dusk hasn't quite fallen, but a few bright stars have burned their way through the canvas of the sky. Caps pop off icy Pilsners, and Aaron Lines' new country hit spills from a black three-quarter ton Dodge, chrome cowboy running boards lit by a row of tiny blue lights.

He's singing about sitting in his Daddy's El Camino with some girl he's been kind of sweet on and how, that particular night, he knew his life was about to change. I never guessed, that second time, when I saw Adrienne at Safeway, loaded down with groceries and offered her a ride. Aaron Lines is so fresh-faced young most of his songs just make me feel old, but this one echoes and echoes again.

A small red car careens around a corner at the crossroads and buzzes up the lane. Dust swirls as the car skids to a stop with the right front wheel on Con's perfect square of velvet lawn. My heart leaps when the driver's door opens. A waif of a girl, a waterfall of black curls curtaining her face. Adrienne?

"Is Danny here yet?" The girl turns and waves to someone behind me. When I hear the tinkle of her voice, nothing like Adrienne's clear low tones, I begin to breathe.

"You okay?" Sadie asks, a line of worry drawn on her brow. "I thought you had a woozy in the kitchen just before we left." I start to shake my head in denial, and then I just shrug.

"I knew I should have fed you something." She hands me a red plastic plate of veggies and dip, and a shrimp concoction loaded with onions and whipped cream cheese, with a pile of Ritz on the side. I set my beer on the railing, take the plate from her hand.

"We might have figured with those two everything would be running at least an hour late, but Wendy's supposed to arrive soon." She takes a sip of my beer and hands the bottle back. "Until then, you can find me in the kitchen."

I watch Sadie hurry across the deck. An aura of efficiency surrounds her and the kitchen help better be ready to work. If they're not, it won't take long for Sadie to whip them into shape.

The girl who's just arrived hurries across the yard, her eyes searching. "Danny?" she asks almost everyone. "Have you seen him yet? Did he call?"

As she passes, I reach for her arm. Ease off the gas, I want to tell her. Take a little time. My hand brushes the blue sleeve of her blouse, but she doesn't feel my touch. I take one step toward the thin line of her receding back when Earl's solid bulk intercedes, blocking my view.

"Did I see your new Buick last week? Out on Grainger's Road? Pretty fancy wheels to be driving on a washboard road like that."

"Not likely," I tell him, although I know it isn't true. I have been out there with Adrienne every chance I get. I thought we'd be safe from prying eyes away out there.

He turns, following my gaze to the black-haired girl. "Sweet. Wouldn't mind a piece of that." He takes a long pull on his Pil. I feel like slugging him, but I think of Adrienne and me out on Grainger's road, and I know damn well I don't have the right.

"Gotta get another beer," I say. It seems like forever that I lean on that rail, looking at the familiar faces and feeling totally alone.

When I see the girl with the black hair get back into her car, I have a sudden urge to flag her down, but I'm trapped in the crowd and she's hurrying to somewhere she can't wait to go. Her red car spins a skein of dust that hangs above the grid road heading north. I blink when I spot a freight train careening down rails silvered by the setting sun.

There are hundreds, maybe thousands, of unmarked railway crossings in Saskatchewan. The rails go one way, the roads the other, and they intersect at level crossings where visibility is clear and you can see either way for miles and miles. I have no idea why the accident statistics are so dismal. When you think of it, it doesn't make one damn bit of sense. There are reflective railway-crossing signs at every approach. You are supposed to stop, check the track both ways and then proceed with caution. But people drive their vehicles over these crossings day after day, year after year, so you lose the sense of the danger there. You do it so often that, sometimes, you might as well be doing it in your sleep.

The red car is gaining speed. So is the train.

My breath comes quick, and a cramp squeezes my chest. Look to your left, I whisper. For God's sake look. The train whistle wails and wails again, but the girl doesn't slow down, not one little bit. She probably has her tunes cranked to the max and her mind on Danny, who never did show.

As she approaches the crossing, I pray to see brake lights, but they never come on. Then, inevitably, the lines intersect and the car disappears.

Thank God, I think, she's made it. She's made it through safe.

A split second delay and then the screech of metal on metal rolls across the prairie like a wave. I catch sight of the matchbox car flipping through the air before it explodes in a grassy ditch a hundred yards east. Like pieces of confetti, bits of shiny metal rain from the sky.

The rest is a blur of people running, frantic phone calls, a few guys running from the deck down to the ditch, although I think they know it's far too late to help, and the seemingly interminable wait until we hear wailing sirens and see the red and blue flash of police cars and an ambulance or two.

Sadie guides me to our car, covers my shivering shoulders with a blanket, offers me whiskey when she finally gets me home. She holds me, breathes softly on my shoulders, and tells me to relax. "I'm sorry," she whispers. "Dammit, tonight, we should have stayed home."

I slump, watch again and again, in slow-motion, the drive toward disaster. I can see it coming but there's not one single thing that I can do.

Tyler's hair is thick and tightly curled and he hates to have it washed, so I've made it a game. He's the shaggy dog and I'm a vet. "Hold still," I tell him. "This crazy dog doctor is on the lookout for big, juicy lice." He barks and paws at my arm and, as I soap his black curls, I pretend to pick lice from his hair and squash them on the edge of the tub with my thumb. "We've got ten big squished ones lined up tonight," I tell him. "Good puppy, sit."

He barks again, and looks up at me through thick black lashes, a grin as big as Texas splitting his face. Fine beige sand has settled on the bottom of the tub.

"Squeeze your eyes closed real tight," I tell him as I pour a plastic jug of warm rinse water over his head, and watch as he shakes his shiny head, spraying water onto the walls and splotching my jeans, just like a real puppy would.

"I think you've turned into a boy again." I lift him from the soapy water and wrap his goose-bumped body in thick blue terry. "And your hair's so clean it squeaks."

I hold him longer than I need to. "Warm enough now?" I ask.

Adrienne pulls faded quilts over two sets of bony brown shoulders and I lean on the doorframe, and watch as she ruffles their hair and kisses their cheeks.

I feel a sudden urge to take her from behind. I want to fill her with my seed, watch her concave belly rise. That part was missing for Sadie and me. Although we both assumed we'd eventually have children, Sadie's period came every month, as regular as could be. We didn't pursue the problem. I guess we thought it would happen sooner or later. And when it didn't, we were settled in and had come to treasure our ordered lives. I never told Sadie about the pang I'd feel when I'd see a tow-headed boy in front of me at the movie, his sleepy head drooped on his father's shoulder. I'm sure Sadie had her moments too, although she never once mentioned them to me. Knowing Adrienne and the boys has stirred up everything for me.

"Go to sleep now," she tells them. "Tomorrow's going to be another big day."

I reach for the switch, turn out the light. "Good night guys," I say. "Thanks for helping me with the barbeque. And for taking me to the park."

"Do you like the crying tree the best?" Jacob's voice is soft and sleepy. "Me and Tyler do."

"Yes, I do," I tell him. "Since the first time I tried it, I've liked it very much."

I take Adrienne's small, soft hand and enfold it in my own. I don't mention anything about the summer solstice having come and gone. And that I've missed my self-imposed deadline which, thankfully, Adrienne knows nothing about. That I'm beginning to wonder if I really have the guts.

A mourning dove calls its plaintive *woo-oo-oo-oo*. I've seen the pair in our backyard, their light grey and brown colouring not a perfect camouflage. Mourning doves are generally monogamous, so Sadie told me, bird book in hand. Ours like to coo just before sunrise, so I know this long night will soon be over. I sit up and listen to the lonesome sound. But I've pulled all the covers off Sadie and when she rolls over, she flings her arms wide.

"Your pillow's soaking wet," she says. "Again." She snaps on the overhead light, pulls a pillowslip from the cedar chest at the end of our bed. She grabs my pillow, strips the soggy linen. "Let's start fresh," she says. "Maybe then you can rest."

Efficient, even at this ungodly early hour, Sadie slips the new pillowcase on, smooths it firmly with her hands and tosses it to me. Soon I am lying beside Sadie again. But never once do I close my eyes until the rising sun bathes the window with a soft, yellow light. Then finally, I sleep.

Black coffee is cooling in my blue Broncos cup, George's lawn mower purrs behind our shabby fence and from my chair on the deck, I can see Sadie's back moving up a row of bushy Harmon beans. When my cellphone buzzes, I almost decide to ignore the damn thing. But it buzzes, and buzzes again.

"Hello," I say, flipping my Samsung open, catching a ray of sun on its small silver face.

"Hi Dave." Tyler's soft lisp flutters in my ear. "Mommy said I couldn't phone, but I cried and cried, so she let me."

"What are you crying for?" I whisper, my eyes on Sadie's back. I hear Tyler's soft snuffle, see him wiping his nose on the edge of his sleeve.

"Jacob won't go to the park anymore," he tells me. "He says he's not going unless you come too."

I cradle the phone, feel sweat on my back. "Tell Jacob the palm tree's lonesome for you guys, so he better get over there and give it a slap. And I'll take you to the park real soon. It's just that I'm kind of busy right now."

His voice is small and sad when he says he will and then says goodbye.

"Bye, Bud," I say to the high-pitched buzz of a dial tone.

Sadie has reached the end of the Harmons and is starting to weed beneath the tomato cages supporting thick branches heavy with fruit. Sweat glistens on her brow and on her firm brown arms. She looks up and sees me watching.

"What's wrong? Never seen a woman work this hard before?" she asks, flashing me a smile. "If it's really bothering you, get off your duff and give me a hand."

Slowly, I fold my phone and tuck it into my pocket. But I don't get up and help Sadie. I sit, lost in the lush greenness of my yard.

"How's your game?" Smoke rises from the other side of the fence and I can see the silver of George's thinning hair.

"Not so good," I say.

"Hmmph."

I want to reach across the fence, touch his freckled arm. Tell him everything. But all I say is that I've got a lot on my mind. A sudden gust of wind knocks over Sadie's latest project, a rejuvenated chair. She hurried off to the Community College one Saturday morning with a bare aluminum frame and came home eight hours later with a navy and aqua woven chair. She loves that chair and she's proud as hell.

It clatters in the cool stillness of our neat little neighbourhood.

"Focus," George says. "That's the thing."

He takes one final drag on his cigarette, and butts it in a flowerpot full of purple pansies. "Better fold that chair. The goddamn wind might just take it clean away."

He stumbles, mutters curses in the dark. "Lose the chair and you're in big trouble, I can tell you that much."

"Right, George," I say and I tuck Sadie's precious chair against the warm white stucco of my silent house.

I think of Adrienne's soft fingers tracing the outline of my lips, her gentle tending of Jacob and Tyler, of the hugs I get from all three when I show up at their door.

And then I think of Sadie, her capable fingers crumbling lumps of packed soil, her gentle touch when she transplants tomatoes, of her quiet smile when I show up with a new garden tool or a packet of exotic seeds.

I hold my head in my hands and steel myself for the sharp snap of George's screen door, a familiar sound that tonight, I know I will find too hard to bear.

BELLY DANCING

SOMETIMES, WHEN I'M HOME ALONE, I LIE buck-naked on the bed and watch my belly dance. I know in my head that it's still a part of me, but watching it bop one way and boing the other makes me feel as if I'm not the real owner anymore. Like you rented out your basement suite and now the renters are making all the rules.

I love saying 'buck-naked', maybe because I'm married to Buck Allen Jarvis. When I tell him I'm going to get buck-naked, my husband just groans.

I'd never thought of my belly as being really beautiful, until that stifling Saturday when Buck and I decided to do something exciting and drove into town to pick up the mail and grab a Dilly bar. Although by that time, I was supposed to be limiting my intake of Dilly bars. So there I was, standing in front of the post office, with the key to Box 10 dangling from my finger, my beautiful diamond cut wedding band feeling very, very tight.

"Wanda! I can't believe I lucked out and ran into you."

Conner is still drop-dead handsome. Some things haven't changed.

"Running into me just now isn't that hard to do," I said, and I patted my huge belly, kind of embarrassed that he see me two weeks before my due date, but kind of proud too. You don't see bellies as big as this one any old day of the week. He told me he was back in town for the weekend, checking in with his folks before he left to go back to school. In Victoria. On the Island. It sounded so exotic to me. School, I thought. Living in such a beautiful place. That's exactly what I should have done.

"That's a magnificent belly you've got," he said. "I feel kind of privileged to have seen it."

Of course, I had no idea what he meant. Did he mean my big belly was magnificent, or did he mean my perfect little flat one, the one he's seen more times than I can count?

"Thanks," I say. "It's been good seeing you again." It was eighty in the shade and I thought I might melt. "But I better go. Buck's waiting in the truck. Air conditioned, thank God."

He touched my arm. "Think of me, once in a while," he said. And then he laughed, the raspy laugh that I have always loved. "Only good thoughts allowed."

Buck revved the Dodge, hard, so I hurried into the post office, opened the little metal door of the mailbox. I heard myself grunt as I squatted to gather the envelopes and I looked around with a flaming face, hoping no one had heard.

I had the letters in one hand and my purse in the other and, somehow, I dropped an envelope as I pulled on the door of the Dodge. You'd think Buck might have leaned over, opened the door for me, but he was busy singing along with some old country song, his blunt, brown fingers tapping the beat on his leather steering wheel. Obviously, it never occurred to him that I might need a little help, or I'm sure he would have offered. At least, I think I'm sure. Anyway, it was no mean feat, retrieving that letter from its landing spot, just under the edge of the four-by-four's chassis. At least I didn't grunt.

"Christ, woman, hurry up. You're letting in a lot of hot air."

I finally lumbered into the passenger seat.

"Speaking of hot air," Buck said, "wasn't that your old boyfriend? He sure had lots to say."

"Nothing important," I said.

But I couldn't stop thinking about Conner once we got home. How he looked so darn good. How he'd come right out and told me I've got a great belly. Conner is the only person who's ever said that to me.

I should have asked for his address. I've got this great collection of belly pictures that no one wants to see. I took the first ones myself, in the bedroom mirror, but when my belly got bigger, I couldn't get the angle right. All I got was the flash in the mirror.

I got Buck to try, but he's a disaster with a camera and the two pictures he took are blurred and fuzzy. You can't tell if it's a belly or a poor shot of the moon. He wouldn't try again. Said it was weird, me wanting pictures of my belly like that. Said he thought it must be some kind of hormone thing.

The best pictures were taken by my sister, Kate, at dusk, in the field, when the sky still had that lovely tinge of pink. There's one where I'm leaning against a gate, my face in deep shadow. The curve of my belly is the full moon caught by my hands and the light is divine. I look like a real Madonna.

Maybe that's one Connor would like. If I just had his address, I'd send him a few. I've got doubles of all the pictures, so he could keep them if he wants.

"Feel this, honey." I take Buck's hand, put it on the side of my beach-ball belly. "Action's happening tonight, and happening fast." His hand rests on my belly for only a fraction of a moment.

"Isn't that cool?"

"Yeah," he answers but he never does ask to feel it again. I rub my busy belly, and I really hope the baby didn't feel that sudden withdrawal.

Buck's kind of hard to figure sometimes, but he's a peach compared to Carleen. Now I find out she's been talking behind my back. I really expected better from my sister-in-law. She's tattled to Buck, said she'd come for coffee and found me lolling around in bed in the middle of the day.

When I heard a knock, I didn't think anything of it, just hollered for whoever it was to come on in.

"Hi! It's me, Carleen."

"In the bedroom," I told her. "Come on down."

I was lying on the bed buck-naked, but I quickly draped one of the baby's little flannelette receiving blankets across my bulging breasts and another across my hips, which I thought was a very tasteful thing to do.

"Wanna watch my belly dance?" I said.

"Uh, no, not really."

"Okay, then," I told her. "It's kind of happening right now, so I guess if you're not interested, you can grab a can of pop or something. There's Coke in the fridge."

She told Buck that I'd virtually kicked her out. Not true at all. She thinks nothing of sitting in her living room watching *The Edge of Night,* and ignoring anyone who shows up between three and three-thirty. She doesn't make coffee, doesn't make eye contact, doesn't say a word.

So if I'm really craving female companionship, or if I need to borrow an egg or cup of sugar or talk about my pregnancy and how it's changed my entire world, I never go to Carleen's until I'm darn well sure she's through watching *The Edge of Night*.

I wouldn't have spent the *entire* afternoon making her watch. Eventually, I would have gotten up and made us fresh coffee, talked about the weather and the awful price of fertilizer, and whether the baby has dropped.

Although it's only seven-thirty, the heat is thick in the kitchen. Far too early for me to be up but, sometimes, I think if I'm going to be a really good wife, I should make Buck's breakfast before he leaves for work. And, besides, once the baby comes, I figure sleeping in will be a thing of the past. At least for me. I'm not too sure about Buck.

My husband is chasing a lone blue Froot Loop around in his Corning Ware bowl. Who ever heard of a grown man who still eats Froot Loops? Why would I think I should get up so early in the morning and cook this man breakfast? A dumb-ass, diehard dreamer, that's what I am.

Clink. And clink.

I lift my sweet, hot coffee, slowly sip. Clink again.

"Could you *please* stop doing that?"

Buck lifts his head. "Kinda touchy today?'

"You know I absolutely cannot stand it when you clink your spoon."

Good old Buck, ex-football hero, never drops the ball. The best defense is a good offence, isn't that what they say? So he asks me what time my appointment is, and if I've thought of asking Dr. Tulley to check my hormones. "Seems to me you're getting really sensitive," he says. "And, besides, spending all your time lying around watching your belly dance is not friggin' normal"

"What's normal?" I say.

At my supposedly final prenatal check-up, Dr. Tulley gets me spread-eagled on his examining table, gently pokes and prods. "Hmm," he says from somewhere south. "The baby has dropped. Fast heart beat. Low slung belly. I'd say a girl." He takes my arm, hoists me up. "And she's pretty well positioned to come into the world. Two days, three at the most. I'll bet you ten bucks."

"You're on," I say. "But you're wrong about one thing. I can tell you it's a boy."

Doctor Tulley is washing his hands. "Humph. Since when did you become the expert? But if you want, we can bet on that too."

I just smile and pat my big belly. Rockford William Jarvis gives a solid kick.

"I'm leaving on vacation Friday, so if you want to collect, you'd better get this process started. And soon."

I feel like killing him. Taking vacation? Now?

I hold my tight belly with my hands, as if it were a watermelon, crisp and firm, and so very, very ripe, it's ready to split. The split thing spooks me, as I have no real idea how this big belly will ever become a person some day, let alone some day soon.

"Please," I say to Dr. Tulley, "the forecast is crappy. Can't you postpone your holidays for a week? Or two? At least until my baby's born?"

I am *so* glad it's me who had a reason for going to town that Tuesday. Really glad it wasn't Buck who picked up the mail. There's the usual array of bills, and credit cards that we've never applied for, with limits of ten thousand dollars we never could repay. But in the bottom of Box 10, I find a little blue envelope addressed to me. Sort of. Susan Jarvis Johnson, in bold black letters, as if my marriage to Buck is almost over and I'm close to being just Susan Johnson again. A script that I immediately recognize. Writing exactly like that on the pile of cards and letters I've stashed in a box. In the back of the attic. Where Buck will never go.

Dear Wanda — or wonderful Wanda, as I used to call you and think you still are —
Been thinking about you and wondering. You sure looked pretty, that day on the street. Somehow, although I knew you married Buck, I'd never imagined you having his kid. Weirded me out a bit but, if you're happy, good for you.

I hope all is well in your world and, who knows, someday our paths might cross again. Stranger things have happened, wouldn't you say?

(Like you dumping me to marry Buck — just kidding — ha! ha!)

Love you forever, Connor the Kid

I used to call him that. Crazy or what? Wonderful Wanda and Conner the Kid. I have heard on the CBC that couples who give each other pet names are much more likely to last. But that didn't work for Connor and me. I reread his letter, turn it over in my palm. The return address is printed clearly and underlined in red.

Maybe this letter is just a feeler. To see if I'd consider joining him out there in Victoria. On the Island. Where everything is green and you would never have to bundle yourself and your newborn baby against a bitter Saskatchewan wind. I run my fingers over the grain of the paper and I wonder if it feels like the fine white sand on the endless beaches at Tofino. Not like I've been there, but I've read about that place.

Vellum. Nothing like the blue-lined paper Buck rips from the phone pad to write his little notes on. Notes that say *don't forget to open the west gate so the cows can get to the trough* or *if you're going to start the lawn mower, open the choke all the way. And don't let the rope snap back. Feed it in slow.* And sometimes, *luv ya, babe,* but those are very rare.

The sun is hot and my feet are pork sausages stuffed into my too-tight shoes. Today, my belly just seems huge and it doesn't seem magnificent, not one bit.

When Conner sees my stretch marks, I wonder what he'll say.

Then I get to thinking. Just because he said I have a magnificent belly, and I've got a real strong feeling he'd like me to write, doesn't necessarily mean he might think having a baby around the house is magnificent too. What if he's still smoking dope at ten in the morning, and I ask him to please not smoke around the baby, and we have our first really big fight before I can even find my way to Woolworth's to buy the giant economy size of Newborn Pampers? Although Carleen says Pampers are far too expensive and are rough as gunnysack on a baby's tender butt. What if Conner's gone all organic from living out West and wants me to use virgin cotton, and wash the diapers by hand in homemade soap, and rinse them in a clear running stream? What then, I wonder? Maybe Buck was right. I should have gotten my hormones checked.

Suddenly, my belly begins to dance, wildly, freely, like there's a real person in there who wants to have a say. High on my left side, I feel one solid kick. Not even close to the belly-dance flutters. This is something more. A kick solid enough to send a football sailing through the uprights, straight and true. Like Buck would teach our son.

I put my lips to the letter, drop it in the mesh wastebasket on a spike near the curb.

"Settle down," I say to Rockford William Jarvis. "We're on our way home."

If I'm there by three, I'll have two whole hours to lie on the bed and watch my belly dance before I have to even *think* about what Buck might like for supper. It occurs to me that my favourite show is nearing the end of its season. In just two days, if Dr. Tulley's right.

Then what? Go over to Carleen's at three o'clock to watch *The Edge of Night?*

JACQUELINE BOUVIER KENNEDY
AND NADINE LOUISE

WHEN JACQUELINE BOUVIER KENNEDY FELL FROM A horse at Virginia's Piedmont Hunt Club on a golden autumn afternoon, people who knew her were surprised. Jackie was an expert rider and her mount was high-spirited, but she'd easily handled high spirits before. The fall, and the resulting bruising from hip to knee, led to doctors' visits for Jackie and extensive precautionary testing.

Jackie's results were as hoped. Blood work normal.

Diagnosis: Simple bruising from the fall.

The girl's bathroom at Benson High is standing room only. I lean on the door and turn my body sideways to wedge my way in. I nudge a short blonde aside and catch a glimpse of myself in the mottled mirror above the four green sinks. My dark hair is perfectly smooth, with an understated flip. I pouffed my bangs this morning but they've fallen a bit, so I backcomb the hell out of them. I *should* say, I am attempting to repair the slight damage caused to my hair by the invigorating ten-block walk from my abode to Benson High. I straighten my short bouclé jacket, check my camel coloured hose to make sure I have no runs. I think of Jacqueline Kennedy and try on her cool little smile.

"Nadine Louise Peters, is that really you?" Cheryl pushes her way out from behind a green cubicle door, touches my arm.

"It's me." I give my hair a final pat. The scent of hairspray and Evening in Paris mixes with the smell of freshly waxed floors and yellow chalk. Grade Ten, I think. Two more years until my life will really begin.

"I'll be screwed, blued and tattooed," Cheryl exclaims. "Turn around, let me look."

Gracefully, I pirouette and Cheryl emits a low whistle. "What did you do, Nadine," she says. "Get your butt reshaped? And your jugs are almost gone. Jeeze Louise, look at those hipbones. Are you starving yourself?"

I have spent the entire summer studying Jackie Kennedy's cool, sophisticated look. At first, I just admired her. After a while, I wanted to *be* her. My naturally blonde hair suddenly seemed crass, my curvaceous body, an insult.

When Noreen Juanita Peters, overcome by a fit of coughing, fell from a stepladder in her yellow gingham-curtained kitchen on a sun-dappled spring afternoon, her daughter was surprised. Noreen was an expert painter and a ladder-climber extraordinaire, easily handling heights before. The fall and the resulting bruising from hip to knee led to doctor visits for Noreen and extensive precautionary testing.

Noreen's results were not as hoped. Blood work abnormal.

Diagnosis: acute myelogenous leukemia. Much more than simple bruising from the fall.

Before my mother checked out of the world, I used to study myself in the full-length mirror at the end of the upstairs hall, searching for similarities between us, as if my looking like her might somehow make her more determined to stay.

"Here," she said to me one July afternoon, when the mercury had hit eighty-four, "I've knitted something to keep you warm come fall." She raised the poncho from her lap, held it out to me, her smile radiant against the paper-white of her skin. The poncho was deep violet, like my mother's eyes.

Her hands were bloodless, her translucent skin revealing the faint map of her veins. Veins so thin the nurses had to poke and poke, wipe their hollow needles and attack again, raising multi-purpled bruises on her stick-like arms. I held the poncho to my cheek. "I love it," I told her. But I haven't worn it. Not one time. Three days after her funeral, when we went out to Uncle Ted and Aunt Jessie's for supper, I took the poncho with me, and I tucked it into the closet in the upstairs hall. Someday, I might be able to look at it again, maybe even wear it, but not right now.

At first, when I began to feel afraid, I tried to memorize the timbre of my mother's voice, the graceful gestures of her perfect hands. It seemed important to capture her core but, too often, when I wasn't in her presence, I came up blank. I could easily recall vials of pink medicine lining the fridge door, where the Coca-cola used to be, the stinging scent of rubbing alcohol that overwhelmed her lilac perfume, even the hard, retching sounds she tried to hide with country music turned full volume. And the cloying smell of death in the upstairs hall, although I didn't recognize it at the time. Worrying about my mom made my head ache, a great throbbing pain. So I turned to fashion magazines, studied the tabloids. Anything to get my mind off the cold certainty in my gut that, one day soon, she'd be gone.

And I found someone, someone alive, someone real. We are alike in many ways, Jackie Kennedy and I, but our strongest similarity is our hunger to be something more. The only significant difference I see is that she had a mother when she was fifteen, whereas I'm fumbling along trying to figure things out on my own.

Sometimes, I miss my mom so bad it's worse than a toothache, but I can't stop thinking about her, just like you can't stop sticking the tip of your tongue in the hole where a piece of your tooth has broken off, even though you know the slightest contact will be worse than a jolt of household current. A jolt you might vividly remember if you've ever stuck a bobby pin into a beckoning wall socket, like I did the year I turned ten. Maybe if my mother had lived long enough, we would have started having those on-going disagreements that Jackie seems to have had with her overbearing mother. As it is, that's just one more thing I'll never know for sure.

Jackie has been strongly influenced by her father, that old rake, Jack Bouvier, and I've been strongly influenced by my father, that old reprobate, Pete Peters. Jack, of course, hung around the track and the club in the East Hamptons, gambling and drinking and raising hell. Pete hangs around the Royal Hotel in downtown Nowhere, gambling and drinking and raising hell. This is new behaviour for my father. It's the way he chooses to cope, so I try to understand. I'm quite sure Jackie also gave old Jack all the leeway in the world.

The lights in the girl's bathroom are footlight bright and I squint as I rearrange my bangs. "Jeez, you really remind me of somebody," Cheryl says, peering at me in the mirror. "I just can't think of who. What's Larry think of the new you?"

I tell her Larry and I are no longer an item. When I began my strict diet and my bosom shrank to a more fashionable size, Larry complained like hell. You've taken the fun out of copping a feel, he said. You've gone from marshmallow boobs to butterscotch chips. Nothing left but the points. Jeez, he said, I can hardly find the damn things. *Oh, begging your pardon.*

Larry protested my extreme weight loss, although the fourteen pounds I shed doesn't really sound like much. He said it pained him greatly to see how thin I had become. So I dumped the bastard. No, I had to terminate our relationship as we seemed to be growing apart.

"Do you mind if I take a run at him?" Cheryl asks.

"Go for it," I say. "He's really not my type."

My classroom is in a dreary basement with only two low windows giving meagre access to the outside world. There are four classrooms available, but enough bodies to fill five, thanks to the baby boom. We are not sure if the winners ended up in the basement, which is really the music room, or if *we* are the rejects. Sometimes, it's best not to know. When we're in our homeroom, we get to listen to music. All kinds of music. Mozart, Chopin, BB King, Ella Fitzgerald. Music most of us would never hear at home. When Mr. Thompson turns up the tunes, I count my blessings. Since I've become one with Jackie, I thirst for culture and quenching that thirst in a town like this is a job in itself.

From my vantage point halfway down row two, I can see two pair of legs outside one of the inadequate windows. The chunky ones are khaki clad, the others long and bare, with no hint of a skirt in sight. Donnie, two seats ahead of me, is squirming in his seat. He leans to the right, trying to get a better view. I wonder if he's popped a woodie. Of course, bodily reactions of pubescent males are of no real interest to me. Not anymore. Jackie would be appalled.

Miss Schmidt swipes her greasy forehead with the sleeve of her navy blazer, sets the English textbook down on the corner of her large oak desk. It must be a real job, removing that telltale oil from her jacket. I bet she has to dab it with dry-cleaning fluid, the kind that comes in little roll-top containers and stinks like crazy. I know, because my mom used it on the lapels of my dad's suit. Sometimes, after a funeral or an anniversary party, we'd stop at the Venice Café for fish and chips on our way home and Dad would be too busy talking and gawking to pay any attention to how he ate his food. So out came the little bottle the moment we got home.

Miss Schmidt should stick to the cotton balls. I know she's got a little stash in her upper right-hand drawer. I saw them one day when I was writing on the blackboard. If she would *always* use them to mop her brow, she could avoid inhalation of those awful spot-cleaner fumes. Oh Lord, I am far too concerned about cleaning solutions these days. Something I had very little knowledge of when my mother was around.

Our teacher turns to the board, still droning on about some boring old grammar rules, illustrating as she goes. When her chalk screeches on the dusty board, goosebumps march down my spine.

"This," she says, "is the difference between a simile and a metaphor." *Nadine is like a rosebud.* She taps the perfect, round writing with her long, blood-red fingernail. "A simile," she says. "Note the word *like*." She taps the blackboard again. "Pay attention," she says. "This will be on your mid-term.

I'm giving you free marks here." She takes the chalk in hand, writes *Nadine is a rosebud*. "A metaphor," she says. "Do you see the difference?"

The guys are snickering openly, and a few are turning to look at me. It's the first time most of them have really looked at me since my mom's funeral. It's as if I've become a ghost myself, and I've ached for someone to look me in the eye. Thank God for Cheryl, who walks beside me down the endless halls.

Donnie raises his brows, wiggles them as he turns to stare. I feel my cheeks go sunset pink, then deepen to crimson, but I lift my chin, and give him a cool Jackie look.

"Boys," Miss Schmidt says, mopping her forehead again, this time with a puffy cotton ball she's pulled from the breast pocket of her jacket. "Settle down, please. I'm trying to help." Two seconds later the bell rings. Miss Schmidt grabs her papers and beats a hasty retreat, the clicking of her high heels as she hurries up the stairs reminds me of my mother's clicking needles when she used to sit in her rocker, knitting angora sweaters for me. But I have eschewed sweaters since adopting my new look. You don't see Jackie Kennedy going around in clingy angora sweaters and faded-out jeans.

Miss Schmidt is young, probably not much older than we are, and the guys don't give her one bit of respect. She usually has a pocketful of cotton balls and they are all convinced that she carries them specifically to stuff into the points of her bra. Those dolts know nothing of astringents. Their minds are consumed by visions of tits and ass. What I mean to say is the male species is hard-wired by evolution to search for a certain body type and when they spot one, subconsciously, they begin to show off. Miss Schmidt, despite her greasy forehead and plethora of blackheads, is one such specimen.

Perhaps that explains the uncontrollable behaviour of the males in English 2E. Sometimes I feel sorry for her. No matter how hard she tries to interest them in their lessons, the boys in this class can be a real bunch of assholes, if you know what I mean.

But Miss Schmidt was remiss in using me as an example without my permission. The males in the class have taken her apt example and purloined the original intent.

"Hey, Rosebud," Donnie whispers. "Rosebud Baby, just wondering if you've ever thought of giving up your dew?" He starts to laugh. Dan joins in, then Doug, then the rest. In my pre-Jackie period, I might have told the whole crowd to go piss up a rope. But they haven't directly addressed me in months, and a flood of gratitude warms me. Slowly, I gather my books. When I'm sufficiently composed, I look at Donnie, his muscular body overflowing his too-small chair. He actually flushes and lowers his eyes. "Sorry I started that," he mumbles.

"Similes and metaphors," I say. "Chapter three, page eighty-two. If you need help understanding, give me a call."

The bathroom is the warmest place in our house. I linger while the bathtub fills and warm steam clouds the mirror. I wipe away the moisture and check my hairline for telltale re-growth. When I began dying my hair, I had no idea how often it would need touching up. There's nothing worse than gleaming, chestnut hair anchored by an inch of dishwater blonde. I turn from the mirror, step onto our big green scale. The needle hovers around one hundred and ten. If I stand closer to the front, right beside the numbers, it goes to one-oh-nine. I slide the scale back under the vanity and add pink bubble bath to the steaming water in the claw-foot tub.

In a cloud of bubbles, I dream my Jackie dreams.

"I saw *Blue Hawaii*," Cheryl says. "With Larry." We are walking down the long hall to the lunchroom. Whispers of "Rosebud Baby" mark our passing. It's been two whole weeks and the nickname seems to have stuck. I'm not too crazy about the name but, at least, the guys in class are talking to me again. And I have Miss Schmidt to thank for that.

When I returned to school after my mother's funeral, a few of my classmates would hesitate in half-stride, as if they wanted to say something, but then they'd drop their eyes and keep on walking. Sometimes I wanted to scream, yes, my mother died and, yes, I know you're sorry, and let's just forget about it and maybe you could goddamn look me in the eye. Cancer isn't a communicable disease, you know.

"I'm kind of off guys right now," I say to Cheryl and I wonder how I ever thought Larry was something special. "Except for Donnie. He grows on you, if you know what I mean."

Donnie and I don't go out much, but he comes over and we hang out at my place a lot. His French kissing does wonders for my psyche and I'm pretty sure it does wonders for his too. After last Saturday, I felt kind of bad, making out for an entire evening. I don't think Jackie would approve. She and Jack probably would have just had tea and talked about books and horses and maybe football, before she showed him out. I hope she doesn't hold it against me. I'm trying, really I am. It's just that sometimes I lose my point of reference, and I feel like I've taken the wrong turn at a crossroads. It's like I've totally lost my map.

I miss things I hardly noticed when my mother was here. The worst is at suppertime. The table was always set for three, and the smell of pot roast or cabbage rolls or stew would make my mouth water the moment I came in our door. "Mom?" I'd call, and above the sound of Loretta and Conway, I could hear her sunny voice. "In here, honey," she'd say. "Just getting these biscuits out of the oven before they get too brown." Now the kitchen is dark when I return, and quiet, and it always seems to be freezing cold.

One day, when I come home to that empty kitchen, the ever-present lump of dread in my belly, I decide to change the way things are. So I lift her cookbook from the cupboard to the left of the stove. I flip to her favourite recipes, marked by spots of oil and chocolate smudges and God knows what all else. I run my finger across those spotted pages, imagine my mother doing the same. Finally, I lay the heavy book aside. I don't really need it. My mother taught me how to melt a walnut-size chunk of butter, stir in two tablespoons of flour, and add approximately two cups of milk, while whisking over a low flame. The result is a base sauce for killer macaroni and cheese. Add thinly sliced Velveeta until the sauce turns slightly orange and tastes good and cheesy. Combine with the cooked macaroni, *al dente* as Jackie would no doubt prefer, in an ovenproof casserole. Sprinkle the top with freshly ground pepper and bake at 350 degrees until the cheese sauce bubbles and browns.

I open the oven door, check the state of the cheese. What my mom didn't teach me was how to keep supper warm for an extra hour while I wait for Pete Peters to come home. It's a problem we didn't have while she was in the world. Just like Jackie, I think, as I add a bit more milk to the casserole and turn down the heat, waiting for my not-quite dependable father to show. I taste a spoonful. The macaroni is still moist, the sauce not yet curdled. So far, I'm doing okay.

The phone in the hall jangles the silence and I run to answer it.

"Hello, dear," Mrs. Cutter says, her voice thready as if she's running short of air. "I'm just wondering how you're doing."

"I'm doing fine," I say. Mrs. Cutter has made it her mission to keep us in casseroles and kindness. It's been three whole days since her last call. "Actually, I'm kind of busy. I was just slicing some bread. Supper's almost ready over here."

"Good for you," Mrs. Cutter says. "You're coping so well. I'm not so sure I can say the same for your dad."

Mrs. Cutter knows, of course, that my father is not yet home. She sits in her rocker on the porch, keeping track of everyone who moves on the entire street. Lately, her beacon has been pretty well trained on 115 Elm. I almost wish someone else in the neighbourhood would die.

"He's been working a lot of overtime," I say.

"Of course, dear. Of course. Well, anytime you're lonely, just come on over. We can have a nice cup of tea." I thank her, slip into talk about the weather and how soon the tulips will be pushing through. Mrs. Cutter's tulips are her favourite topic and she's easy to distract. When she finally runs down, I replace the receiver and wipe my brow with the checked apron I threw on over my new jeans.

Mrs. Cutter is being kind, I remind myself. And she's probably lonely, too. A wind gust lifts dirt from the curb, whirls it in a blur of brown. I let the curtain fall across the glass. Dad, I whisper, please come home.

I remind myself that Jack Bouvier was smoke in the wind, but still, he could do no wrong in Jackie's adoring eyes. My dad's been smoke in the wind himself for the last few months.

It's not how he really is, so I'm trying to cut him some slack. "Help me, Jackie," I pray. "Please." And I rearrange the salt and pepper and the butter dish, refold the gingham napkins I've placed beside our plates.

The back door slams and Dad steps in from the porch, running his stubby fingers through his thick greying hair, rubbing his bloodshot eyes. "Sorry," he says. "Stopped for one after work and I lost track of time."

"Yeah, I gathered." I place a black wrought iron trivet on the table, and bring the bubbling casserole from the oven with Mom's mismatched oven mitts. "I think this is still okay."

"Mmm," he sniffs the air. "You're getting to be quite the little cook. Just like your mom." I pull out his chair and, as he sits, he stirs a wave of stale smoke.

About bloody time you showed, I think. And in case you haven't noticed, you're not the only one around here who's lost. When I open my mouth, Jackie taps my shoulder, shakes her head, no.

"Thanks," I say. "I'm glad the casserole wasn't ruined. I wasn't really sure how long I could keep it warm." With my mother's silver berry-spoon, I slide a generous scoop of macaroni and cheese onto my father's plate.

"A bit more?" I ask as I put a dab of macaroni and cheese on my own plate.

Jackie smiles her perfect little smile. We watch as my father eats, but something blocks my throat and I have to chew and chew before I attempt to swallow. When we're done, Dad washes the dishes, and I dry. He says nothing about the half-eaten glob of macaroni I've left on my plate.

I fold the checked towel, hang it to dry on the oven door handle. "Good night." I kiss Dad's cheek, my legs suddenly shaky with fatigue. "Think I'll hit the sack. Maybe read a bit before I go to sleep."

Jackie loves it when I read.

I wash my face with Dove. When a sudden cramp hits, I seize the sink. *Shit*, I whisper. *Not again!* The vanity doors are crooked and one hinge is loose. I pull on the porcelain knob. Nothing. I whack the door, yank again and, finally, it gives. My hand rustles through the rubble inside until I feel the box. I pull it out, look inside. "Oh no," I groan. "Don't tell me."

If my mother were here, *she* would be the one to visit the druggist, pick up the offending goods, and walk nonchalantly to the till. But she's left the furtive purchase of Kotex and bottles of Midol up to me. When I go to the Rexall drugstore on Main, I pray that no one will walk in when I'm at the till, counting out my bills. I'd die if anyone saw me buying Kotex, or toilet paper for that matter. I am absolutely certain that Jackie never purchased sanitary napkins in her entire life. And the purchase of toilet paper is something one just does not discuss in polite company. It's supposed to be there, one of the things we all take for granted in life.

I wonder when Jackie will tell little Caroline the facts of life. How do you pick the perfect time to warn your daughter about cramps and the possibility of waking up at night in a pool of warmth, sick with the knowledge you've been bleeding in your bed? Too soon might be scary, and I already know what too late is like.

I hope Jackie tells Caroline while she's still quite young. Maybe then the idea will grow with her and it won't come as such a shock.

I rummage through all my drawers, finally find a back-up supply, thankful for my habit of overstocking when I finally do get up enough nerve for the Rexall run.

The two o'clock bell has not yet rung. Miss Schmidt's face glows with grease. "Boys are dismissed early today," she says, straightening the books piled on her desk, her downcast eyes lingering on the green felt pad. "Girls, please stay in your desks." The guys grab their books and binders, heading for the hills, before she changes her mind. "Confidential session," she adds. Laughter and loudness fill the doorway and flow down the hall in waves. Thanks a lot, I think. Now they know for sure.

Miss Schmidt closes the classroom door, stands at the front of the class, and clears her throat. "I'd like to talk today about the responsibility of becoming a woman," she says, a red tide rising on her graceful neck. "Something you're all going to be dealing with soon." She stutters, haltingly offering information about ovulation and eggs and, most especially, how sex between a man and woman is a sacred act that should be saved for marriage. It's up to us to make sure we remain chaste, because boys are more apt to push for sexual experimentation. She quickly skims across the scanty information on birth control, as if it were a dangerous thing to know.

No doubt my mother meant to tell me all this a long time ago. But she didn't get even the chance to forewarn me about menstruation, let alone birth control. I finally got the goods about the dreaded monthlies from Cheryl when I called her, sure that something was terribly wrong. Sure that I, too, was about to die. She got a real belly laugh from that one. Lucky for her she's been such a good friend or I would have hung up on her without a second thought.

My mind wanders to my mother. I don't have a picture of her, pregnant with me at the age of nineteen. Too bad, I think. A picture would be nice.

About the only picture I have of both my parents is in a black metal frame on my bureau. Mom's blonde hair looks almost like a halo, partially obscuring her face. She's a little on the plump side, not very tall. My dad used to tell her not to worry, that he's always liked his women round and firm and fully packed. The wind is ruffling my mother's flared skirt, lifting her wavy blonde hair. I hold the picture closer, and notice for the first time that my mother looked a little like Marilyn Munroe.

She was always the one behind the camera, so there are lots of shots of Dad and me, and almost none of her.

I hold the snapshot closer, tilt it to catch the light. I run my fingers across her face, stare into her violet eyes.

"'Night Mom," I say, and place the picture on the bureau, beside my Mickey Mouse clock. I wish she were here so she could go to the Rexall drugstore tomorrow and pick up the feminine supplies. Who knew, before she was gone, the things I'd have to figure out? Then I feel guilty, wishing her back to buy Kotex for me. Whatever would Jackie think?

It makes me feel guilty that I have more pictures of Jacqueline Bouvier Kennedy than I have of my own mother, but I can't help myself, I study them all the time. Every night, I turn to my thick, blue scrapbook and try to decipher Jackie's secret smile. Her hair is never messy, even when she's just stepped down from Air Force One. When she wears pink, as she often does, it makes her hair look even darker, deepens the mystery of her eyes. I love her saucy little pillbox hats, the fact that she's the first wife of a president to bare a bit of leg.

John F. Kennedy is a handsome man. In every picture, he's standing close to her. John-John and Caroline are usually there too, standing in front of their mom and dad. Jack's left hand rests on John-John's shoulder. Jackie holds Caroline's hand.

It's a wonder she didn't break when she miscarried Baby Patrick, not just from losing the baby, but from having the details splashed all over the front pages of every newspaper in the land. Some of the headlines called Jackie fragile. I think those reporters totally missed the mark. Look at this picture, the day she went home from the hospital. You couldn't say she looks anything close to radiant, but she's composed, pale, and reserved. The headlines say that despite her loss, she's holding up well.

I wonder if that's what people are saying about me.

"Good night, Jackie," I say, and I run my fingers across her clear, composed face. I fall asleep with the scrapbook tented across my chest.

Mostly, Donnie and I hang out at my house. I've been so tired lately, even lasting through the early show is more than I can bear. Tonight, while we watched *Bonanza*, it felt good to rest in the circle of his arms. He kissed me. Lightly at first, then he tried pushing with his tongue. I stood up, turned on the overhead lights. I can't take his French-kissing frenzy tonight; he might just wear me down. For some reason, my resistance is kind of low.

"Time for you to go home," I say. "I've got a ton of homework to do."

Donnie slouches against the pillar of the verandah, moonlight glinting in his sea-green eyes. "Lover's moon," he says. "Too bad we're letting it go to waste."

"It's not wasted," I say. "It'll light your way. Two back alleys and you're home."

"Yeah," Donnie says, his shoulders slumped and his eyes hidden by his flop of hair. "Lit by the lamp of the poor."

He's feeling sorry for himself because, although we've just spent three hours together, he didn't get even close to copping a feel. There was a moment, when Donnie was holding my hand and Pa Cartwright was beside himself because he'd been too hard on Little Joe, that I thought maybe making out might raise my sagging spirits for a while.

Then I thought of Jackie, and kissing like crazy seemed a crass thing to do.

Dad and I have been invited for Sunday supper to Uncle Ted's farm, fourteen miles out of town on a gravel road. Mostly, people have kind of eased off inviting us for Sunday's and holiday suppers, but Uncle Ted and Aunt Jessie are steadfast in their kindness.

"Do you want to drive?" Dad asks, and I look at him, surprised out of my mind. I won't be eligible for a learner's license for six more months.

"Not now," he says, "but once we're off the highway."

"Sure," I say.

"Driving on gravel's a skill," he says. "Something you should learn. To keep you safe." It has never entered my mind that my father might be worried about keeping me from harm. I look at him, see that the lines around his eyes have deepened and the black undertone in his hair has turned entirely silver. His face wavers and blurs until I only see his outline. He grows thinner, taller and his metal-grey hair morphs to black.

"You mean the world to me," Jack Bouvier is saying. "Even when I wasn't there to make sure things were going okay, I thought of you all the time. Surely you've always known that, Jackie."

The snap of my father's leather fingers call me back to the world, to my dad and me, sitting in the driveway in our blue Chevrolet. "Nadine, snap out of it," he says. "I didn't mean to scare you. If you're freaked out about driving on gravel, just say so. Really, I just thought it would be a good idea."

Our mid-term marks are posted on a list outside our homeroom door. The crowd is thick, the girls edging to the front anxious to see how high they've placed, and most of the guys hanging around near the back, not really eager to see. There's no shame in being next to last, but last kind of singles you out.

"Jeez, Rosebud," Tom says, "I thought you were studying Donnie these days. And he's not into bookwork, if you know what I mean. How'd you pull this off?" He points to the wall and I stand on my tiptoes, see my name second on the list.

"It's nothing," I say. "Applying yourself to your studies does wonders. And I've been reading a lot."

Jackie reads voraciously. Before she fell in love with Jack and ended up as the First Lady of the United States of America, she aspired to be a writer. When she has the time, after the children are grown and she and Jack have retired to Hyannisport, I bet she'll be knocking out bestsellers hand over fist, while he's out there coaching all those little Kennedys in football etiquette or racing his speedboat across the bay. Or maybe she'll be an editor. Whatever it is, I know it's going to be about books. And not those trashy romance novels, either. She'll be dealing in literature. Real Literature, if you know what I mean.

Tom looks at me like I've just landed from Mars. "Reading?" he says. "That's not what Donnie says you and him do."

"He," I say. "What you and he do."

The only disappointment for me on the list is my mark in math. It stays at a stolid sixty-two percent no matter how hard I try. I've even gone to old Stinkbreath for extra help. I should say I asked Mr. Davidson if he had time to go over some concepts I had failed to grasp, and he kindly agreed to help me out. Although I went for extra help every other Tuesday for two months, it didn't do one damn bit of good. I *meant* to say, perhaps I am numerically challenged and should hire a tutor. Or, I can do as Jackie has done and marry myself a piss-pot full of money. An unlimited chequing account would be the best solution for my math problem. If it worked for Jackie, surely it could work for me. A piss-pot full of money, I think, and shake my head in disgust. What I meant was someone fun, and handsome, someone wild about me. A man who just happens to be rich. Someone like JFK.

Class is a state of mind. Jackie has it; she was born with it. Maybe I can never get it right.

I have taken up equestrian pursuits. In my world, that means I go out to Uncle Ted's on the weekends and help him fork manure out of the barn. After that, I get to figure out how to ride old Jake. It's nothing like Jackie's English riding lessons or her purebred horses in the paddocks at the club.

Jake's a sweet horse, sway-backed and slightly stubborn, but I'm finally getting the hang of riding him. At least I can slip the bridle on without a half-hour wrestling session and I've learned how to squeeze my knees to get him to turn. What I haven't learned is how to stop him when he's decided he's had enough. He just puts his head down and gallops hell bent for leather to the barn. All I can do is hold on and duck when we go through the door.

I meant to say the horse knows when he has reached his limits and one should always take one's cue from the animal. After all, rapport is most important.

The barn is dark and cool. Dust motes float in the alleyway, lit by sun shining through square windows high on the wall. Uncle Ted appears from behind a stack of bales and pats Jake's lathered neck. "Did she work you too hard, old boy?"

"I didn't," I say as I slip from the saddle. "It's just when he's ready to come home, I can't hold him back."

"Nothing wrong with that," Uncle Ted tells me. "Kind of like that myself. Come on, let's get ourselves some lunch. Aunt Jessie was baking a chocolate cake last time I checked."

I try, but I can't eat my cake. The chocolate is so dark, the icing too thick and sweet. I pinch small pieces into my palm, let my hand trail beneath the table until I feel Laddie's gentle lick.

The soft country music drifting from the blue plastic radio fades and is gone. But the sweet voice humming along with the music holds the tune. Mom? I think. Mom, is that you? A pot clangs against the porcelain sink, and my eyes pop open at the sound. My head is resting in my hands and my elbows are planted firmly on the faded oilcloth. I quickly lower them to my sides. Jackie would be appalled.

Aunt Jessie is rubbing her hand across my shoulders. "If I didn't know better, I'd swear you just took a nice little nap, sitting straight up."

"I was just daydreaming." I pick up my plate, take it to the sink. Aunt Jessie's arm slips around my waist and she gives me a quick hug.

"Imagine," Aunt Jessie says. "You coming out here all the time. Helping Uncle Ted." She touches my hair. "You've got a kind heart. Just like your mom."

"You think so?" The sink is full of bubbles. Jackie's smooth face smiles at me from the largest one. When I reach out my finger to lift the bubble, it bursts and she's gone. My reflection in the kitchen window highlights my chestnut hair, smooth and sleek. I look just like Jackie, I think.

A sudden sharp pain, like a distance runner's stitch, pierces my side.

Things have changed on the home front and I don't know why. I know that Jackie made excuses for Jack Bouvier for years and I was doing okay, following her lead. Now, in what seems the blink of an eye, Pete has done a one-eighty, coming home on time, tidying the house, cooking supper. The good thing is he's so busy humming and tidying, he doesn't notice when I scrape my supper into the garbage, virtually untouched.

In our yellow kitchen, the absence of my mother is like a black hole and carrying on, eating supper there as if nothing has changed, seems terribly wrong.

"How about we have some company on Sunday for a change?" Pete is running the iron over the collar of his baby blue shirt, one of his best.

"Aunt Jessie and Uncle Ted?" I slip my plate into a sink full of Lemon Joy. "I guess it's about time we paid them back."

My father clears his throat, the iron stalled in his working-man's hand. The smell of scorching cotton fills the kitchen. "Actually, I have a friend," my father says. "Nannette. I'd like you to meet her."

I stare out the kitchen window, see a fragile killdeer flapping in the grass near the willow tree at the edge of our lot. A fat tabby cat watches from the top rail of the fence. The bird is trying to draw attention to herself, away from her nest and her young. As the cat pounces, I look away.

"I've got plans with Donnie." I swish my plate beneath the gushing tap. "Cheryl, too." My dad's face crumples, like a Dixie cup crushed by a fist after the water's been drained.

"Your shirt," I say, and he looks down, sees the smoke rising from his collar. He lifts the iron, stares at it like it's an alien being.

"Shit." He offers his shirt. "Do you know what to do?"

Beneath the sink, I find a spray bottle of vinegar and water. I spray the collar quickly, something I remember seeing my mother do. I am not sure what this will do for the scorch marks, if anything, but at least it kills the smell.

My father? A friend? I think of Jack Bouvier, of the strange and exotic women he must have known. Did he call them his *friends*? I wonder if he introduced any of them to Jackie. I wonder if she felt bombed out, like I do right now. I bet her belly never rolled with sudden cramps.

"I thought I could cook us up a feed of jambalaya," he says. Dad is dabbing the damaged collar with a white cloth and he pauses, turns to me with hopeful eyes. "And maybe after we could play some cards. Or Scrabble. Nannette plays a killer game of Scrabble."

I think of my father, sitting around a kitchen table somewhere playing Scrabble with a woman I've never seen, and saliva floods my jaw

"Maybe sometime." I swallow, swallow again. "But not just yet."

Jackie comes to me. She perches on the side of my bed and I feel the shallow indentation of her elegant body.

"Men crave female company." I look at her beautiful face lit by blue moonlight. "You needn't worry," she says and she tucks the sheet around my shoulders. "My father introduced me to his friends all the time. Most often, it doesn't mean a thing."

I wonder at her strength. All of her duties with the president and the children and, still, she makes time to come to me. I hope she's not too tired in the morning. I hope the nanny keeps John-John and Caroline occupied so she can sleep. I hope she takes her breakfast in bed.

If Jackie can do all this for me, I cannot for the life of me figure out why my mother can't make more of an effort. If she would come to me, just one time. Maybe we'd make the most of our bonus moments, and we'd talk about things that matter. It's all well and good for Jackie to say my father needs female companionship, but I'm not one bit sure what my mother would think. I helped her in and out of the high, hydraulic bed that she finally gave in and let Dad move into the living room. I bathed her face every morning before I went to school, combed her peach-fuzz hair, but never once did I ask what she was thinking or how she expected us to act if things went west. I didn't even have the courage to ask her if she was afraid.

I stare at the ceiling for hours, but my mother does not come.

What does come is winter, the snow blanketing our already silent house, making the cold kitchen seem colder still. But sometimes there are hours, even entire days, when we seem almost okay. Last Sunday morning, Dad opened her cookbook too, and tried his hand at Eggs Benedict. I told him they tasted fine, but that he shouldn't make it too often. "This is loaded with calories," I said, as I used the last bit of my English muffin to mop up the rich sauce, "and cholesterol too."

So he's trying, he really is, and I decide that maybe I ought to try a little too. But I almost choke on my orange section the morning I tell him I might finally be ready to meet his friend. "Next Sunday would be fine," I say.

He turns from the toast he's smothering with loganberry jam, beams at me like I've given him a gift. "Nannette will be so pleased," he says. "She's been anxious to meet you and I think you'll hit it off. She's very nice."

"Yeah, you said." I stir sugar into my blue coffee cup. "Just don't count on me hanging around all evening. Donnie and I are probably going to take in a show." I sip my steaming coffee and it scalds my tongue.

On Sunday, when Nannette walks into our kitchen, I fold into my sturdy chrome chair, clutch the grey edge of arborite so hard my fingers cramp. She's got blonde hair and dark blue eyes. She's short, a little bit plump.

"Pleased to finally meet you," she says and holds out a soft little hand. I see Jackie in the shadows, offering her own hand, slowly and deliberately, so I'll know what I'm supposed to do. I make it through the small talk and all the way to dinner, but when it comes to Dad's special jambalaya, I can't eat a lick. Jackie frowns at me, raises two smooth fingers, but I can't swallow one bite, let alone two. Not tonight. Even for her.

I don't talk to anyone, even Cheryl, about the really big things, like how I feel about Nannette and my dad. But I do tell her about the Kotex problem, how I hate going into the Rexall drugstore. Cheryl shakes her head.

"Jeez Louise," she says. "You poor little thing."

I don't much like being called a poor little thing, but I do like what happens the next time I go to Cheryl's.

Her kitchen is cluttered, untidy as could be and her mother is sitting at the table smoking Player's Plain. The sink is full soap bubbles and crusted dishes and her mom hasn't wiped the table. Crumbs are everywhere.

Cheryl's mom fishes two packs of Player's from a brown paper bag, and then hands the bag to me. "Your supplies," she says. "I buy 'em all the time for Cheryl. From now on, I'll pick up extras for you."

I feel like kissing her but, instead, I tuck the Kotex into my purse. "Thank you," I say. "Thank you very much." I hand Mrs. Johnson a five, but she waves it away.

"My treat," she says. "It's the least I can do." Cheryl's mom suddenly seems like one classy lady. I guess either you've got it or you don't.

It rained last night, a soft spring rain, and the greening grass is strung with a necklace of diamond dew that glitters in the sun. Like a ghost, I float around Aunt Jessie's kitchen, pouring out my Corn Flakes slowly, adding the milk, careful not to make a sound. I leave my unwashed dishes in the sink. Aunt Jessie will be pleased when she sees the cornflakes clinging to my bowl, the sparkle of sugar I didn't take the time to rinse. You're too thin, she told me last night at supper. Far too thin.

My bedroom at the farm is robin's egg blue and there's a sheepskin rug on the floor. The bed is a four-poster pine, the sheets are crisp and the quilt is heavy. When I'm lying there awake, I'm never afraid. Last night, when I came up the wide stair, I walked right past the bedroom door, drawn to the closet at the end of the hall. Its varnished door was silk beneath my palm, and I bowed my head and took a deep breath. The door was warped at the top right corner, and I had to tug hard before it gave.

My Aunt Jessie is an organizational wonder. Her closet shelves are neatly lined with rolled towels and perfectly smooth sheets, and sweet smell of linens that were dried on the clothesline outside. On the top shelf, there are three square boxes, labelled Thanksgiving, Christmas and Easter, Aunt Jessie's handmade decorations, carefully stored in them. My breath caught in my chest. Please God, I whispered, let it still be here.

I should have had more faith. Aunt Jessie has taken especially good care of my poncho. I find it wrapped in clear plastic on the second shelf. I lift it and unwrap it carefully, hold its softness to my cheek. When I slip it on, it feels like a whisper across my neck.

I fell asleep holding my poncho, totally dreamless until Jackie showed up. Or *was* she a dream? Close up, there were hints of blue beneath her eyes, and she stifled a yawn as she bent in the moonlight to tuck me in. For a moment, she didn't notice the poncho . . . But then she picked up a corner and ran her fingers over the even stitches. "It's so incredibly soft," she said and she touched my cheek lightly, just once. "Almost like a hug."

I blew her a kiss. No more visits, I told her. She smiled at me, began to shake her head.

No, I mean it. You have to look after yourself. For the children. And the president, too.

As I rolled over and pulled the poncho closer, I smelled my mother's soft scent. For a flickering moment, I felt the brush of her familiar hand across my brow.

For too long, Jake's been cooped up in the barn and the warren of corrals outside. This morning, he's standing at the fence, eyeing up the greening grass. It's not shirtsleeve weather yet, but it's getting close. The poncho will be perfect for days like today.

I know Uncle Ted's been too busy preparing for spring seeding to ride old Jake, and I wonder if Jake's been lonely. I fill a pan of oats, and he lifts his head, looks at me with his winter-weary eyes.

"Yep," I tell him. "We're going for a ride."

I turn Jake west and we gallop full bore. When he stops in an open meadow, I slip off his lathered back, let the reins fall. I squat in the scrubby grass, part it gently with my fingertips. I find a mound of crocus, five flowers in all, and then another. In a few days' time, they will paint the prairie in shades of purple but, right now, I feel as if they're blooming just for me.

I pluck two tiny blossoms, caress them — velvet on my fingertips — and then I weave them carefully into my hair. When I finally remount, Jake stands like a statue.

For the first time ever, he's taking his lead from me.

A Fun House Reflection
of My Own Sad Face

MEMORY GHOSTS GLIDE ALL AROUND THIS TOWN and I've always been frightened of coming back. I left home at seventeen, not nearly soon enough.

I've balanced on the deck of a drilling rig in the middle of an ocean, worked through blinding sandstorms and horrific heat in Yemen and Syria. I'm the guy who takes charge when the drilling goes bad and she's about to blow. One cool, calm lead hand, that would be me. So why is my heart now pounding, my breathing jagged and my hands cold and damp?

The white clapboard facade of St. Stephen's church, on the corner of Second Street and Main, is curling, and I have to duck when I enter through the door. I suppose, back then, building budgets were tighter and you just made do. Plus, our generation is taller than the last. Probably something to do with adequate nutrition, or lack thereof.

There's a wide centre aisle, for brides or coffins, and two side aisles, formed by rows of three-person pews angled to the walls. I know it's not the usual arrangement, but I am hoping Mother and I can sit along the side to avoid the staring eyes. Crystal blue light from a high window blankets the altar like frost, and I fight the urge to kneel. Instead, I bow my head and massage my brow. I jump when a missal falls from the lectern, thuds on the hardwood floor. A small statue of the Virgin Mary is tucked into an alcove near the front of the church and, suddenly, I see Ralph's lined face tucked into the crook of her left arm. He badly needs a haircut and he looks real sad. Ralph, I want to say. Why? Why? But somewhere a door creaks and then the pastor glides across the blood-red carpet and offers his hand. He blocks my view of Mary and, when he finally sits beside me, Ralph's face is gone.

"My condolences," he says.

"Thanks," I say, and pull out Mother's list. She's decided to let me handle the business end of this, as if having balls and a beard makes it easier for me than it is for her. Not that she's driving herself mad with questions or guilt. She has always believed firmly in God's divine plan. Right now, I envy her absolute certainty that Ralph is in a better place.

The minister and I go through the list, point by point. When we've covered everything — how many pews reserved for family, which of the psalms are appropriate, who's to do the eulogy — the pastor says "Shall we take a moment to pray?"

I shake my head, no. He stands up quickly, his gown swishing as he turns to walk away.

"There's one more thing," I say. "Can we play Ralph's favourite song?"

The minister turns out to be the old-fashioned kind, and won't hear of letting the King croon, "Wooden Heart" for

Ralph. He tells us that the soloist does an excellent job, and suggests "What A Friend We Have in Jesus". Old high-pitched hymns like that will give a guy a headache every time. Just my brother's luck. Even his funeral isn't going to turn out the way I know he'd like it to be.

The old home place is ten miles from town. I drive there alone. I need to see it again and I don't need my mother along, filling me in on what year this happened, what year that. The woman is a walking history book, full of dates and events so long in the past I've never heard of half the people she's always going on about.

I suppose the same thing will happen someday when I try to tell my kids, when I finally have them, about my brother, Ralph and what a nice guy he was, how he never said one bad thing about anyone. Not once in his whole, entire life. Maybe they won't ask what happened to him, why he died at the age of thirty-nine. Let's goddamn hope.

The Beamer whispers to a stop near the cargana hedge that straggles around the edge of the yard. The windmill still stands, but three blades are broken and the rest are gone. The rain gods have been generous and the grass is thick and aching, Irish green. I stumble against a hunk of crumbling foundation at the northeast corner of the house. When I finally get my bearings, I walk the perimeter, marking the ghostly remains with a trail of crumpled grass. The walls have fallen in on themselves. The cellar is full of broken boards. Signs of life are nearly obliterated, but the air is heavy with dreams.

The grandfather clock in the front hall is bonging a solemn nine. The roast has curled and dried, the fluffy mashed potatoes turned to globs of glue. Still, we wait, hunger rolling across our bellies in painful waves. My brother and I have already milked Betsy, and Mom is assembling the two million pieces of the separator when our father's truck chugs up the lane.

He shuts the door of the Chevy too precisely, so it makes a harsh metal sound. He holds himself too carefully erect, walks too slow. "Another quota," he says. "Trucks lined up for at least a half a mile." The sickly-sweet smell of rum wafts on the air.

Mother's jaw is set as she dishes up the ruined meal.

"You don't have to act like you're Mother Theresa," our father says. "A man should be able to take a sociable drink once in a while. Keeps the customers coming back. Christ Almighty, at least put a smile on your face. I haven't killed anyone."

He grabs for her waist as she plunks the milk jug in front of him, but she's too quick, evades his bumbling touch.

She sits ramrod straight at the opposite end of our plain, pine table, cuts her beef into small pieces. She chews slowly, swallows hard, as if there's something alive fluttering in her throat.

Ralph and I are as quiet as the dead. We don't want to do anything that might set him off.

He picks at his food, and pushes the dry beef with the edge of his knife. In the mound of potatoes mother has plopped on his plate, he barely makes a dent. Finally, he checks his watch and wobbles to the living room. When we hear the CBC news begin to blast, we disappear onto the porch.

Ralph stands beside me and I crank the handle of the separator, my muscles screaming at the first four turns. But once I get some momentum going, the handle almost turns itself. We watch the cream begin to trickle from the spout at the top, ears soothed by the steady *whir-whir-whir*. When my arm starts to feel like a long, wet noodle, I nod at Ralph. He moves closer and takes over the crank from me without missing a beat.

Eventually, the milk pouring through the spout slows to a thin dribble, and finally stops. I lift the bucket, fill a Rogers Syrup pail full of warm, sweet milk. Mounds of fluffy foam top the pail and I wait for it to settle so I can add a little more. Ralph and I carry the pail between us as we walk down to feed the kittens that live in our barn.

The kittens twine around our feet, push their furry bodies against our bare ankles and yowl. When we pour the milk into a battered pie plate, they scratch and scramble, pushing for a place. We watch as they drink, their hot pink tongues flicking out and in.

Ralph picks up the smallest kitten, its belly swollen with milk, and wipes the foam from its stubby whiskers. He tucks the little orange ball of fluff right beneath his chin. The kitten's sudden purr tickles down my spine.

"Do you think he'll be asleep when we get back?" Ralph asks.

I can feel his legs start to quiver as he stands beside me in the dark.

"We'll stay here a bit," I reply. "By the shape he was in, it shouldn't be long."

I move in close, my leg against his until he feels the warmth of my body and finally, he's okay. The soft, slurpy sound of kittens lapping milk lulls us almost to sleep. But then I look up, and see a dark shadow swinging from the beam our father insisted be so high and so strong. I blink and look again, the shadow is gone. A sudden shiver chills me. "It's time," I say to Ralph and I pick up the empty pail.

Those nights we spent huddled in the barn left bigger scars on Ralph than they ever did on me. The old man was all huff and puff and bluster, so all I really did was figure out how long to stay out of his way. Sure, he'd cuff you a good one if you got in his way or said something that ticked him off, but the blow was always weak, as if he really didn't have the heart. I learned soon enough that if you called bullshit just once, he'd leave you alone.

But Ralph let the fear settle in his bones.

I try to imagine the reason why, all his life, he longed to come back. Did he dream an ordinary life and came back home to make it real? He phoned me, when the old farm came up for sale, again. The house was near to falling apart when we were still boys, and I couldn't imagine how bad it would be after all these years. The only decent building on the place had been the barn. But Ralph had all it all figured out, how much it would cost each of us, how long before we'd own the place, free and clear.

"We can rent the land out at first," he said. "But I'm moving back. I'm going to build a solid little house, plant a lot of trees, fix up the old homestead, just like the Old Man always planned."

He was so excited that it took him a while to notice the silence on my end of the line.

"You're in, aren't you?" he asked, a catch of hesitation finally finding its way into his voice.

"No way," I told him. "Not on your life."

The roofline of the barn is as straight as the day that the rafters were raised. Ralph and I pitched in at the barn-raising bee, at least we thought we did. The old man put us on the working end of a wheelbarrow until his patience ran out, which took only a smidgen of our day. So mostly, we carried pails of icy water from our sand-point well down to the thirsty carpenter crew.

We set up the trestle table and helped our mother carry trays piled high with beef and egg-salad sandwiches on home-baked bread. I cut big slices of her double chocolate cake and slid them onto plastic luncheon plates, and Ralph scooped mountains of ice cream like a man possessed.

"Really, Ralph," Mother said, when she finally noticed the level of ice cream left in the pail. She flicked the back of his head with her hand. "Will you ever learn not to dive into things like there's no tomorrow? Ice cream will keep quite well, you know."

Ralph just grinned. Then suddenly he stooped, slurped up the pool of ice cream that he'd spilled on the flowered oilcloth. He winked at mother and, although she tried to turn away quickly, I know I saw the ghost of her smile.

"Time you boys got back to some real work," she said. "Down with the men."

For the rest of the day, we picked up stray nails and stacked odds and ends of wood. But mostly, we watched as our old man organized the building of the barn. One thing he insisted on was that the main beam had to be double thickness, and raised extra high.

When someone said it wasn't necessary to build it as solid as that, his cheeks flamed as fast as powder-dry prairie when someone drops a match. He stopped sawing and his eyes got icy. He said it was his goddamn barn and he'd build it the way he goddamn pleased and he didn't need any cut-rate carpenters telling him how.

The crew was deathly quiet when they finally raised the beam.

All I know is Ralph must have developed a hell of an arm if he threw the rope up there all by himself.

The weathered boards of the barn, pinked at the edges by the pure, soft light, look like velvet. My fingers ache to touch them. I walk to the barn, place my open palms on the big sliding door. The wood is slivered and hard, bitter on my skin.

My hand is tingling, like it was the night I touched Susie Sorensen in the Lion's park across from my grandpa's house, when I was fifteen and she, three days past thirteen.

The town had a curfew back then. When the whistle blew at dusk, every kid knew it was time to head for home. So I'd go home to Grandpa's and tell him good night. I'd wait until I heard the tap of his cane on the bedroom floor, the creak of his sagging springs and, when I was sure he was settled, I would edge up the stairs and let myself outside. Grandpa was a carpenter, and a good one too. Neither the stairs nor the screen door made a single sound.

I found a piece of gravel, flicked it at Susie's window. One time, two times, three. Finally, her sun-bronzed face appeared in the window as she eased up the sash. "What's up?"

"Come on," I whispered. "Full moon tonight."

Last Saturday, when he was too drunk to notice, Susie and I stole three beer from her brother's half-empty case, and hid it in a garbage can behind her old man's garage.

Susie eased out the window, first one long leg, then the other. Her white nightgown was gauze and lace, ruffled by the breeze.

"What are you waiting for?" she asked, taking my hand. Maybe she didn't realize how pretty she was and that she'd forgotten to get herself properly dressed. She led me, as if I were a blind man, across the freshly mown lawn. I stopped by the green garbage can and Susie grabbed the lid. It had only been two hours since I'd dumped in all four trays of Grandpa's precious ice, but the cubes had already melted to darkly stained murk. Susie plunged her hand in, and came up skunked.

"They're gone," she said, turning to me. She looked like an angel, the gauze of her nightie luminescent in the silver of the moon.

"Shit," I said, "some son-of-a-bitch must have found our stash." I grabbed her hand. Her palm was cool, still wet. I tucked it under my arm, and pulled her closer to me.

"Let's go anyway," I said. "Howl at the moon."

The park was deserted, the swings moving in ghostly rhythm to the whisper of the wind. Susie sat on the merry-go-round and started to push it around, foot trailing in the soft, fine dust. I stuck my hands in my back pocket, felt six jujubes I'd forgotten all about. I hopped on, sat down beside her and handed her two reds and three blues. The black, my favourite, I kept for myself. I could hear Susie sucking on her candies as she leaned into my arm. The silver of the moon was ensnared in the sticky sweetness at the edge of her lips. I leaned over, pushed her back onto the deck of the merry-go-round. First fast, then slow, I licked those lips. When she turned her head away, I rolled on top and pinned her down hard. Jesus, I thought, she's definitely not just one of the guys.

Susie had tagged along so often, we paid her absolutely no attention. She was smart enough to stay quiet on the sidelines and keep her mouth shut. But one day, when someone drew a circle in the dust and we pulled out our marbles, Susie dug into her back pocket and came up with a beautiful tiger's-eye glass.

"Do you mind if I play?" she said. Matt and Tom both shrugged.

"She's hanging around watching anyway," Ralph murmured. "Makes me damn nervous. Let's get her in the game." So I moved over, made some room.

"When you're playing with the big boys," Matt told her, "you better remember you're playing for keeps."

Susie just smiled and squatted beside me in the dust. That game of marbles brought out a killer instinct I'd never seen in Susie before. She won my cobalt blue shooter fair and square, but when she scooped it up and rolled in it the palm of her hand, I almost asked her if she would please give it back. She would have too. Thank God something made me look around, notice that the guys were watching what I'd do.

"You can have 'em all," I said, tossing her my purple velvet Crown Royal bag, lumpy with marbles. I heard the crunch of glass as she caught my pass. "There's gotta be something more interesting to do with my time." I stood up casually, hooking my thumbs into my belt loops, as if I didn't give a damn.

Bad enough to lose your best shooter, but to lose it to a girl? That day changed my view of little Susie, changed my whole damn world.

The merry-go-round wobbled as she tried to roll away. I felt the secret transformation of Susie's sturdy body, saw her teeth flash as she tried for a smile.

"Hey," she said, raising her head, trying to look me in the eye. I put my fingers over her mouth, traced the outline of her lips. She went quiet beneath me, like a rag doll that someone had forgotten to pick up and take home.

I could almost see through her gauzy nightie, and my right hand discovered its own way to see.

"Don't," she said and she pushed my hand away. She stayed cool, not even vaguely tempted by my clumsy teenage moves and the silver of the moon. Her absolute calm made me see red. "Cock tease," I hissed, sitting up, turning my back. "I'm gonna tell the whole world that you've been fucked for sure." Susie touched my shoulder and I turned around. "What's gotten into you?" she whispered, her blue eyes dark. I gave the merry-go-round a good hard spin. She was crying softly when I walked away, but I didn't look back.

I told the whole town and, at the time, not one person questioned what was true.

Teenagers in towns tend to run in packs. When they turn on a member, it's a dangerous time. I thought of owning up, of admitting Susie hadn't done one damn thing, except to trust a guy like me. But I didn't have the courage. The approval of the pack was vital to me.

Susie denied my accusations over and over, but no one listened. The more she protested, the worse it got for her.

When Ralph asked me one night if I'd really fucked Susie, I threw my half-full beer into the embers of our campfire, got up and walked away. "She just doesn't seem like that kind of a girl," Ralph hollered at my receding back. "And if she really isn't, I'd hate to think my own brother would do something so low, especially to a friend."

Mother has written me the details of Susie's hard life, more than I ever needed to know. She married too young and I've heard that her husband is as useless at tits on a boar. She checks groceries down at the Co-op store, has raised her three boys pretty well alone. I've thought often enough about Susie, my childhood friend, and how I fucked her over good. When those bells toll tomorrow, I hope she doesn't show.

The windmill creaks. For a moment, I think the blades are turning, but it's only the movement of the clouds as they scud across the sky.

I try to figure out what it was that called to Ralph, drove him out here, but a murder of crows, high in the branches of the poplar trees begins to caw. I don't get the draw. Never did, I guess. Suddenly, I can't wait to get back to town.

The Beamer purrs to life. Even the washboard gravel can't spoil her smooth ride. When I turn onto Main, I drive real slow and idle past the Co-op, the old brick post office and the false clapboard front of the hardware store. The Starlight Café sign swings in the breeze and I angle-park outside.

The plate-glass window, edged by some kind of climbing vine, is brightly lit. Four old guys sit in an orange vinyl booth close to the door. One of them slaps down a deck of cards. Another leans in, makes a slow, deliberate cut. Two cards drop, so he reshuffles, cuts once more. One of them gimps to the counter and refills his coffee cup.

The screen door is ragged and flies flit in and out. Willie Nelson croons "Georgia", his mellow voice soothing in the stillness of the night.

Deke was the Chinaman's boy. The youngest of the ten, born in the Union Hospital at the edge of town. Straight A student, and he spoke English better than most of us did. When we saw him on the street, we pulled up the corners of our eyes with the heels of our hands, pitched our voices high. "You orda Chinee food? Fly lice? Chickie baws?"

When he tried to kick us in the shins, we shoved the little bugger down into the dirt.

When we found out how easily Deke could dip his hand in his old man's till, he suddenly had a host of friends. Someone always suggested that we load his beer and then lose him before we headed out of town, but I didn't mind Deke. As long as he kept us in cool ones, I made sure to ask him along.

His old man caught him red-handed one Saturday night. I've always wondered what kind of Chinese torture made him spill the beans, because keeping us as friends was as important as breathing to Deke.

The cops pulled us in.

"Oh God, don't tell me he was stealing," we said. "From his own father? The kid must be crazy. We sure never asked him to supply us with beer. If we'd known he was buying it with stolen money, we never would have touched the stuff."

Ralph said we should level with the cops, but we bullied him to silence. He was always kind of timid, so it wasn't hard to do.

Charges were pressed, but the only one they stuck to was Deke.

We never thought of him as a person. We talked about sex and girls all the time, but no one asked Deke if he'd ever jacked off in the centrefold of a *Playboy* magazine. Not one of us ever invited him to our house, although we spent half our lives hanging around his in the Starlight Café. Of course, we'd been to his living quarters up the narrow stairs, but down in the café is where the family really lived. Homework in the right-hand booth at the back, supper at the long green counter, washing dishes in the kitchen after close. The café was the place Deke could always, always, always, find his mom and dad.

I'm waiting on the steps the day he goes away. Deke's father pulls the car up in front, leans over and opens the door. His suit shines at the elbow and his neck above the white of his collar is dried-out leather, wrinkled and brown. A wing of black hair shadows his deep-set eyes, already focused on the long road ahead. Music drifting from the jukebox wraps a soft shawl around us, but Deke and I both begin to shiver in the hazy August heat.

"It's time," I say to Deke. As he starts down the steps, my fingers brush his back.

I wave as Deke's small face fades from my sight. I keep on waving until my arm feels brittle, like strands of blown glass. I hope going to reform school doesn't wreck the rest of his life. I hope Deke realizes he's finally got a friend.

Memories are a sinkhole, icy cold and deep, and when I finally fight my way to the surface, my sheets are always tangled and damp and I can't get back to sleep until I turn on a light. I'm haunted by Deke, my Chinese friend.

Matt and Tom and I go down to the Starlight one night after Deke has been gone for a week or two. Ralph, as usual, has to tag along.

"Can I take your order?" his little sister asks, her enunciation true and clear. We change our orders twice as she squints under the fluorescent lights, painstakingly printing on her little yellow pad.

"Give the kid a break," Ralph says, when Matt decides to change his one more time. "And, anyway, we haven't got all night."

Four icy Cokes sit beading on the counter. Deke's mother peeks out, sees us sitting there. The swinging doors crash open and she starts to shriek. "You bad boys," she hollers. "Bad ones. Out. Out light now!"

I've heard that Deke runs the café now, just like his old man did, but there's no way I can walk in there and order up a Dinner for One, although I long to huddle in the safety of an orange vinyl booth, plug a dime into the jukebox and play some Elvis songs.

Through the dusty window, I see the cronies deal another hand of crib. "Fifteen two, fifteen four, fifteen six, and a pair is ten." The counting is a litany I've never quite forgotten. A guy with a few long grey hairs smoothed across his shiny scalp pegs quickly, before anyone takes note. Hell of a start, is what I know he's going to say. I step on the gas, let the night black me out.

The square of yellow light from my motel room window guides my fumbling fingers as I lean on the door. My room is fairly new, and still smells like plastic, not smoke or old grease. The key clicks the lock open first time I try. A square of tightly folded paper rests on the carpet inside the door, the small, precise writing more familiar to me than my own. I unfold the tight little note. Mother would like to meet for breakfast at the hotel by eight o'clock sharp. I'm not really interested in breakfast, and, if tomorrow didn't start until it was already over, it would be just fine with me

If I could get his keys from the cops, I'd probably find a big stack of Mother's letters, addressed in her careful hand, somewhere in Ralph's old desk. He saved that kind of thing. Letters, wedding invitations, newspaper clippings, the postcards I sent from London or Paris, Brisbane, wherever I happened to land. I'll bet the farm that Ralph's got every card I ever sent him, back when I used to keep in touch.

Why didn't I call, when I knew he'd come back home? Because I can see Ralph as clearly as if I were right there in his room.

His armchair, its soft, brown corduroy a caress for his aching back, creaks as he moves. One small lamp pools a soft yellow light. He gathers the flurry of unopened bills, flips through them one by one, then stacks them neatly and sets them aside.

From the bottom drawer of grandpa's scarred oak desk, he lifts a bundle of letters and cards, fans them on the emerald felt of his desk pad. He runs his hands over the little pile of papers like they were treasures from the deep.

He picks up a pen, writes his last note.

Dearest — My dream of coming home has now turned to dust. I guess I'm not a real farmer after all. The bank is losing patience and there's still no sign of rain.

I have always felt that some vital piece of me was missing, maybe that's why I spent my whole life longing to come back. The day I bumped into you again in the produce aisle at the Co-op, I felt that missing piece click firmly into place. I'm sure you felt it too, but sometimes, things just don't . . .

The line grows squiggly, staggers off the page.

The day is too perfect. Warm sun, high clouds, light little breeze. When I've settled Mother into the back seat of the Cadillac, I finally break the news that I'd far rather walk. My legs are aching to run, my slight body gone sluggish and slow. A few blocks won't help much but, maybe if I walk fast enough, I'll at least breathe deeply, finally draw some oxygen back into my lungs.

Mother starts to protest, but when she sees me raise my hand to twist and tug at long-gone locks of curly hair, she realizes the state I'm in. I broke my nervous habit of twisting and tugging before I started grade one at Vista Valley School. And I haven't had hair for more than ten years. "See you there, dear," she says. "I'll wait by the stairs."

The hearse is at least twenty years old but it's been polished to a mirror-like gloss. As it pulls away, I see a fun-house reflection of my own sad face. Blindly, I follow as Ralph sets the pace, four short blocks, his square, bulky body still moving slow. The cracks on the sidewalk blur, begin to snake up and down, and my stomach starts to clench. Someone lightly touches my arm. I stumble, look up, straight into Susie's blue eyes.

"Take care," she says. Her white dress is gauze and lace, ruffled by the breeze. She takes my hand, leads me like a blind man across the fresh-mown lawn. She guides me through the crowd to my mother, places my hand on her eighty-year-old arm. Susie strokes the top of my hand with a feather-light touch before she disappears.

Mother almost stumbles on the first step, where the cement has crumbled from years of assault by the alkali soil. I tighten my grip and we start to climb. Four more steps.

People in the foyer part to let us through. The minister raises his arms. It's time to go but my legs start to quiver, like Ralph's used to do when we were boys, hiding out together in the barn.

Someone moves in close, his leg against mine, until I feel the warmth of his body and, finally, I'm okay. The soft, snuffly sounds of a church filled with people whisper in my ears.

"It's time," Deke says to me, and his fingers brush my back.

ORDINARY LIVES

THERE IS NO LOGICAL REASON FOR MY handbag to contain three letters from a man I've never met. A man who's doing twenty-five years in a Louisiana jail. I try to imagine what the mailman must think. A post office box would have been a much better idea.

I hope our postie never runs into Dave and strikes up one of those idle conversations that can wreak havoc on ordinary lives.

Chimes tinkle and I look up, but it's not Desiree walking through the door. I should have known. We are both what they call 'emerging' writers, although I am already forty and she's not far behind. We meet monthly to critique each other's stuff, and to encourage each other to keep sending out stories, even though both of us could paper our guest rooms with rejection slips. I start looking forward to our next lunch almost as soon as our current one is over. Sometimes it's absolutely necessary to get out of the house and carry on a conversation with a person whose line of sight is higher than your belt buckle.

Desiree has no idea how much finagling I have to do to free up even an hour and a half. It's become a lot more complicated since Mother got a life. Not that I expected her to be around to babysit Carlie all the time but, lately, she's got plans every time I call.

My green tea still appears thin and pale, so I stir it briskly as I wait not so patiently for Desiree. There was a time in my life when men would ask if they could join me when I was lunching alone. Not anymore. I am average height, but I used to wear the highest of heels to maintain the illusion of the longest of legs. Now it's runners almost all the time. My chestnut hair is not quite as lustrous as it once was, a side effect of pregnancy I could have done without. The waitress hurries by, the decadent aroma of dark chocolate heavy in her wake. I deny my instant urge to order a cheesecake or a double fudge brownie. Since Carlie, I'm a little on the chunky side.

My eyes are my only distinguishing characteristic. One is a deep crystal blue, the other semi-sweet brown. My husband says it's disconcerting and that it's hard to maintain eye contact with me. It's like looking at two different people, is what Dave says.

The aroma of Jerry's special chili permeates the air. I love the smell of the exotic spices, and my mouth waters as I contemplate the unusual taste of cinnamon in the beef. Yellow block letters on the blackboard above the counter state digestible prices — two dollars for a cup, three-fifty for a bowl. Extra for the bun.

Jerry's is a trendy little place in an untrendy, workingman's town. I hope he makes a go of it here. It would be nice to see an underdog come out on top for once.

I know for sure that the hardhats on Dave's crews wouldn't come within a mile of Jerry's. Too many sprouts on his sandwiches, they say, not enough meat. And the mustard!

Full of little seeds and it tastes like hell. When Dave offers to pick up sandwiches for his crew if they're heading out of town on a job, they all want Subway. The guys all think Jerry's gay, is what Dave says. I wonder if they think being gay is something you can catch, like the measles or the flu. All I really know about Jerry is he makes the best brownie I've ever tasted. Almost sinful, I'd say.

Three walls in the bistro are painted a pleasing shade of pumpkin, and the fourth is deep chocolate brown, the colour so true I fight a sudden urge to walk over and lick it. Two elderly ladies are playing checkers on a low table beside the sofa. Magazines litter the top of an old sewing machine and more magazines are piled on the treadle below. An antique apple crate screwed to the back wall holds paperback fiction — authors like Margaret Atwood, Carol Shields, Bonnie Burnard. Nothing by male fiction writers, I'm puzzled to note.

I reach into my bag and finger the envelopes, bound tightly together by a blue rubber band.

I check my watch again. Twelve-thirty-five. I drink the last of my tea, stare at the leaves, but I can read nothing there. The smell of cinnamon is everywhere, sweet and somehow bitter too. I think this might be the end of the road for Desiree and me.

Jeopardy, Dave calls and I come in from the kitchen, wiping the last of the dish suds from my hands and onto my jeans. Dave builds houses for the wealthy, palaces actually, and his forty-three year old body is buff and brown. He lifts his plaid lap blanket and I slip in beside him, lean against his muscled arm.

"Carlie's asleep," he says. "She only lasted halfway through *Are You My Mother?* tonight. Thank God." He stretches wide and I admire the flex of his muscles, the rise of his chest.

"One of my guys didn't show up this morning and I was on the working end of a wheelbarrow for at least half the day. I'm totally bagged."

"You work too hard," I say.

But Dave has already hit the volume button and Alex Trebeck fills our small living room, his voice so loud I almost miss the phone. "And the category you've chosen is After-after." What in the world, I think, is After-after?

"Osiris was the Egyptian God of this." Alex flips his index card over, looks expectantly at the contestants. A chubby woman with horn-rimmed glasses is smiling smugly. Beside her, an athletic-looking college type guy is rubbing his brow with the forefinger of his right hand, his eyes tightly closed. The guy I'm rooting for, on the far right, is staring into the lights, eyes wide and blank.

"Hello," I say, the receiver in my hand but my mind with Alex Trebeck. The plumber from L.A. has a slim lead. Quick, I think, what is after-life? Spit it out. Come on! Say it.

"Hi, Joan," I hear Buddy say and I know right away my brother wants something from me. He never calls just to talk. "I was thinking about Mom. I'm kinda' worried. This crazy idea she's got about packing up her life and hitting the road seems so out of character. Somebody should talk some sense into her, don't you think?"

"Really?" I say.

"Maybe you can bring it up somehow," Buddy says. "You know, tell her we're concerned. Make sure she's not going off half-cocked."

"I'm even not going to try," I say. "I'm going to show up there on Friday and help her pack her things, just like she asked."

Our seventy-four-year-old mother has found her soulmate on a lawn-bowling green in Florida. She'd mentioned Albert's name last winter in her letters home, but I didn't know it was serious until she came back to town and put our childhood home up for sale. She and Albert are planning to tour the southern states in a Winnebago, starting the end of October and coming back sometime in March.

When she told me, I almost said, "what about Dad?" But I managed to swallow those words. My memories of my father are shadows, wrapped in white mist. Mom has always talked about Dad like he'd just left the room for a while and would soon be back. Sometimes, her stories about the things he would do or say, or what he used to like, irritated me and I felt like screaming, telling her that he'd been dead and gone for years. But now I realize she was trying to keep him real for Buddy and me. And maybe for herself.

But hey, if she's finally letting Dad go and plans to grab a little happiness while she still can, good for her. Still, the soulmate thing threw me, I have to admit. I think it threw Buddy too.

"Are you coming to help?" I hold the phone close, almost whispering. I have a pretty good idea how Buddy will reply. He's always left the hard stuff for me. With a name like Buddy, what can you expect?

"I'm kind of busy," he says, "but I'll see what I can do." I hear the rasp of his cigarette lungs. "At least find out about the guy. Maybe he's a no-good. After her money."

"Buddy," I say, my fingers drumming the sofa arm, "you know damn well there's not much money to be after. So let's assume Albert loves her madly, just like she says."

I hang up quickly when the plumber bets all his money on Final Jeopardy. Of course, he blows the question and now he's shaking Alex's hand, a sickly smile fixed on his face.

I walk to the picture window. The full moon is shining blue, the leaves on the trees shivering in the ghostly light. I fold my arms across my chest and turn back to our cozy room.

"Come on, honey, it's time we hit the sack." Dave groans as he tosses the throw aside and takes my hand.

The new owners of Mom's house talk her into pushing the possession date ahead two weeks. I have no idea how we'll ever weed Mom's stuff down so it'll fit into the storage space available in a Winnebago, and I imagine Albert will come with a few possessions of his own.

True to form, Buddy doesn't show. Just like the fabulous disappearing Desiree, I think. I wonder how it is that I'm surrounded by totally unreliable people. Except, of course, for Dave.

Apparently, Buddy hasn't bothered to call, so Mom keeps expecting him and she goes to the window every time she hears a vehicle approach.

I shudder to think how many times Buddy has left Dave high and dry on the jobsite, when he wakes up too shaky to snap a line or mud a single brick. Buddy is an artist with brick and mortar but he's got the artistic temperament too, a trait that doesn't fit with deadlines and anxious owners wanting their places completed a week before the contract says. Guys like Buddy walk all over people like Dave.

Mom is peering down the street again and I can't stand it anymore. "I think Buddy got called in to work this morning." The lie slips out smoothly. "Didn't he phone?"

"I believe he may have," Mom says. "Early this morning, I think. But it seemed like a dream. I've been so tuckered out from all this packing."

So while I sort and pack, Mom spends hours sifting through piles of books, boxes of faded pictures, Dad's old tools. "Do you think Buddy might like to have his crescent wrenches?" she asks. "Do you think he might like this old straight razor? It's still in perfect shape. I think the handle might be real ivory."

When I decide to tackle the kitchen, I start by dumping the junk drawer onto the grey arborite of the table. I run my hand over the grooves in the chrome near the corner, the ones I inadvertently made with a bread knife when I was sawing two thick slices of Mom's homemade bread. One for Buddy. One for me. Suddenly, the smell of fresh-baked bread fills the kitchen. My mouth waters. I almost expect to see six brown loaves cooling on the bread rack. But the counter is bare, even the coffee canister emptied and packed.

I focus on the jumble of lids and string, nails and screws, can openers, odd knives, a pair of rusted scissors. I shake the drawer one last time. An envelope is stuck in a groove at the back of the drawer.

I tug until it comes free. Inside the yellowed envelope, I find a black and white snapshot of two little boys on a big roan horse. I study the snapshot, and finally decide that one of those boys is my father at about the age of twelve. The other is younger, and he's hanging on to my dad's waist, clinging to him as if he were about to fall.

"Who's this?" I say.

"You'll have to come here, dear." Mom is standing on a chair, reaching for a pair of dusty Red Rose tea kittens curled on a shelf.

"You should leave that for me," I say.

I offer my hand and, surprisingly, she takes it. "Oh, dear," she says, when I hand her the picture. "Oh, dear." We sit on her flowered couch, which will soon become a garage sale treasure for some poor soul.

"Who's this?" I say, pointing to the picture of the smaller boy. "The other one's got to be Dad."

My mother draws a deep breath. "It's your Uncle Bennie," she says. "Four years younger than your dad."

"What? Dad had a brother?"

"They were left alone," she says, "at an early age. First their father died from that awful flu and, a few weeks later, their mother too. So they had to fend for themselves while they were still closer to being boys then men. Your dad was so lucky, getting on steady at the hardware store. He often said landing a full time job saved his very life."

I have never imagined my father desperate, or young. I picture him beside the open ended metal bins at the hardware store, patiently sorting nuts and bolts, washers and nails, returning the wayward ones to their proper place. I see his solid shoulders, square beneath his fisherman knit sweater, the green-shaded lights suspended from the tin ceiling emitting shafts of yellow, their rays probing his thinning hair. My father is forty-nine. The oldest he ever got to be.

He methodically fills the shelves with new stock: soft leather gloves, denim coveralls, stiff and grey. I can smell new leather and, from the hot metal of the light shades, the slowly roasting odor of bluebottle flies. Finally, he looks up, notices me standing on the wide stairs at the back of the store. The balcony above me is home to my father's office, where he spends endless hours. A ledger is open and papers are piled everywhere.

"Time for you to head home," he says, and pulls a gumball from his hip pocket, blueberry blue, my favourite kind.

"Thanks, Dad," I say, and I lean against the counter, rolling the gumball in my hand until my palm is stained. Then I pop it into my mouth, lick blue from my hand.

"Scoot now," he says. "Tell your mother I'm running a little late."

I stand outside the screen door and watch as he bundles up a parcel, hands it to Mrs. Hankins, who had taken forever to decide what to buy. When he opens the door for her, he sees me lingering. "Home now," he says. "Really. I won't be long."

She's turning the picture again. "Benny wasn't as lucky as your dad. He wasn't really bad, but he was a wanderer, couldn't settle into anything. Times were hard," she says, her eyes far away. "I think sometimes Benny went hungry. Maybe that's why he turned to petty crime."

Benny loved the trains, she tells me. When he could afford to pay, he bought a ticket and travelled passenger coach. When he couldn't, Benny rode the rails. He'd even figured out how to slow the train.

"Imagine this. There used to be a steep grade just west of town, near the trestle bridge. Benny would grease the rails with fresh cow manure and wait there until a loaded freight train came along. When the steel wheels hit the manure, the train lost traction. Your father used to sit on the back porch and watch for the smoke. The train would spin out, and slow right down. Benny could jump the train then and find a place to hide."

My mother's face is creased in a smile. "Ingenious of him, really, to figure that out." She takes a deep breath, looks me in the eye. "He only stole from people with plenty of money," she says. "Men who sat in the club car flashing their cash. If they were polite and respectful, he left them alone."

Mother rubs her finger across the picture, stops on Benny's left leg. "I think he did okay," she says, "as far as pickpockets go."

I try to imagine.

"He'd show up once in a while, with only his valise," my mother said, shaking her silver head. "But he was always clean, wore a crisp white shirt and little black bow tie. And he always had his own bar of soap. He'd ask if he could rinse out his clothes. Of course, I did it for him. Pitiful really. One undershirt, two white shirts, one short-sleeved, the other long and frayed at the cuff. Two pair of black woolen socks. Of course, he must have had underwear. But he was a gentleman. I never washed his shorts."

"Mom," I say. "Why didn't we know?"

"Benny hopped a freight one October morning, at least that's what he told your father he intended to do. Said he was going to Vancouver. Saskatchewan winters were too long and too cold, he said, hard on his gimpy leg. He said he'd send a postcard, one with the downtown Vancouver skyline lit up like a Christmas tree." Mom stops for a moment and folds her hands. "He never came back," she says. "Your father was at the lumberyard that morning, but still, I'm sure he stood outside, watched for the plume of black smoke to the west. I think he had some sense of foreboding, because he began to watch for a letter almost right away. We never did get one and I thought it might kill him, the not knowing."

She turns the picture over, rubs it across the cotton of her dress. "I couldn't stand to see your father waiting day in and day out, so I talked him into putting Benny to rest."

"How did you?" I ask.

"We arranged a memorial service for Benny, as if we knew he was really gone. Just your father and I, and old Reverend Pringle."

"Tell me more," I say.

"Not much to tell. He was clean, he was quiet. He came and he went." She rubs her fingers across the picture, turns it to the light. "He had a pronounced limp. From the polio when he was a child. He always said if he hadn't had such a noticeable limp, he could have been a successful bank robber. But he was too easily identifiable. Restricted him to being a small-time crook. So it was a blessing in disguise, that wasted leg."

She puts the picture in Buddy's pile. "Maybe your father never really got over losing Benny," she says. "We didn't talk about it. Not at all. Maybe all the wondering wore a hole right through your father's heart." My mother takes off her glasses, polishes them with the edge of her checked apron. "Maybe that explains why he left this world too soon."

I stand up, suddenly disoriented.

I was seven and Buddy was ten. All that summer, he talked me into trouble, then disappeared like a morning mist. I had to return a box of jawbreakers Buddy and I had lifted to Sam's corner store and explain to Sam that Buddy had just forgotten to pay, lying like a fool, while Buddy waited in the alley outside. I didn't own up and apologize for stealing, like our mother had insisted Buddy do.

"Do you want to be on Sam's shit list forever?" Buddy had asked as we walked to the corner, and I shook my head. He'd rewarded me with his hundred-watt smile. "Thanks for not ratting me out," he said.

I remember why I've always called Buddy's easy grin his con man smile.

"Let's take a break for a while," I say to Mom. "I'll make some tea."

In the harsh florescent light of the kitchen, she sits in her usual spot, and when I turn to light the stove, I feel a squeezing in my chest. When the tea is steeped, I pour Red Rose into two silver birch cups and slide one across the table to my mother.

"You okay?" I ask.

"Yes. But I have to admit, this is hard. When I found your father's broken pocket watch, it nearly made me weep. Do you remember how he'd polish it before we went to church on Sundays?

"No, I don't." I've tried, really tried, to remember, but mostly, I can't.

My mother reaches across the table, briefly touches my cheek. She has always been a stiff-upper-lip type of person, not given to impulsive hugs or any touch without a reason, like the dreaded spit washes on my ten-year-old dirt-smudged face.

Maybe all this talk of Uncle Benny has finally breached her impregnable wall.

"Lots of memories here," I say. "For both of us." I turn my cup in my cold hands, wonder if I should proceed. "You were a good mom," I finally say. "You did everything for Buddy and me. I know you tried to do double duty, and Buddy and I never gave it a thought. What you'd lost."

I think of Dave, his steady ways, how he helps with Carlie all the time, so unobtrusively that, sometimes, I hardly notice him at all. Carlie will be blessed with clear memories of her father giving her horsie-back rides, reading her bedtime stories in her pink bedroom, tucking her in. Sometimes, I think I remember my father's voice, feel his gentle touch, but I am never sure.

"Do you remember how your father and I used to argue?" my mother asks. "I was always worried that you and Buddy would hear."

The shadows moving across the bare walls of this almost empty house dip and waver, and I can feel an ending, for my mother, and for Buddy and me.

"No, I don't," I say. "Did you argue a lot?"

"Some," she says. "Or maybe a little more. It took us a while to grow together. He was so stubborn and, maybe, so was I."

She takes another sip of her cooling tea. "With Albert, it was totally different," she says. "When I saw him for the first time at the potluck supper, I had the strangest feeling I'd met him before, that I knew everything about him."

I'm glad she doesn't say anything about soulmates. It would have been more than I could stand.

"Well," I finally say, "we better carry on if we don't want to be here half the night."

A half hour later, I give the kitchen one last look to see if I've missed anything. The envelope is propped against the Barkerboard backsplash, and I pick it up, smooth the creases with my fingertips.

St. Tammany Parish Jail is stamped across it in red. *Inmate Correspondence Not Censored.* There's a return address in the left hand corner. It ends with *Prisoner 28, Cell Block 2.* Uncle

Bennie's handwriting, I wonder and I slide the envelope into my purse. Did my father find him after all?

Every morning, I get up at six to make Dave's breakfast before he leaves and I always pack his lunch. Today, it's roast beef on whole wheat with lots of lettuce, easy on the mayo. Homemade gingersnaps.

"Have a good day," I say as I kiss him goodbye. "Come home safe tonight."

After I've bathed Carlie, I try to comb her frizz of yellow hair. She cries and pulls away, so I kiss her, apologize. "Mommy's sorry," I tell her. Let's get your coat on and we'll go to the park. Try out the high slide."

Carlie's blonde head bobs as she holds the garbage bag and Janet stuffs it with fallen leaves. Janet is a good neighbour and I wonder why I haven't spent more time with her, instead of wasting my days with Desiree. Desiree's like a morning fog, sometimes coiling close, sometimes leaving just a hint that she's been anywhere near.

I love watching my daughter, love knowing that Dave's white shirts are waiting in a jumbled pile on the basement floor. The basement is cool, dimly lit. I pick up Dave's shirt, scrub its collar with Sunlight soap. I think of Uncle Benny, his pitiful pile of laundry, his whole life folded inside the battered valise. I wonder what really happened to him and why my parents didn't try harder to find out. Maybe he's still out there somewhere, chasing his dreams. Some days, my life seems so dull, so small and contained. Some days I can't even remember what I dreamed I would be.

When I send the first letter to the St. Tammany Jail, I am well aware that Uncle Benny's probably long gone from this world and quite possibly never was an inmate there. But I think Dad kept that envelope hidden for a reason and I give in to my curiosity about Prisoner 28, Cell Block 2.

What do you say? I have no idea, so I just write a few details about my life. That I'm a stay-at-home mom, in the process of learning to be a writer. I don't call myself a writer yet, I say, but I hope to, someday soon. I send along a picture, me leaning against the old maple in our backyard. Dave took it last Sunday after we'd raked the leaves. Leaves as big as a bricklayer's palm cling to my shirt and yellow sun shines on my face through the scraggly leaves that still cling to the tree. I look happy, and about as close to beautiful as I'm ever going to get.

A month goes by before the postman delivers the letter. *Dear Joanie*, it begins.

When I was thirteen, I decided I could not stand my given name. Joan. To me, it said steady, dependable, hard-working. It said nothing about dancing in the moonlight, nothing about chugging beer around a campfire, about miniskirts and long, long legs. I told my friends and family I wouldn't answer to Joan any more. "Call me Joanie," I told them, "or don't call me anything at all." Of course it didn't stick.

Dear Joanie, I say aloud.

Please allow me to introduce myself. My name is Bill McMurtry and I am happy to have received your letter. It's been a long time since I've had any contact with the world outside. I am an avid reader, and it intrigued me to hear you are a writer. (I realize you say you are learning to write, but by the composition and content of your letter, I've decided you're a writer already and shall refer to you as such.)

Thank you for including the picture. I think you are very beautiful. Beauty and brains, what a combination! The purpose of my letter is in hope of finding someone to write to. I am thirty-nine years old, six feet tall and 195 pounds, with blue eyes and black hair — although I shave my head. Working out in a cell is challenging, but I do it anyway. My teeth are straight and, despite my inclination for adventures that place me in jeopardy, I come from a good family. Unfortunately, I am doing this time alone, as my family is no longer. I surmise that you have a significant other in your life, but hope that you will be inclined to write to me.

My life has been filled with many adventures, such as travel (I have even been to Edmonton, Alberta) and many people have said to me I should write a book on my life. I am a multiple bank robber, but came from a family of privilege. I was starting my third year of college towards a bachelor's degree in chemistry (I wanted to be a teacher) when a catastrophic event happened in my life, which sent me in a direction that preceded my outlaw life. I have morals and values that I tossed aside in the heat of the moment, but I have asked forgiveness and believe that perhaps I will be given another chance.

I apologize for rambling on. Let me close by saying that perhaps divine providence has directed your letter to my cell. Take care, Joanie.

I wish you the best of luck.

Sincerely,

Bill

For some reason, I hold the letter to the light, as if it holds some hidden message. Finally, I hide it in a fake leather suitcase in the back of the closet. This man is obviously not my long lost uncle, but his gratitude at receiving a letter is really sad. Should I reply? Should I not? I know I am playing with fire.

I'm stretched out on the grass, my bathing suit pulling at my hips. The yard has been baked by the relentless sun and there's no relief to be found, so I've given up on the shade and decided to work on my tan. I watch Carlie swooshing back and forth in her blue plastic pool, and consider joining her.

Dave's work truck rattles up the drive and I check my watch. Two-fifteen? I hope everything's okay. When he lopes around the corner of the house, he's grinning. No big disaster on the worksite today.

"Could I interest you babes in some real beach time?" he asks. "Out at the park?"

He peels off his sweaty shirt. "We got the Sorensen house done," he says, "two days ahead of schedule. And the cement work's not completed for the Wilson one yet. So we're at a standstill."

Dave spends his summers measuring and sawing, hoisting rafters, and hammering buckets of nails. Carlie and I have learned to entertain ourselves in the backyard, at the playground, sometimes at the pool.

"Are you two going to sit there gawking, or are you going to pack us some grub?" Halfway up the steps, he stops to unlace his boots, and I admire the muscles bunched on his brawny back.

"We're coming." Carlie hops from the pool, leaving footprints on the sidewalk as she runs helter-skelter for the open door. "Wait. Wait for us."

When we hit the highway, I roll down my window, savour the rush of air across my sweat-slicked arms. My hair whips across my cheeks, tickles my neck. Carlie leans against me, singing a tuneless song. "Mom," she says, sitting suddenly upright. "My guitar. We forgot."

When the doorbell rang one Saturday morning before I'd finished my first coffee, I was surprised to see Buddy standing there. I almost asked him where he'd been and why he hadn't, at least, called if he wasn't going to show up at the job site for three days running. Instead, I said, come in, how are you, what brings you out so early?

He was holding his old guitar. "Brought Mathilda over," he said. "For Carlie. Won a new one in a poker game." A curtain of hair obscured the hard-living lines on his face. I wanted to reach out, push that hair back in place.

Carlie will love it, I told him, but she's not even up yet. Have you any idea what time it is? When he looked at his watch, Buddy's eyes widened and I realized he hadn't even been to bed.

"Come on in," I told him. "Since you woke me up, you can darn well stay for coffee. Tell me what's going on in your world."

Buddy's shadowed eyes cleared. "I'm pretty sure you don't really want to know," he said, "but the coffee sounds good. Really good right now."

So Buddy and I sat in my yellow kitchen, sipped our coffee, talked about the weather, about Carlie and kinder-garten, how his garden was coming along, anything but what I really wanted to say. And when Carlie stumbled down the stairs, Buddy held out his guitar.

"Brought you something," he said and she rushed to his side, leaned on his long, thin leg. She reached out, ran her baby-fat fingers along the frets.

"For me, Uncle Buddy?" she asked. "For me?"

Buddy's old Ovation now has a place of honour in our dining room. Carlie picks at the strings, nags me for lessons, but I told her she has to wait until her hands get a little bigger.

"Can we go back home and get it? Can we please? Uncle Buddy told me I could play it around the campfire, just like he used to do."

"There'll be lots more campfires," I tell her. "For now, you just sing. You've got a good voice. Pure and clear and true."

So Carlie, easily distracted, launches into "You Are My Sunshine". Dave weaves in and out of the summer traffic. My daughter's voice fades into the rush of the wind. When I wake up, sweet pine perfumes the air. I offer to help Dave pitch the tent, but he turns me down. Really honey, he tells me, this is a one-man job.

Carlie calls a stray puppy into our campsite, so we walk around, hoping to find its owner. It's a cute little mutt, maybe a Boston Terrier cross. "Did you lose your dog?" Carlie asks from the perimeter of each site. I know she's hoping this dog is a stray and that she'll be able to take it home. "No," the man in campsite number ten says. "But if anyone asks, I'll tell them a cute little girl's taking good care of their dog."

Carlie beams. I'm sure she thinks the puppy will soon belong to her. Then we hear a cracked voice calling. "Here, Lizzie. Lizzie, come to Papa. Come on home."

The dog jumps from her arms with an excited yap, yap, yap.

"I think that little puppy's found her home," I say. "The poor little guy must have been kind of scared, wandering around alone."

Carlie sniffs as a tall man strides around the corner, the puppy snuggled in his arms.

"Are you the folks who found my Lizzie?" he asks and when Carlie shakes her head, yes, he thanks us again and again. "She's the only company I have now," he tells us. "Camping's not the same since I lost Estelle."

I tell him that we're glad we could help, and I pat his arm for a moment, before we turn to leave. "You keep right on camping," I say. "I bet Lizzie just loves it out here."

As Carlie and I walk, darkness gathers in the swaying pines, and cedar smoke drifts in the air. I count my many blessings, count double for Carlie, and for Dave.

"Let's go roast some marshmallows," I say to her. "Daddy should have a good fire built by now."

Later, when Carlie's zipped into her sleeping bag and Dave and I are sitting by the fire, I lean against him, take one last sip from my wine, and turn my face to a night sky peppered with stars.

"We are so lucky," I say. "Imagine if you could never see the sky. And you were only allowed outside for a half hour once a week." Dave pulls me closer as a shiver runs through my body.

"Listen to the silence," I say. "Imagine a place where you listen to rap videos, wrestling, the worst of the soaps, all day long. Volume always cranked too high."

"You imagine too much," Dave says.

He takes my glass, sets it on the ground.

Dear Joanie,

I thank you profusely for your kindness. You have no idea how even the anticipation of your letters shortens my days. You ask me if there's anything I need. Of course there is. I need to be held on dark nights when ghosts and goblins roam about. Seriously, if you can send me some reading material I would be most grateful. I've been studying geometry, the make-up of the physical world and its integration with the metaphysical. I'm missing On Growth and Form, *by D'arcy Thompson and anything you have on the layman's guide to the string theory. Books have to be soft cover and must be sent by a bookstore or publisher. Also, I'm open to anything else you think I should read.*

I spend my days trying to find things to do. It's boring here but I have lots of time for legal work and study. And cards. I am the cribbage champion of Cell Block 2. I sometimes feel the title might be worth my life. The fellows here don't take losing well but, nevertheless, I have to admit I take no small amount of pride in this accomplishment, paltry as it may seem.

My appeal lumbers along slowly, as most things in the so-called justice system do. I sometimes think judges in this country are chosen by their past successes in hog-calling contests and the lawyers get their degrees at the local Wal-Mart store.

But I am learning. In the meantime, I live on hope.
Your letters make it possible.
Yours truly,
Bill

The phone shrills, makes me start. "Mom," Carlie says, pulling away from my busy fingers. "Thmarten up. You're pulling my hair." She's lost her two front teeth, and her lisp is pronounced. The tooth fairy left five dollars for her first tooth, three for number two. Now she's hoping all her teeth will go and she's wiggling a third tooth with her fingers, a line of silver drool darkening the front of her shirt.

"Sit still for just one more minute," I say. "I'm almost done." I give her braid a final twist and grab the phone on its third ring.

"Hi." Desiree's voice, and I am surprised. I'd left messages on her answering machine for three straight Mondays, and when she didn't return them, I kind of wrote her off. "It's me. Could we get together for lunch? Get started again?"

"Desiree," I say slowly. "It's been a while." She starts to babble about her latest stories, how they seem to flow from her pen. "It's like they're writing themselves," she bubbles. "You've got to read them, tell me if they're any good. They're coming so easy it makes me nervous."

"Okay," I say, and I twist the phone cord until it's a hopeless tangle.

"Are you writing much these days?"

Carlie has opened the fridge and grabbed the glass pitcher of Kool-aid I mixed up not ten minutes ago. I can see a lake of green all over my freshly washed floor.

"Carlie," I say, my hand over the receiver, "wait one minute. Momma will help. Sorry," I say into the phone. "I'll call you back later. I've got a disaster in the making. I've really got to go."

Yeah, Desiree, I think, I'm writing a lot, but it's nothing I really want critiqued. I'm writing almost every week to a convict in Louisiana. He knows a lot about what I think, how I feel. All about my hopes and dreams. He even knows how I look.

He's given me suggestions on easy ways to improve the soil in my garden and he's researching plants native to zone three so I can have a beautiful, yet maintenance-free yard. He doesn't know one damn detail about Carlie or Dave. If I told him about that part of my life, I'd really feel like I was committing adultery. It's bad enough the way it is. Can you think of a literary genre that encompasses letters to convicts? Letters where you pour out your heart?

"You seem kind of zoned out lately," Dave says. He's drying the dishes, something he rarely does.

"I'm just tired," I say. "Must be the dreary weather. Cloudy days make me want to crawl in a hole and pull it in after me."

He takes my soapy hands, blows the bubbles from my palms. "As long as everything's okay," he says.

"Well, for one thing, Buddy's all worried because he hasn't heard from Mom for awhile," I say. "He keeps phoning me, as if I should know what to do."

"I'm sure she's just fine," Dave says. "Enjoying her honeymoon on wheels all across America. She's probably forgotten about Buddy and you. Amazing the things love can make you do."

I'm afraid to leave the house. What if the mailman delivers a letter and I'm not here to intercept it? What if Dave sees the envelope, asks me about the return address of the St. Tammany Parish Jail?

Through the small squares of my kitchen window, I see Bill walking to our house like he belongs at 1230 Winnie Street. His black hair is cut short and slicked back and his body is thin and so, so white. Dave is painting our new front door a rusty red, and his square shoulders dip as he leans to rest his brush on the rim of the pail. Then he straightens, and I hear his friendly voice. "Hi," he says, moving down the step and extending his hand. " Thought I knew everyone around this town, but I guess it's not so. Are you looking for someone? Anything I can do to help?"

Oh, no, I think. Please, God, no. I have been so damn careful and Dave has no idea.

When Desiree calls again and wants to get together, I tell her I haven't written a thing for the last three months. I tell her I'm busy trying to get back on track with my writing and that as soon as I've got something decent, I'll give her a call. It's just so hard to get away right now, I say. Especially since Carlie's started playschool. I tell her I'm beginning to feel like an unpaid chauffeur.

What I don't tell her is I feel like a fraud.

Dear Joanie,

When you've been in jail as long as I have, you kind of run out of news. So I've been ruminating about things in life you don't forget. On the top of the list, of course, is your first sexual encounter. Mine was in Branson, Missouri, and I was on a school band trip in a chartered bus. It was from the Bluebird Line, padded seats, air conditioning, the whole ball of wax.

I was scheduled to perform a saxophone solo during the final competition at Branson High. Our director, Dickhead McLeod, had worked very hard to shape us up, and we were poised to take first place.

You probably don't want any more details, but I missed the solo and McLeod expelled me because I didn't show.

It was a pretty easy choice for me. A duo with Mary Anne Mason in the back of the empty Bluebird bus or a saxophone solo on the stage of a jam-packed gym. Like I say, some experiences you never forget.

Another that's stuck with me forever, and I think it's the penultimate as far as thrilling goes, is the joy of bagging a brand new Beamer, or a Jag, turning up the tunes, seeing the countryside whipping by so fast everything's a blur. The adrenaline rush will almost take off the top of your head.

In one of the photos you sent, I noticed an old Chevette parked in what I assume is your driveway. The car itself was blurred, but it didn't look to be the kind of car for a woman like you. So I guess you already know what it's like to drive a piece of shit. So do I, because I tried it in another life. And, I must say, after driving a Beamer, those economy models absolutely suck. I've been pondering this and I've decided to share some information with you. You can consider it my first gift to you, and do with it what you will.

A guy I met in here who used to 'shop' for cars in Houston and bring them to New Orleans told me this. Luxury car dealerships (the big ones, try Calgary, I think that's the closest one for you) have a keyboard on the wall with all of the keys to their demos and best trade-ins.

The caliber of used cars at those luxury dealerships is unbelievable. Imagine being rich enough to trade in a perfectly good car with hardly any miles. Most of those cars have probably been owned by old peckerheads too chicken to put the pedal down more than half way.

Anyway, the pegboard is usually in a convenient place on the showroom floor so the salesmen have easy access. So, pick out your car, be sure it's parked where leaving the lot is easy, then pick a busy day, lift your keys and drive away. It's easier if you slap on different plates near the edge of town. Also, it helps if you know someone in the licensing bureau. You might just want to store it out at Buddy's acreage, just drive it around when you visit. (Only if Buddy knows how to keep his mouth shut, of course. You'd be the best judge of that.)

I am still waiting to hear on my latest appeal. Remember, I told you my hair is black but I shave my head? Well, I've stopped. I figure if I win my appeal and actually get to walk in the world again, I want to blend in, not draw undue attention to myself. You might meet me on the street and not even give me a second look.

Love

Bill

PS: If I lose my appeal and you get a car as per the above, maybe you can drive my getaway car. (Ha! Ha!) Maybe we could find somewhere unique in your country that's neither in Saskatchewan or Quebec. I've been doing some armchair travel and I've found some pictures of a really cool spot. Tofino, BC. Ever been there? Apparently, it's a wonderful place. The writer says the ocean there gives real meaning to the word 'awesome'. It's something I'd love to see. Who knows? It might be soon!

I fold the letter, tuck it into the back pocket of my jeans. The thermometer just hit eighty-two and Carlie is whining to go to the spray pool. I bribe her with a grape Popsicle and tell her to sit on the back step in the shade.

"The grass is getting too long," I say. "Work before pleasure."

Carlie's purple moustache grows bigger by the minute. She's focused on her Popsicle, intent on catching every drip.

I wheel the lawn mower from the shed, open the cap, and check the gas. It's full, of course, bless Dave's meticulous heart. I pull the rope and the lawn mower purrs.

I don't love my Chevette, but I think Dave does, at least a little. He glides out from under the passenger door on a redwood dolly, a wrench in his hand. "Checking things out," he says. "Have you noticed your car's pulling to the right a little bit?"

Of course, I've noticed but, as usual, I haven't done one damn thing to rectify the problem.

"Good thing you've got good old dependable Dave," he says. "How 'bout you get the worker bee a beer?"

Dear Bill,

I've been thinking about the information you sent me on 'acquiring' a car. It's not as if illegal acts have never been done in my family before. (Although I, too, come from a good family, despite it not being one of privilege — your words. I do save the letters, you know!) Have I ever mentioned my Uncle Bennie? Although I never met the man, he was instrumental in my contacting you. Long story. Probably a sad one too.

I look forward to your letters although, sometimes, I have to admit, they frighten me. I can see you clearly in the musky dankness of Cell Block 2. I walk with you to the commissary (once a week!), and I count out money for a pack of Player's Plain, priced exorbitantly high. I ask if you've thought of quitting.

You tell me that the anticipation of your next cigarette gives you almost as much pleasure as the smoking itself. It's how I mark my days, you say. Two cigarettes in the morning, two in the afternoon, one just before lights-out.

Your letters paint pictures of exotic places you have been, foreign cities as familiar to you as the back of your hand. Strangely, I sometimes feel I have walked those streets beside you.

My life seems so ordinary compared to yours. Confined as you are, your mind takes you places I have never heard of and cannot even imagine. Like Tofino, BC. By the way, I did go to the library and research the place. I think you are right to want to see it. Inside my little house on the endless Saskatchewan prairie, where caragana and Manchurian elms are the trees of choice, I dream the scent of soft cedar, smell saltwater tangy in the air. When I awake, it takes me a moment to realize where I really am.

Some days, when I'm browning round steak to put into the crock pot for my Swiss Steak Surprise, deciding what my husband might like for dessert (you're aware that I do have a husband and I feel extremely disloyal even mentioning him), I stand outside myself and watch from what seems to be a great distance.

I feel a vague pity for the woman I used to be, before my contact with you opened a wider window on the world. But sometimes, I envy the rhythm of her days, a slow, steady rhythm that could lull you to sleep.

But enough of my rambling. I hope you are well and that your appeal is moving forward. I'll let you know what I decide about the car.

Yours truly,

Joanie

PS: I'm glad to hear you're no longer shaving your head.

When Dave goes to bed at night, he gets horizontal and he's gone, just like that. Maybe it's his job, hard physical labor for eight to ten hours a day, and lots of fresh air, but sometimes I think it's his remarkably clear conscience.

But tonight, when I'm having trouble sleeping anyway, he's tossing and turning like paper in the wind and, twice, I've had to push him aside so I can reclaim a little slice of the bed for myself. He rolls, cocoons me again.

"Don't," he moans. "Too high. Oh no. Don't."

I wonder if he's talking to one of the guys on his crew, maybe some careless kid jerking around on top of a ten-foot scaffold. The fact that he could be held liable if anyone on his crew gets hurt on the job and he's found negligent doesn't do a thing to settle my mind.

"Don't worry about it," he always says, "my men are smart and I train 'em well. Nothing bad's gonna happen as long as I'm around."

There's Buddy to worry about, too. Two days out of the last six, Buddy's been late for work. And when he finally does show, his hands are so shaky he can barely add sugar to his coffee, let alone lay a straight line of brick, so Dave says. Now he's almost behind schedule on the Tessier house in the new subdivision above Pike Creek. And he's too damn kind to blame it on Buddy, although I know the fault is mostly his. I hope it's not the amazing disappearing Buddy who's haunting Dave's dreams.

He groans and I butterfly my fingers across the square of his shoulders. A phantom breeze pushes the curtain aside so moonlight floods our room. The light etches Dave's muscled back, pools on the floor beside our bed. The wide fir, stained green and varnished until it shines, reflects shards of the moon into my wide-open eyes.

He flops onto his back spread eagled. A train whistles once, twice, then once more. I can hear its engine chug as it struggles up the grade on the west side of town. The whistle wails one last time, fainter, further away. Uncle Bennie, I think, where did you really go?

I drop Carlie off at the sitter at 8:00 AM. If my mother were home, she'd have offered to babysit. But she's God knows where, somewhere in America with her soulmate, Albert. So I'm on my own.

Carlie's tired this morning, and so am I. She's making a fuss so I take her in my arms, carry her like I used to when she was a toddler, when she used to wrap herself around me as if she'd never let go.

"Mom," she says. "You're holding me too hard. You might break me."

I set her down, study her delicate little body as she straightens her Barbie doll backpack, reties the laces on one of her new pink runners. "I won't break you," I say. "Never. Not me."

I haven't even opened Bill's latest letter. It's tucked in my purse, in a zippered compartment. I fish for it, unfold the letter and read as I drive. Dangerous behaviour, I know, but not nearly as dangerous as what I've been doing the last few months.

Dear Joanie,

I spend my days studying, working on my appeal and, of course, taking all the counselling sessions I can, so the Parole Board will be convinced I have mended my wayward tendencies.

Your letters are a breath of fresh air, delightful to read and, most importantly, totally dependable. Others have written once or twice, but no one has stayed the course. Not like you.

Have you thought of sending some of your stories out for publication? The last one you sent me was excellent, in my opinion. And believe me, I've become an astute reader. What else is there to pass the time if you don't happen to enjoy wrestling on full volume all day long?

Here's something to chew on. I once met a troupe of British actors in Hull, Quebec. I was up there on business, the nature of which I will leave to your considerable imagination. The troupe had just completed a Canadian tour. They worked in conjunction with acting schools in each of the provinces, developing and performing plays. I was told that most of Canada is pretty bland, but there were two provinces unique in the country, Quebec and Saskatchewan.

I lift my eyes from Bill's letter, skim over flat land washed by monochromatic shades of brown. Today, even the sky is pale, boring to the eye. I don't know diddly about Quebec, but if you were driving the Trans-Canada highway through this part of Saskatchewan, I'm pretty sure you'd only stop for gas if the needle slipped past zero into the red, and you were absolutely sure you were about to suck air.

But I know better. The first summer Dave and I were crazy in love, we used to take a picnic lunch and a six-pack of Pilsner, roam the countryside in his beat-up Chevy truck. You could never predict when you'd top a small rise, come upon a hidden coulee, or a sudden ravine. The landscape may appear flat and boring, but it's full of hidden secrets. My face flushes as I think of the places Dave and I have lain together — beside a small spring-fed creek, icy cold, that we used to cool our beer while we made hurried love, under a spreading elm, by fragrant sagebrush in a rolling pasture, even by the collapsing picket fence of a forgotten little graveyard where our lovemaking was hurried, intensified by the tilt of the mossy headstones nearby, and the encroaching ruin of the place. Afterward, I wandered the graveyard, traced moss-covered names with my fingertips, and tried to imagine lives already lived.

The clarity of memory surprises me. It's been a long time since Dave's made time to wander the countryside with me. He's intent on making a name for himself, building dream homes for others, and ensuring a shot at the good life for Carlie and me.

My palms are sticky. The crispness of Bill's letter pulls at my fingertips and I lay it aside.

I glance at the highway, make sure I'm still inside the lines. I wipe my sweating hands on the upholstery, pick up Bill's letter. Three quarters of the way down page two, I find it, *two provinces, unique in the country, Quebec and Saskatchewan.* I run my forefinger across Saskatchewan, pick up where I left off.

These actors said the problem for writers coming from such places is not so much in finding stories — they are plentiful — but being able to write these stories in such a way as to make them believable. It might be a matter of absolutely overpowering the reader with your conviction. Like that point you reach when you're no longer afraid of your guitar.

Goosebumps dimple their way along my arms and I shiver despite the heat. What, I think? *No longer afraid of your guitar?* I refold the letter. It crackles as I fold it, the paper fragile. Maybe just like Bill? I step on the gas, watch the wheat sheaf on the Saskatchewan border sign recede to a blur of yellow.

After four hours straight driving down #1 Highway West, I fight my way to downtown Calgary. The trip from the outskirts takes almost as long as the trip from home. I park the Chevette directly across from the double doors of Carter's Motors, under the shade of a big oak tree.

My eyes are blinded by light glancing off the windshields of what seems to be acres and acres of cars. I walk into the showroom, locate the key case on the wall, near the water cooler and not far from an exit door.

I ask for the key to the ladies' room, thinking it strange that they've locked the bathroom, yet the keys to expensive cars are hanging in clear sight, just like Bill told me they'd be. The man is truly amazing. He's told me all about the makeup of the physical world and it's integration with the metaphysical, how, if I do the geometry perfectly, I can build a pyramid in plain sight, invisible to everyone else. He said the ancient Egyptians perfected the practice and there's lots of pyramids out in the Sahara that no one has ever been able to see. He said once I'd built my own, I could hide my Lexus there, and take it out only when I felt the urge for dangerous speed. Dangerous speeding is something I haven't longed for much, at least not since Carlie was born. But now that he's written it down, I have found myself wondering just how far and how fast I could go.

I open my purse, spill my pile of letters on the black granite of the vanity inside the luxurious Ladies Room of Carter's Motors. I hold my hands under the gushing water, inhale the sweet vanilla scented air. And I think of Bill, on his narrow airless bunk, cradling my latest letter in his sunless hands.

And I see Dave, sitting on a sawhorse at his worksite, his lunch kit open on his knees. He lifts his ham and cheese sandwich, checks beneath it to see if I've sent a little note.

I tuck the letters into the side pocket of my purse, straighten my pencil skirt, and tuck in my beige linen blouse. When I dressed this morning, I tried to dress rich, so I wouldn't stand out in this place.

"Thank you," I say to the receptionist when I return the washroom key. She reaches for the black tag without giving me a second glance. I walk around a shiny Lexus Prestige sedan, the carpet beneath my feet thick and soft like a sponge. I have to make a conscious effort to lift one foot, then the other. For a moment, I lean on the heavy glass of the wide double doors, take a deep breath and step outside.

I walk among the beautiful cars as if I'm walking in a meadow of metal flowers. I run my hand along the side of a poppy-red Lexus Sportcross.

My new life is almost unimaginable. I'm dazzled by the diamond sand, the azure water, the emptiness of the beach. On a beach this beautiful at home, you'd be fighting for space. But this isn't home, I tell myself. At least not yet. I pull into a patch of shade beneath a spreading tree, the species totally unfamiliar to me. They're not poplars, of that I'm sure. The Lexus is loaded with inflated tubes and air mattresses, striped blankets and a red picnic hamper, full to the brim. It has handled beautifully on the twisting rutted roads, and I pat the dash as if the car were a valued friend. I turn up the stereo to drown out the giggles of three little girls. Carlie's quick to make friends wherever she goes, not a bit like me. Belize is a country I'd never even dreamed of, and here we are, Carlie and me. Sometimes, when we're sitting in the wicker swing on our wraparound deck, I can't believe we're really here. The deck is a great place to hang out, although the house is in a sad state of disrepair. Nothing like the home I left behind. Sometimes I miss our little house on Winnie Street with its postage stamp yard. And I always miss Dave, with his dependable ways.

A whistle pieces the air, brings me back to Carter's Motors. I hear myself humming a reggae tune, notice that the pink polish on my ring finger, left hand, is chipped and is in desperate need of repair.

My Lexus is situated near the end of the second row, with an open run to the front gate. I love the red, but I decide it's too bright, too easy to spot. The car beside it is a soft olive green. Camouflage colour, I think. I lean against the driver's door and look inside.

"Would you like to take it for a test drive?"

"Not today," I say and try to ignore the young man's crestfallen face. "I'm just looking."

I scope the place out thoroughly and then I return to my Chevette. I train my eyes on the patchwork of expensive cars in Carter's lot. After a while, they all begin to look the same.

I adjust the tinny radio. When an old Wilf Carter song laced with loss and longing scratches my eardrums, I think how nice a CD player and a really good sound system would be. I open my window, thinking air conditioning would definitely be a plus.

Then I flip down the visor, and try on Buddy's con-man grin. But in the depth of the shadows, there's no mistaking my eyes. One dark chocolate, semi-sweet brown and one bright crystal blue. Easily identifiable, that's for sure.

I reach into the side pocket of my purse and pull the letters free. Slowly, I tear them into tiny pieces. I lean out the window and open my hand. Caught by a sudden breeze, they form a curtain of confetti, briefly obscuring my view.

CARNIVAL GLASS

"IF YOUR TURDS FLOAT," CLAYTON SAYS, "IT'S a good sign. Means you're getting adequate fibre." He's sitting at the antique dining room display on the right-hand side of Gemma's Treasure Box, near the big front window. A walnut console radio murmurs a Hank Williams song and Clayton's sausage fingers tap the beat.

Brenda looks up from polishing an antique silver filigree bowl, the blackened cloth limp in her hand. "Pardon?"

"It's not easy these days," he continues. "Too much processed stuff. People have got to change. Get back to the land." He places his black cowboy hat on the table above one of the green and gold Limoge place settings.

"Like you?"

"Well, I ain't there quite yet, but I'm working on it." He rises, his hand resting on the ladder-back chair. "I'd like to buy this."

"I'm sorry," Brenda tells him. "I can't sell just one and break up the set."

"Begging your pardon. What I meant was, I want this whole display. Table, chairs, dishes, tablecloth. The whole shebang."

Brenda's green eyes widen. "All of it?"

"Yep. I'll bring the cash next Tuesday. Just don't go selling off any of my stuff. That cranberry bowl caught my eye. Reminded me of sitting around my momma's table for Sunday supper." Clayton picks up his hat, holds it over his heart. "I long to taste coleslaw like she used to make. Kept it in a big old crock in the cold room downstairs. Fermented it, I think. Might explain it being so danged good."

The cranberry bowl is carnival glass, highly collectible and hard to find. Gemma's Treasure Box is two miles off the main highway, and although its presence is well marked by Allen's hand-painted signs, there still has to be a draw. Brenda thinks her reasonable prices, good strong coffee, and homemade baking just might do the trick. So purchasing the carnival glass was a splurge. She'd agonized over investing so much in a single piece.

"That dish alone is three hundred dollars," she says.

"It's a steal," Clayton tells her, "if it makes me think of Momma, the way she used to be. Before sour gas seeped from our fields, and right into her brain. We didn't see it coming, that's for dang sure. Once I realized how bad it was and went to the library to study up on it, I found out that that damn gas starts to affect you at as little as twenty parts per million, before you can even pick up the god-awful smell. But I have to admit, we were swayed by those big royalties. Not one thing else."

Clayton has relocated to Langford, Saskatchewan, from High River, Alberta, and Brenda's heard lots about his grandiose plans to revitalize their dying town. The coffee shop is abuzz with the news that the deeds to five derelict houses now bear Clayton's name. The plan, he told Brenda one day, is for him to get everything fixed up. Soon as I'm done, he told her, my kids are moving out here. It was the sour gas in Alberta, he claimed, that finally drove him out. Goddamn stuff is even getting into the food chain; he could feel it in his bones. Of course the government's going to say everything is tickety-boo, but the old bones aren't fooled. You could smell it everywhere, he said. So it stands to reason sour gas was permeating the plants in the garden and, sooner or later, those fleshy leaves sucked it in, right down to the roots. Made a man afraid to cut into a baked potato or chomp on a cob of corn. And the water. Hell, hydrogen sulfide follows the line of least resistance, so you can bet it followed the piping straight down into the well. Water started to taste like a stagnant slough smells. Sometimes worse.

Brenda nods. She can quote the statistics, too. Anybody who's tuned into the local talk show or picked up a paper in the last few months knows more about the environmental pros and cons of oil and gas exploration than they ever would have imagined. There have been endless reports. The ones commissioned by the oil companies insist that careful and considerate exploration in the Sand Hills won't harm the ecosystem in any discernable way. Those driven by die-hard conservationists decry the tracks of a single drilling rig munching at the fragile base of the Sand Hills. Brenda is at a loss as to what might be the truth. Anyway, she's been too busy getting ready for her grand opening, fretting if she's advertised widely enough, and fussing with her displays.

She picks up a porcelain cup and holds it to the light, imagines Clayton's thick fingers wrapped around its delicate handle. "Are you sure you want these?" She sets the cup down gently on its matching saucer, dotted with blue forget-menots. "I've got some bone china mugs with nice big handles. Might be a sight more comfortable for you."

Clayton shakes his head. "I want it just like you've got it set up. It's perfect. Just perfect, I'd say."

Brenda is boggled by the scope of Clayton's purchase, but she's grateful too. She knows firsthand how hard it is to be strapped for cash month after month, spending half your time figuring the least you can pay each creditor to keep them off your back. And she realizes some of her neighbours might be saved by the money they can get from letting the seismic companies cross their land or, at least, allowed to hold on for one more year. Brenda's not sure what she and Allen would do if a fast talking land man came to their door with earnest reassurances of how the oil companies care deeply about preserving the land, especially if he had a substantial cheque in his hand.

She loves the Sand Hills, their great rippling dunes painting purple shadows in the scrubby sage. She used to take Deanna there on Sundays, with a picnic and a crazy carpet. Deanna would spend hours sliding down the gilded dunes and Brenda used to slide too, until the walk back up to the top wasn't worth the lickety-split ride. When her legs began to scream, Brenda would find a bit of shade and admire her daughter's determination.

It's been too long since she's sat mesmerized, staring at the waves of sand ruffled by the wind. The hills advance and recede, sometimes four or five feet per year. There were times Brenda imagined she could hear them sigh with the futility of it all.

The white tails she'd sometimes spot were beautiful, the Sand Hills and its pockets of scrub trees a perfect habitat. From her quiet spot beneath a scraggly tree, Brenda once took an amazing picture of a buck poised at the top of a dune, his magnificent rack tilted as if it might be picking up signals from God himself. But she's heard the deer aren't so plentiful out there anymore. And that's just the start of it, the conservationists say.

She turns her thoughts from the Great Sand Hills to her cozy little shop. She holds the carnival glass to the light, admires it for a moment. If it has to be sold, at least it's to Clayton. Allen says she's going to make a poor business-woman because she has a tendency to get way too attached to her stuff. Gemma's Treasure Box is a business, not a hobby, and she means to contribute to the coffers of their struggling farm.

Clayton stands, sniffs the air. "Still sweet," he says. "Sure hope people around here have enough sense to appreciate what they got. And keep it that way."

"I can't decide what's right," she says. "If you waved big bucks around this country, you'd have people scrambling to book the first rig. Times have been tough for at least ten years. Folding money's hard to find." She straightens the silverware at the place setting of Limoge opposite Clayton. "Speaking of big money, do you want the silverware too? You might be surprised at the sum when I add it all up."

"Consider it sold," he says. "This dining room is perfect for the house I'm setting up for Bob."

"Has Bob ever been here?" Brenda folds a sheet of paper in half, writes *Entire Display Sold* in black jiffy marker and tents it on the table. "Maybe if you took him on a tour of the Great Sand Hills on a warm fall day, he'd fall in love with the place. Or have him come in hunting season. You might just get him hooked."

"Oh, he'll be hooked, all right," Clayton replies. "Just like I was the first time I took a deep breath out here. Nothing sour hanging in the air. Not yet, anyway. And I aim to educate people so they'll fight to keep it that way." He drapes his canvas riding coat across his thin shoulders, tugs on a reddened ear.

"Course," he says, "exploration companies are telling anyone who'll listen that the gas around here is as sweet as a baby's breath. It's why I can't go down to the coffee shop anymore. Called one of them city slickers a liar and kind of started an altercation. Got myself kicked out for life. I gotta admit, I'm kind of lonesome now."

Brenda shakes her head. An altercation at coffee row? What next, she thinks. What comes next?

Clayton shifts his hat from one hand to the other, rolls its soiled brim. "But don't you worry, Bob will be coming out soon. Once he comes, the rest will surely follow."

Brenda raises a brow.

"You know how that goes," Clayton says. "Oldest one sets the pace. The rest mostly follow. Comes with the birth order, I think."

Brenda checks the pictures on the wall by the cash register. Deanna is fine-boned, blonde, with a porcelain kind of beauty, nothing like Brenda's sturdy stockiness. Her two little boys are leaning into her, one on each side. Kurtis resembles Deanna, but Carson is a dead ringer for his grandpa — solidly built with an easy stance and no hint of shadows in his hazel eyes.

Poor Deanna, first, middle, and last child. In her childhood photos, she's sober and thoughtful looking, always alone. One child might be easy for the parents, Brenda thinks, but maybe it's hard for the child. She's noticed how Kurtis and Carson look out for each other, how Carson shadows Kurtis wherever he goes. Those little boys have such fun together. A pair beats a single, she thinks, in more than a poker game.

Clayton clears his throat and tips his hat to Brenda. "I thank you for the sustenance," he says. "Those rhubarb muffins are manna from the gods." He turns at the door. "I know danged well Bob and the rest of them will be chomping at the bit to move out here. Probably before I get those houses habitable. So I better carry on."

The wind clutches the tails of his coat, lifts the long straw hair that hangs from beneath his big hat. He looks like the scarecrow she's built to safeguard her corn. She stands at the wide window, watches his beat up International until it's a rusted speck on the canvas of the vast Sand Hill sky.

When Brenda drives toward the town from the east, nothing looks awry. But from the west, her eyes become confused and dart from house to house. A small bungalow north of the church shines bright lemon yellow, its neighbour glowing a vicious lime green. The two-story wreck next to that is painted peacock blue. At the top of the hill, an orange clapboard story-and-a-half glows like the embers of a banked-up fire. On the corner, an eggplant-purple shack turns blank eyes to the pot-holed highway and the traffic dodging by.

The yellow house boasts two new windows, the green house, a new front door. But all of the houses are half-clad, with siding missing, broken porch railings, or half the chimney crumbling onto cracked shingles that cling to steep-pitched roofs. All are in various stages of undress, like busy whores on a Saturday night.

The sky is grey and threatening rain. When Clayton's not busy removing siding and installing windows or hauling bundles of shingles up to a roof, he spends most of his time at Brenda's shop. She pours freshly brewed coffee and prays the rain will hold off until Allen finishes the barley on the Stengland place. She's watching the clouds darken and roll.

"The cheap bastards won't even *think* of giving me a break on electricity rates," Clayton says as he breaks another rhubarb muffin onto his plate. "You'd think they'd encourage entrepreneurs like me. But hell, no, they want full price." He clears his throat. "What do you think?"

"I suppose," Brenda says, "if they gave you a break, they'd be setting a dangerous precedent. If you know what I mean."

"But I'm saving this town from total decay," Clayton insists. "And I'm planning to have electric heat in every house. Think of the bucks the power company would be raking in eventually. No matter how high my heat bills might be, there'll be no gas lines snaking poison into any property of mine. Natural gas is one thing, but, wherever you find it, sooner or later you're gonna find sour too. The bastards never tell you that."

Clayton pushes back his chair. "Power company should be happy to give me some kind of a volume discount deal. Not tell me I gotta pay the same prices as everyone else."

Brenda tops up Clayton's coffee and pours herself a cup of Red Rose tea. "Maybe you need to invest in some good wood-burning stoves. Stock up on cedar posts and chop up all the dying elms and birches. God knows, there's enough of them around town."

The drought of recent years has taken its toll. Even established trees can stand only so many years of being constantly thirsty. Half the trees in the countryside have literally died of thirst. Brenda brings her cup to her lips, blows on the tea and breathes in the steam. "I've got a couple enamelled

Colemans in excellent shape. There's nothing like the heat from a crackling wood fire. But you've got to have lights. That family of yours isn't likely to be happy sitting around in the dark."

"Yeah," Clayton says. "I guess you got a point." Thunder rolls across the darkened sky. "Have you heard anything about oil or gas companies nosing around? One of the RM's is looking into changing the zoning out there so exploration can go. Don't those damn fools realize how fragile the ecosystem is?" He slams the table with his ham-sized fist.

"Easy on the china." Brenda straightens a cup. "Actually, I didn't know a thing about fragile till you came along. All I know is I used to spend entire days out there with Deanna, riding crazy carpets down the biggest dunes." Brenda smiles, lost for a moment. "I have to admit, the Sand Hills have always seemed pretty solid to me."

"Well, they're not." Clayton pulls out a polka-dotted hankie, honks long and hard. "Wind erosion is already bad. Think what'll happen if they let rigs in. They'll be chewing up the scrub grass and flattening the sagebrush. Riggers work hard when they work hard, but there's lots of down time. Nothing worse than rig pigs with time on their hands." He honks again. "First thing you know, they'll be taking pot shots at the pronghorns. Probably wouldn't think twice about picking off a burrowing owl. And those poor birds are already on the endangered list."

Brenda thinks that Clayton might be on the endangered list, too, if he goes around town talking against the looming development of gas and oil. He hasn't exactly rallied a crowd to his anti-development stance and local businesses and farmers are already counting on spin-offs if the oil activity goes.

"And drilling for gas is the worst activity they could possibly allow. Those bastards use water like there's a never-ending supply. We're damn close to being a desert already. Town foreman told me the level in the well dropped fourteen inches in the last two months. Pretty soon the water'll be even more precious than the gas and oil."

Brenda picked up the cranberry bowl, held it so it caught the sun. A red shadow fell across the table and onto Clayton's craggy face. Is there no place, he ranted, where a man can be safe? Don't they know what will happen to the air? Brenda set the bowl down, but the red tide on Clayton's face remained. It took a full pot of coffee and two pieces of sour cream pie to finally calm him down.

Allen hangs his cap on the hook by the back door, and shucks out of his dust-laden coveralls. He washes his hands in the kitchen sink, then turns to Brenda. "Saw Clayton's truck turning west on the grid." he says. "Driving like a bat out of hell. How did he seem today?"

"The usual."

"I'm starting to wonder if he might be dangerous," Allen says. "I've heard lots of talk. His neighbours aren't thrilled, that's for sure. Course, who would be, if you had to look out your living room window at those eye-watering hues he's chosen for the houses? And there's not a one where he's really finished the job. Makes me glad we built on the farm."

Brenda dishes up the chili and hands Allen a brimming bowl. "I think he's harmless." The faint smell of garlic permeates the air. "A little eccentric, maybe, but lonesome, is all."

"Well," Allen says, "I guess as long as he's a paying customer, there's no good reason for me to run him off."

Allen's done all the carpentry work in readying the antique shop. He's even milled the woodwork for the windows and doors when they couldn't find period trim. He's not quite finished, of course. But Brenda didn't mind and she went ahead with opening anyway. Now she's got time to ponder, imagine different colours on the antique tin he has yet to attach to the ceilings. She's partial to a soft yellow or cool, pale-green, maybe with a thin copper glaze. Nothing like the vivid colours Clayton seems to love.

Clayton pads around the shop like a nervous cat. He picks up a footed pinwheel crystal candy dish for at least the fifth time.

"You're strung as tight as a fiddle today," Brenda says as she pours strong coffee into his cup. "Come on over, sit yourself down. Or else I've got to get up and start pacing too."

Clayton sits, taps his toes as he fiddles with the handle of his greenware mug. He takes one sip, then pushes it aside.

"Coffee too weak?"

"Nothing wrong with the coffee. Might just be the way I'm feeling today."

Brenda is sorting through a box of trinkets that she'd bought for a dollar at the auction sale on Wednesday night. Sometimes she finds real treasures buried in a box of junk but, so far, she's found nothing that catches her eye. She tosses a chipped glass ashtray into the trash.

Her fingers find a yellowed ivory hair catcher, smooth and rounded, but squished, like someone has pushed on a rubber ball. The lid has a hole in the centre and she lifts it with her forefinger, twirls it around. In Victorian times, women used hair catchers to salvage hair from their brushes. She marvels at their patience. She's read that selling hair was a lucrative business. She's not sure what the buyers used it for. Stuffing upholstery or cushions, maybe.

"Here's something that might interest you," she says. "Look at this. Maybe Cassie would like it for her dresser." She hands over the catcher. "What do you think?"

When Clayton reaches for the hair catcher, Brenda notices the state of his hands. They're red and raw, his cuticles ragged and swollen.

"What did you do?" she asks, "Get paint stripper on those hands? They look like they're about to bleed." She rummages in a cabinet by the cash register and comes up with a tin of Watkins salve "Let's see if this old salve lives up to its claims." The tin is rusted and battered, but when she hands it to Clayton, he opens it for her with one quick twist.

She sits beside him at the square pine table and rubs the thick, stinky salve into his work-worn hands. "There you go," she finally says. "This stuff's supposed to work magic. I guess we'll see."

She slips the ivory hair catcher into a crumpled plastic Co-op bag and hands it to Clayton. "Here," she says. "For Cassie's chiffonier. This one's on the house."

For Cassie, Clayton has purchased an entire burled oak bedroom suite, from the sleigh-back bed to the ornate dresser and massive chiffonier. The porcelain knobs on the dressers are decorated with delicate yellow roses. That's what has sold him on the set.

"Yellow's always been Cassie's favourite colour," he says. "I think I'll paint the inside of her house the same sunflower shade I used outside."

Brenda adds up the cost of the bedroom suite along with the quilts and runners Clayton has picked. He leans against the counter, touches the pictures of her grandsons that hang on the wall beside the cash register.

"Nice looking little guys," he says. "They'll be playing with Cassie's boys before too long."

"That would be something, wouldn't it?" Brenda's cash register dings. "Eight hundred dollars and change. Not bad for an entire bedroom, including bedding and blankets and the patchwork quilt."

Clayton pulls out his fat leather wallet and counts out the cash.

"Pleasure, as always," he says. "See you next week."

Brenda's been too busy to get into town. Allen's been the one to pick up the mail, and stop at the coffee shop to find out what's going on. But she needs baking soda for the pumpkin cake she's got half-mixed, and Allen's hauling bales, so she dusts off her hands. She'll have to run her own errands today. The stock at Turner's Lucky Dollar is sometimes old, and always expensive but, when she's caught short, she has to pay the price.

She wipes her hands on her apron and fishes in a canister on the counter. Her fingers sift through bobby pins and paper clips, nuts and bolts and, finally, find her key ring, a blue plastic fish she got from the boys. She hangs her ruffled apron on a hook by the door, slips into her shoes. Brenda actually remembers to check the level in the gas gauge before she fires up the Ford.

When she turns off the highway, Brenda stares in wonder. The sunflower house sports new cedar shakes. Wide windows, framed by white shutters, sparkle in the sun. A new picket fence outlines the yard, and the earth in the garden is freshly turned. The straggly caraganas have been carefully trimmed, like the moustache of a dapper old man. She pulls over, steps from the truck.

"You lost?" Clayton's voice is raspy with disuse. She looks up, sees his solid outline above, in the orange harvest sun. "Hang on a minute," he says and scrambles down the sturdy ladder. He takes a large silver key from his pocket and opens the new front door. He steps aside, bows low, and sweeps her inside with his hand.

As she steps across the threshold, Brenda feels like an actor in an elaborate set. The old-fashioned roses twining up the walls are a perfect foil for the tufted burgundy chesterfield Clayton had hauled home from her shop. Antique side tables flank the sofa and the matching chair, embroidered runners are neatly placed. An old rag rug warms the floor of burnished pine.

"Beautiful," she breathes.

Clayton dusts his coveralls and lowers himself to the couch. He pulls a blue envelope from an inside pocket. "Maybe not beautiful enough," he says and he hands her the crumpled paper.

She smoothes it against her solid thigh, moves closer to the bay window where the light is good and strong.

Dear Dad — how are things? We hope you're not working too hard. Things have kind of turned around here and we're all doing better than fine. I got a job operating the Mobil battery west of the farm. Makes for a nice little bonus at the end of the month.

The twins are in Peewee AA hockey and Glenn started high school in High River last week. I hate to tell you this, but there's no way I can talk Estelle into moving them now.

But it sounds like you got a deal on the houses, so you should be able to turn them around for a pretty good buck. Especially with all the oil and gas activity that's supposed to be happening out there. You can hear the buzz all the way to Calgary. Too bad you didn't buy a piece of the Sand Hills. You might have ended up rich. That would be something in this family, wouldn't it? Looks like we missed the boat again.

Take care and we'll have to talk real soon — Bob

She looks up at Clayton's shattered face. "But I thought ... "

"So did I."

Brenda looks around the snug little house. Her hands flutter at her side. "Cassie would have loved this place."

"There's still hope for my Cassie," Clayton says. "There's still hope yet."

Brenda has no idea how she'll be ready for the annual Fall Supper before Sunday at five. She has a twenty-two pound turkey to thaw and roast, and the Community Club expects each member to bake six pies. The women compete for the flakiest crust, rolled so thin you can almost see right through the pastry. And no canned pie fillings allowed. There's an unwritten law against store-bought stuff, although Brenda has noticed a few suspect pies coming in from the younger members. Brenda's not one to take shortcuts so she's feeling under the gun.

Besides, Deanna got called in to assist at an emergency C-section and her sitter was down with the flu. When she called to see if she and Allen could watch the boys, Brenda couldn't figure out a graceful way to say no.

Her grandsons love Gemma's Treasure Box, but she doesn't dare let them run loose in there. Too many precious things sitting around and too much restless energy banked in their sturdy bodies, especially Carson's. Kurtis she'd trust. She can feel the reverence when he lifts a cup and saucer, turns a piece of crockery to check the name on its bottom. His eyes get far away. She's sure he's an old soul, remembering events or people from long ago. But when the two are together, they definitely need a chaperone.

The boys had asked if they could go in and take a look around, but she told them to play outside. Their 'please Gemma's' fell on deaf ears. She promised that, later, when her chores were done, they'd work on the new dining room display she's been planning, to fill the empty space from Clayton's buying spree. She didn't let herself see the disappointment clouding their hopeful eyes.

She forms a ball of pastry, and begins to flatten it with her rolling pin. When she hears Clayton's truck rattle up the lane, she draws a sharp breath. There's no way she can sit around and drink coffee today.

"Hi, Clayton," she hears Carson say. "Wanna play with us? Gemma's busy baking pies and, besides, she's kind of grumpy today."

Clayton pulls something from his pocket. From her kitchen window, Brenda sees three heads bend and she wonders what they're checking out. She slides two apple pies into the oven and, when she checks the window again, Carson and Kurtis are rounding the chicken coop with Clayton bringing up the rear.

The community hall is buzzing. Somehow, ArcView Oil has skirted the environmental issues peculiar to the Sand Hills and moved in a drilling rig. It's not exactly in the hills, but its niggling right at the edge. There's been talk of lateral drilling and how a person might as well take whatever money they're offering because, if you don't, they'll just set up across from you and drill right under your yard, if that's where they've decided they want to go.

Brenda has seen the bright rig lights from her kitchen window late at night. She's felt the fluttering terror of the ferruginous hawk and the endangered owls. Kangaroo rats scurrying for the safety of their sandy holes have tickled her chilly toes. From the yellow square of her kitchen window, she's sensed dark shadows moving in the night.

Some nights she'd actually seen lights shifting out there in the hills and wondered aloud what they might be. Blackfoot warriors, Allen had told her, seeking souls compelled to return to the Sand Hills, the most eastern edge of their ancient hunting grounds. When we were boys, he said, we used to find lots of arrowheads out in those hills. Entire tribes out there, dwelling in their phantom villages shifting like the sand, hunting ghostly buffalo and tending ghostly fires. Still searching for something, he said, something they lost a long time ago.

And even though scrubbing her and Allen's supper plates in the iridescent suds had warmed her hands, she was glad to feel his sinewed arms encircling her not-quite tiny waist.

"Come on," he'd said, "enough of telling of tales. It'll give anyone the heebie jeebies. Time to go to bed."

And so he'd led her up the stairs, and she'd pushed all thought of ghostly riders and drilling rigs nibbling at the sacred edges of the Sand Hills entirely out of her mind.

But now she keeps her kitchen window closed up tight and every morning and as she walks to Gemma's Treasure Box, she stops like a pointer and sniffs the breeze. So far, she hasn't smelled anything sour in the air, but she wonders how Clayton has taken the latest news.

She checks for empty salad bowls on the tables assigned to her and Marilyn, wipes the vacated places, and quickly resets the cutlery and cups.

"Great meal. You can't beat coming out to these little towns."

"God, did you see all the pies? And this is real whipped cream." Compliments swirl around her head.

Brenda checks her watch. Not quite seven. She's been watching for Clayton's spare form, hoping he'd be in the next group of hungry customers coming down the stairs.

She and Marilyn have been clearing and scraping dishes, but there's a lull for a moment and they've finally caught up. "I'm taking a break," she says, as she unties her green gingham apron and wipes her hands on its skirt. She moulds a piece of wrinkled foil over the pie plate she's filled with mashed potatoes and gravy, turkey and dressing, turnips and creamed baby peas.

She slips a generous piece of apple pie onto another plate, balances one in each hand. "Hope he's hungry," she mutters. "He better be."

Brenda peeks into the kitchen, sees Allen elbow-deep in suds. She stuffs two paper napkins edged with dancing turkeys into her hip pocket. "If Allen asks, tell him I've taken a plate down to Clayton. I can't believe he didn't show."

Marilyn is cutting a pumpkin pie. She glances up, waves the knife. "Don't worry," she says. "Just go. I'll handle things here for a while."

The air is crisp, with an edge of winter reaching from beneath the barley wind. Brenda pulls her poncho closer and feels the warmth from the pie plates puddle in her palm. Golden harvest light tints Cassie's yellow house to amber, makes the siding glow. There's no answer when she knocks firmly on the green front door.

"Clayton?" She knocks once more before she steps inside.

She's drawn to Cassie's cozy kitchen by the familiar words of a Hank Williams song. She slides the cooling plates onto the scarred maple table and glances to her left. The double enamel sink is littered with shards of green and gold Limoge and blood-red pieces of carnival glass.

"Shit," she whispers, and fumbles for the knob on the RCA console that Clayton has polished to an ebony shine. Her voice rises in harmony with the sudden howl of the wind. "Clayton?"

Her fingers spread wide and she fumbles her way along the newly smooth wall as if she's suddenly lost her sight.

A Perfect Intersection of Vectors

PAPA LOOKS THINNER. HOW LONG, I WONDER, since I've been to the farm. Four weeks? Five? I could borrow Raymond's car, but I hate to ask. I know how much he'd like to come along and I'm not ready to take him home to meet my folks. Not quite yet. Mr. Johnson, down at the shop, has a nice new Hudson and he's offered, too. But if I took him up on his kindness and maybe tore off a muffler on those rutted roads, it might change things at work. The way it is right now, I sew perfect seams, he pays my wages, and we get along just fine. Best to leave it at that.

"Molly, my girl, you've sure fixed the place up nice."

I look around my snug apartment and know what Papa says is true. The hours I spent scrubbing, the layers of wallpaper I soaked and removed. It all seems worth it now. The only room untouched is the spare bedroom. I kind of liked the yellow wallpaper roses twined around the white trellis background, so I left them alone.

I want to hug him for even noticing my efforts and, maybe, too, because the lines on his face seem deeper today, his shoulders not so square. Instead, I lift the crocheted cozy from my teapot and pour him another cup of tea.

"Thanks," I say. "I guess some day I'll get used to the stairs. But at least up here, I hardly ever hear Miss Parsons. Only when she's tuned in to *The Bickersons* on Saturday night. She's more than a little deaf."

I glance around my snug kitchen. Its walls are painted a colour I call Contentment Blue and the placemats are quilted bits of Sun-drenched Sunday. I know it's crazy, this compulsion I have to re-name the basic colours, call them something other than blue and yellow, green or red. I do it when I'm tailoring, too. It's much more fun sewing a jacket of Passion Plum than plain old purple.

Cripes, maybe I *have* been living alone too long. I didn't plan it this way, but with so many of the boys off to war, there are lots of women like me. Most of us are working at menial jobs, doing what we can to contribute to the war effort but, really, we're just marking time, waiting for the war to end. For things to get back to normal, if they ever will.

Papa clears his throat, pulls at the collar of his worn flannel shirt.

"It's kind of small but it's perfect for me," I say. I don't want to tell him in case it hurts his heart, but *this* place is home.

He takes a sip from the teacup, its Spanish Lace pattern incongruous in his roughened hands. "I was wondering," he says, "if you'd consider boarding the girls."

I breathe out, slow.

"Looks like a record-setting winter. Lots of days the snow's so deep they can't get to school. And it seems to me they're taking every chance they get to stay at home. They can't keep up, even Mary Ellen can't, missing every other day."

I look outside at the drifting snow, banks of it like peaks of whipped cream enfolding the spindly legs of the town water tower just across the street. I imagine my father harnessing the horses, slugging through wind-hardened drifts with hay and water for his herd of red Angus cows. And feeling guilty when it's too cold or the snow's too deep for Laura and Mary Ellen to walk the mile to school. And maybe spending a little longer on those chores, outside, where life is as simple as it always was. The extra chromosome that came with Carl has complicated our Momma and Papa's entire life.

"I hate to ask," he says, his gaze fastened on my blue and white gingham tablecloth. "You've made yourself a good life. Nice and quiet here."

What can I do? I touch his hand.

Laura and Mary Ellen are sixteen and seventeen, although Laura seems younger, and it seems I hardly know them. I didn't realize when I got a job and left home how much of their growing up I'd miss. At twenty-four, only seven years older than Mary Ellen, I feel as if I've always lived in a totally different world than theirs.

When I left, they were nine and ten, just a pair of kids. I wonder how it will be, living with them every day?

Two days later, when Papa brings them to town, their faces are shiny with excitement. When he finally leaves, they kiss him hard. "Tell Momma we'll be fine," Mary Ellen says. "And for goodness sake, keep an eye on Carl. Momma just lets him do anything he wants. He's turning into a real little scamp."

Papa slips me a twenty before he leaves. "For expenses," he says. "I know the power bill, for one, will be higher with the girls around."

"Papa, really, I can manage." I've already planned to take on some custom sewing on the side, away from Keep-U-Neat Cleaners and Tailors. As long as I put my hours in, I'm sure Mr. Johnson will say it's absolutely okay.

I try to push the twenty, folded and creased, back into Papa's restless hands.

"No, take it," he says. "Take this too." He drops the key to the locker plant into my hand. "Help yourself to whatever you need. The damn thing is full as usual. Besides all the meat, your Momma has more than a few packages of frozen garden stuff stored there. You'd be helping us out if you could take it down a package or two. Besides, those two might look like bits of nothing, but they eat like a pair of stevedores."

Momma will never afford a fridge for her kitchen if Papa doesn't pull his purse strings a little tighter. I know the locker plant is cheap and reliable storage, but a locker full of frozen meat isn't too handy when you live ten miles from town. Poor Momma. I wonder how many times she's had to improvise because all of her meat and vegetables are safely frozen in their locker in town.

So, I'm about to tell Papa we can get along just fine on our own, then I notice the net of lines tugging at the corners of his ice-blue eyes.

"Thanks, Papa." I fold my fingers around the key, and the money too, and then I hug him hard. "Don't worry, they're in good hands."

"I know," he says. "Locker number is twenty-four."

It takes us a while to work things out, Mary Ellen, Laura and I. I had come to cherish my oasis of quiet and order. Laura and Mary Ellen are sudden summer whirl-winds, incessant talking machines. But the first two weeks are safely behind us now, and, so far, no murder and not much mayhem. But still, they're slightly wary and maybe getting a little homesick too.

"Join hands, please." A magnificent round steak stew bubbles on the stove, thanks to Papa's bursting meat locker and my recent possession of the key. I even made biscuits with cheese, their favourite.

Laura looks first at Mary Ellen, then at me.

"Really," I say, "give me your hands." I lean across the table. When I lift Laura's hand, I feel as if I'm holding the delicate bones of a hummingbird.

"Humour her," Mary Ellen mutters, taking hold of us both in a businesslike grip. "Old-maid crazy. She's lived alone too long."

Twenty-four is far from old, I'm about to tell Mary Ellen and, since I've met Raymond, my old maid standing is in jeopardy as well. Then I notice a grin tugging at the edge of her mouth so, instead, I bow my head. "Thank you, dear God, for this precious time together. Guide us please."

Laura and Mary Ellen dawdle over the dishes. I can hardly wait until they go upstairs, and I have the silence of my living room, and the escape of a good book.

Maybe later I'll tune in Benny Goodman on my new walnut console, a gift I've recently given myself. It was an extravagance, but I believe the salesman was right when he told me sound that sweet is worth the price. One extra payment a month might be a stretch, but it's only for a year. But tonight, I don't care one bit about music, I revel in blessed solitude. When I finally go to bed, I tiptoe to the girls' room and, for a moment, watch them as they sleep. I bend to kiss them good night. Mary Ellen stays quiet, dreamless, but when I kiss Laura's cheek, she mumbles softly, and on my lips, I feel the sting of salt.

෴ ෴ ෴

Mary Ellen has pulled her curly hair back into a glorious haystack, the colour of coal, not straw. Darn her for being so much prettier than me, and God, please forgive me for even *thinking* that. I love my sister, really, I do. She leans closer to the mirror and dusts the base of her eyelids with purple powder. Her eyes are amazing, big and round and bluebell blue. She doesn't really need to do anything to make them noticeable. I wonder what Papa would think.

"Here, Laura," she says. "Try a little. Works wonders, it really does." She lightly dusts my eyelids, and I blink. "Hold still, if you want this *on* your eyes, not *in*."

At the last minute, Mary Ellen has taken off the dress Momma made and thrown it on the bed. She's borrowed one of Molly's black pencil skirts and a cardigan set, too. Of course, she assures me, I would have asked, but I can't. Molly's already gone to work.

Mary Ellen is excited about her first day in grade twelve at the big, city school. She's not even nervous about starting in when the year's half done. Maybe because she has this knack of fitting in. But I am dreading the day. The very idea of a room full of sixteen-year-old girls I've never seen before fills me with dread.

My yellow dress, its square neckline outlined with a chain of dainty daisies, is still lying on the bed. I loved this dress when Momma was sewing it for me. Momma's an excellent seamstress too, when she has the time, which isn't often anymore. I feel her cool hands on my shoulders, turn, she tells me, turn again. She tucks and pins, making minute adjustments where I can see absolutely nothing wrong. I see her, bony knees hard on the lino, her mouth full of pins. "Square up those shoulders," she says. "It will make you seem tall." I am a model that day, twirling for Momma in our sun-warmed kitchen, but now I am not so sure. What does she know of city fashions? What do I?

"Hicksville," one of the girls from my class said to another, that first day at Benson High. "Jeez, did you see the nice white knee-high socks? No competition there." I sat stone silent behind the cubicle door, waiting until those giggling girls had finished checking their makeup and their hair. When the coast was clear, I fled. I was ashamed of my cotton dress, my new white knee-highs. And ashamed of myself for being ashamed.

Momma tried so hard for me. She really did. But the damage has been done.

"Wake up, sleepyhead." Molly's hand is soft on my cheek. She touches the path where a tear has slid from the corner of my eye to my ear. Slow leaky tears that I can't seem to stop. "What's this?"

And so I tell her about the enormous mistake of my white knee-highs and my troubles with the girls at school.

Her face softens and, for a moment, I think that maybe she, too, is going to cry. Instead, she sits beside me on the bed, and begins to roll down one of her nylon stockings. I hear the silky whisper. She rolls the second nylon even more slowly, as if she's saying goodbye to a dear old friend. When she's finished, she folds them flat, and pushes them into my hand. "Here," she says. "Garter belts are in my dresser, top left-hand drawer."

The phone has been ringing. I open one eye, pull Molly's crocheted throw tighter and hear a soft thud as my science notebook slides to the floor. Studying is about the only thing that puts me to sleep these days. And I don't want to wake up, not quite yet. The couch is so soft, the afghan so warm.

I wonder where Mary Ellen is and why she's not picking up the phone. Finally, I roll from the couch. Maybe, just maybe, someone could be calling for me.

"Hello."

"Hi. It's Sophie. Can I talk to Molly?"

"She's not here just now," I say, my voice thick with sleep.

"Where is she?" Sophie, sharp, impatient. "Will she be back before five?" Although I know exactly where Molly has gone and approximately how long she'll be, I decide it's none of Sophie's business. So I tell her nothing. Nothing at all.

"She just stepped out."

"Well, tell her I called and it's real important. And she should get back to me as soon as she can."

I look at my arms, pocked with goosebumps, the fine blonde hairs standing on end. I first met Sophie when Molly brought her up to the apartment for tea. She and Sophie and Raymond had just come home from a movie. Now that I've been around her a bit, I'm pretty sure that Sophie had just asked herself along.

She goes way back with Raymond and she doesn't mind making a big deal of it, like 'do you remember when this happened, Ray, do you remember that.' I figured out real quick that she was staking her claim, making sure we knew she was around long before Molly ever was. She's made it real clear that her family is old money too, like Raymond's. It doesn't make a lick of difference to him but, to Sophie, I think it matters a lot.

"She's down at the parish hall," I say, although that big fib floated to the tip of my tongue just at this moment, . "Setting up tables for a funeral lunch. I have no idea how long she'll be."

After I hang up, I make the sign of the cross. I am not a habitual liar, but something about Sophie gets under my skin. Let her think Molly must be a fool or, maybe even, some kind of saint. Let her *really* wonder what Raymond could possibly see in a girl like that.

I wander back to the living room, pick up my splayed notebook and reread Mr. Woodard's introduction to vectors.

Vector diagrams can be used to describe the velocity of a moving object during its motion. Technically, Position is a point and Velocity/Acceleration are vectors. For example, the velocity of a car moving down the road could be represented by a vector diagram. In future studies, vector diagrams will be used to represent a variety of physical quantities such as acceleration, force, and momentum. Be familiar with the concept of using a vector arrow to represent the direction and relative size of a quantity. It will become a very important representation of an object's motion as you proceed further in your studies.

There was a moment, just before I drifted off to sleep, that I'd felt a glimmer of understanding, but as I reread the notes, my mind goes totally blank. Poor Mr. Woodard, trying to teach grade eleven students facts that we're not even vaguely interested in, knowledge for which we can see no earthly use. Vectors mean nothing to me.

"Your Eggs Benny are almost ready," Molly calls from the kitchen. She knows Eggs Benedict might be the only thing to entice me from my Sunday-morning bed.

I hear the pipes knock loudly, then Mary Ellen's laugh. Lucky her. She loves mornings, while I have to drag myself from my dreams. Lately, for me, restful sleep *begins* with the dawn.

I raise my arms, stretch like Momma's favourite calico cat, my fingers testing the temperature of our room. It feels like the inside of Papa's meat locker, and I fight the urge to snuggle down, cover up my head.

Damn, I think, I sure could do without church today. As soon as I think it, I wonder how many Hail Marys I'll need to get myself back to even. I'm always down a prayer or two it seems.

Molly has sewn me a blouse for the school dance next Thursday night, and I'm not sure I even want to go. The girls in my grade are still a closed group to me. But if I do get up my nerve to go, and some guy they've already tagged happens to ask me to dance, it won't help me make friends. It seems that now my life is so complicated, so hard to figure out.

The blouse has a flattering scoop neckline above a hand-smocked bodice, and it's my favourite shade of blue. Ice blue, like my eyes. I turn, checking the mirror, admiring the fit.

"Here. Try this." Molly tosses me a scarf, shades of cobalt and midnight shot with blazes of white. "Your neck looks kind of bare."

I loop the scarf around my neck, but something is wrong. Molly's beautiful scarf sags like a half-mast flag flying over a wreck.

"Come here, you dope." She reties the scarf, arranges it so one end drizzles just below my collarbone and the other is flung casually back over my shoulder. Then she turns me toward the mirror, her hands warm on my shoulders.

"It's all about arranging your accessories so they look effortless," she says. "Don't worry. One day, everything will fall into place."

Molly's got an eye, that's easy to see. So far, watching her has done nothing to improve my fashion sense. But I've noticed that Sophie studies Molly, too. While my sister is adding a final dusting of blusher to her cheekbones, or checking her lipstick before they head out the door, Sophie will hold something of Molly's up to herself and crane her neck to check her own reflection in Molly's mirror.

Last Friday, when she tried on Molly's new cashmere sweater, I noticed it gaped very unattractively across her chest. You never see Sophie nibbling on junk food or candies, so I wondered, for a moment, how she could possibly be gaining weight.

"I think this mossy shade of green is much better on me," she said, to no one in particular.

It's kind of creepy. Like she's trying on Molly's personality, as if, maybe, Molly's the person *she'd* like to be. More than kind of creepy. Very creepy, I'd say.

My days here at Molly's are good except, sometimes, I really miss Momma and Papa, and I always miss Carl.

But at night, when I close my eyes, I see shadows move in the darkness. When I was tucked under the eaves of Papa's house, I used to see pinwheels of colour, starbursts of light. No wonder I've started having such trouble drifting off to sleep. I've thought of talking this insomnia problem over with Molly, but she'd probably just tell me I'm lonesome for home. She'd tell me to use the time to good purpose, maybe say an extra prayer. But I've already tried adding ten Hail Marys, and it hasn't helped a bit.

So I rely on science, math, and chemistry. Tonight, I've gone through my chemistry formulae three times and, finally, I'm starting to drift, almost gone. Maybe one more time through the list, starting, of course, with silver — AG.

If nothing else, I'll ace the test.

Thud. I feel it. Hard, like a sack of potatoes dropping. I swear it shakes the bed. My eyes jerk open to darkness, with only a sliver of blue light seeping in from beneath the tightly drawn shade. My heart is hammering so hard against my ribs I think they must surely break. What? What?

I tumble from the bed, snap up the shade. There is nothing to see but a swirl of snowflakes beneath the streetlight. A sudden huff of wind flings them up from the street and into the frosty air.

"Mary Ellen, wake up." I tug the shoulder of her nightgown but she rolls away, the worn flannel slipping like silk through my frantic fingers. It's freezing in our bedroom at the top of the stairs, and puffs of my breath hang in the air.

I grab her shoulder, roll her toward me. "I'm scared."

Mary Ellen half-opens her pansy eyes. "Get back into bed, you ninny. It's too cold for nightmares tonight." She rolls over and pulls the quilt snug around her shoulders. I slide in beside her, curve my shaking body to hers. Soon the wheeze of asthmatic breathing fills our little room, but the familiar sound does not lull me quickly into sleep.

I listen for the crunch of footsteps on the snow, the squeak of the apartment door, for Molly's soft laughter and the murmur of Raymond's deeper voice, even for the silence that would signal their goodnight kiss.

If she was home, she would make me hot chocolate, sit beside me on the bed. Molly would never just roll over and go back to sleep. But I hear nothing and, finally, drift into an uneasy sleep.

It was Molly who taught me to keep my papers organized and how to file everything so the information you need is at your fingertips. Her recipe box is a thing of beauty. She's actually glued a clothespin to the inside of the right-hand cupboard door so that, when she bakes, she can pin the card she's using out of harm's way, and her cards are not all splattered and dog-eared like Momma's. Used to bake, I guess I should be saying now.

I wish she'd have left us stained and grease-spotted cards because, then, it would be easier to choose the ones she used the most. And, without Molly's little notes stuck to the cupboard door telling us what meat we should defrost for supper and where to find certain ingredients for a stew, Mary Ellen and I are often at a loss. So we eat a lot of tomato soup. And salmon sandwiches.

Molly would never have imagined the kind of file I'm keeping now. I call it my Sad File and I've taped it to the inside cover of my science book. Mr. Woddard says there are all kinds of natural laws where everything makes sense and every action creates a corresponding reaction so, in the end, things even out. At least I think that's what he's trying to teach us. He believes that there is some kind of order in the universe. I don't know what I believe, not anymore.

When Molly was killed, I felt like I'd stepped into a dream and all I wanted to do was wake up and find everything as it was. But I couldn't. The *Cold Creek Gazette* covered every little detail of the night she died, how the investigation was proceeding, and who said what on the stand. I *had* to read it.

The paper lay like a diamondback rattler, coiled on the kitchen table. Some sick compulsion made me want to smooth it out, study its every detail. I've clipped every single article, slipped them into my growing file. I've added some of the cards and letters that people sent us, too.

If I leave everything next to the Laws of Science, maybe something will click and those pieces will align themselves into some kind of picture that I can understand.

I even study the clippings during Mr. Woodard's class but, so far, nothing has helped me to make sense of the events leading up to my sister's death.

Sad File — Item #1

Cold Creek Gazette — *February 10th (Staff Special) Molly Lanigan, twenty-four, of Condy, came to her death from injuries suffered when at 12:10 AM Feb 2nd she was struck by a car. Miss Lanigan had been in a coma for the two days previous to her demise.*

I wonder why the news coverage of Molly's accidental death wasn't more complete. And I wonder if the investigation might have gone differently if she'd been the mayor's daughter or the daughter of the town's fire chief, not just some unknown girl who worked in a tailoring shop downtown.

Sad File — Item #2

Laura — please turn off the kitchen lights before you leave for school. Don't forget! The City bill is already high. Water and sewer are dear enough and leaving the lights on only makes it worse — love Molly

I don't know why I've kept this. Maybe because it's the last thing she ever wrote, at least to me. Her handwriting flows like script, but the content of her note is so ordinary that reading it almost makes me believe she's going to come home after work and give me heck about the lights because this morning, I forgot the lights. Again.

Sad File — Item #3 LANIGAN INQUEST CONTINUES:

Raymond Dunn, while walking home from a dance with Miss Lanigan, said he noticed a car approaching the intersection. The couple kept walking, he said, because they knew the street had a stop sign and he thought the car would stop. It wasn't until they were a third of the way across the road that Dunn realized the car would hit them, he said. Dunn was thrown to the ground and, in striking Miss Lanigan, the car dragged her for about forty feet. The car did not stop at the intersection, Dunn testified.

Sophie Conrad, one of the car's occupants, testified that, after stopping at the intersection, Chuck Harmon had remarked on the poor visibility and that he had been driving with one window down in order to more clearly see the road.

Miss Conrad testified she had heard a thud and said she thought they had struck something, possibly a dog. Harmon said he'd go back to prove they had not. Circling the block, they returned to the scene of the accident and found Miss Lanigan.

In the margin, in my own cramped hand. 'A thud?'

In grease pencil, I've underlined the part where Sophie says she thought they had stuck a dog. Those words make my stomach sick. And I cannot actually believe anyone, especially Sophie who was *supposed* to be Molly's friend, would say such an awful thing, or that a reporter would print it in the paper. Thank God Papa has stopped bringing the paper home. He buys it and reads it right here at the kitchen table. It seems as if sitting here, at Molly's table, eases his heart somehow. But when he finally leaves, the paper stays behind. He says it's too hard for Momma to read the details of the accident. So at least she missed the part about the dog.

I take a crumpled paper from the Sad file, smooth it with my hand. My vector diagram is a mess, arrows everywhere. The position, where Molly was hit, must have been fixed. But the velocity and acceleration vectors vary, depending on who is testifying. How could all three of those damned vectors line up that night? And why?

We're doing whatever we can think of to get by. In Momma's case it's praying and believing even harder in the promise of eternal life. I'm stuck rearranging the events of that night, of questioning the premise that God has a plan.

Of course, Mary Ellen is sad, but she's also one for action. When she told me today was the day to tackle the sorting of Molly's room, I wanted to tell her, no way. I didn't want to disturb one thing, but Mary Ellen had that steely look in her eye.

"Sure," I said. "Let's get it over with." The only good reason I can think for doing this is that if Mary Ellen and I sort through Molly's things, Momma won't have to.

Molly's room seems to be bursting at the seams in one way and, in another, as empty as a stage when a play has suddenly closed and left town.

Piles of clothing on the bed are folded neatly, and Mary Ellen is just now threading a needle. She has found one pearl button slightly loose on a spring-green sweater. Finding something of Molly's that's not already perfect is a miracle in itself, but it's also given Mary Ellen something. One last task to do for Molly, an offering of love.

I remember a conversation I overheard once, Momma and Mrs. Allen talking over tea. As Momma poured from her Silver Birch teapot, she spoke of a boy who had gotten into one of those stupid fistfights that sometimes erupt outside little town halls over nothing, when being terribly tough is the only option. A fist had knocked him flying and he came down hard.

Mrs. Allen shook her head. Poor fellow, she said, dead when he hit the steps.

He needed a haircut, that blond boy did, Momma said, and it was his sister who went to the funeral home the night before the service to cut her brother's hair. She'd been cutting it for years. She couldn't let him leave the world needing a haircut so badly and she couldn't bear for anyone else to give him that final trim.

A morbid pair, I thought. Such awful talk over a cup of tea. I didn't understand. But now, watching Mary Ellen fold and stack, sometimes holding a sweater a heartbeat too long, I get it. Really, I do.

Molly's clothes smell of Tide and sunshine, and frost, crisp from the line. The ladies down at the Goodwill store won't have to approach these bags gingerly and hold their breath like they do with some of the stuff that ends up there.

I wanted to keep everything, leave her room just as it was, but Mary Ellen said, no. Molly would never agree to us hoarding her things. Think of all the people she can help. It would give Molly a great deal of satisfaction, Mary Ellen said, to know she's still helping others, even now, after she's gone. I wonder how Mary Ellen can be so sure.

But Mary Ellen has a practical streak, because she's set one dress aside. It's brand new, never been worn.

It makes me smile to think of Molly and her compulsion to buy or sew beautiful clothes. I think she'd rather have had a smart new dress than supper sometimes.

"I think we can take this one back." Mary Ellen checks the tags, still attached to the collar. "Expensive. And it's no use letting twenty-five dollars go to waste." She looks at me, as if she's expecting me to put up a fuss.

"You'll have to do it." I pick up the Sad File, and leave Mary Ellen to finish in Molly's suddenly unbearable room.

It had been over a month between the time Molly bought the dress and Mary Ellen and I returned it. Imagine, Mary Ellen, asking me.

"Please," she said. "It won't take us long. And I can't go alone."

Since Molly died, I haven't stepped foot into Christie Grant's Department Store. I can't bear the Ladies Department, full of reds and purples and blues. Can't bear the thought of Molly's sparkling eyes.

"Maybe it's been too long. Maybe he's not going to take it back," Mary Ellen whispers. Mr. Christie takes the purple bag and vanishes behind double plate-glass doors. But soon he reappears, walks to the women's section and hangs Molly's dress on a sale rack at thirty percent off.

"Doesn't seem right." He shakes his head. "I miss her. Miss her stopping by."

No doubt the sight of Molly's unworn dress reminded him of all the times she'd come into his store to check out the newest styles and colours, and how he regularly talked her into buying. He'd often given her a discount, even on his brand-new stock. He knew she could go home and sew up a dress almost like the one she'd just tried on. She was that talented with a needle.

I think Molly's death has been hard on poor old Mr. Christie too.

The dress was navy, with lime green trim. It had a little mandarin collar and lime green buttons marching down the front.

"Your opinions?" Molly had asked the day she brought it home, taking it from the distinctive purple bag of Christie Grant's Department store.

"Looks nice," I said, looking up briefly from my science book.

"I'll model it," she told me.

Molly's light touch across my shoulders. "What do you think?"

I could not believe my eyes. The dress, which had looked kind of ordinary, now looked smashing, to say the least. It clung to her curves as she walked, swung from her hips when she turned.

"How do you always pick the ones . . . did Mr. Christie?"

"Nope, I spotted this one right off. You have to develop an eye. I'll teach you. It's easy, once you begin to see."

Now she's not here to teach me anything and I don't believe I will ever truly see.

Too bad she didn't wear her new dress that final night.

"I'm saving it for Valentine's Day," she told us. "Raymond's made a reservation. In the dining room at the Skyline Hotel. I've got a feeling it's going to be a really special night."

"Special how?" Mary Ellen asked.

"Guess you'll have to wait and see." But she smiled when she said it and I wondered if she and Raymond had already talked about an engagement ring. But surely, Molly would tell us if she knew. I remember thinking that marrying a guy like Raymond would be real good for Molly. But if Molly married Raymond, whatever would happen to Mary Ellen and me?

I see her lying like a discarded rag-doll in the street, her coat crumpled against the whiteness of the snow. I do not know where the red of her long woollen scarf stops and the red of her blood begins. I see one bare foot, blue-white, I think, from the cold. The other foot is still clad in her new black patent shoe, the heel a good two inches higher than the sensible ones she usually wears.

Before she and Raymond left the house that night, Molly had done a little twirl in the kitchen for us, her full aqua skirt lifting and then settling again, like the wings of a bird about to take flight.

"What do you think?"

I believe she was asking Mary Ellen and me, but it was Raymond who answered.

"It's perfect," he said. "We better get going. I'll go start the car."

Molly held out a shapely leg, rotated her ankle so we could admire her new black patent shoes. "It's a short walk. Plastic windows aren't exactly made for driving on nights as cold as this."

How I wish Raymond had insisted they drive his new convertible. Freezing cold or not. Damn him and his stupid car. If he'd had a lick of sense, he would have bought a Ford sedan.

Molly picked up her small beaded purse, folded two Kleenex and tucked them inside. I heard the snap of her purse closing, Wilf Carter on the radio. "No cloddy winter boots for me tonight," she said, "but I guess I'd better make some concession to the weather." And she wound a long red scarf around her neck. "Now, I don't care if Prince Charming himself turns up at the door looking for a last minute date. You girls get out the crib board or a book. I don't want either of you going out tonight."

Raymond held her coat and she slipped into it like a shadow. For a moment, I thought he was going to pull her close, but he only dropped his arms and sighed. Sometimes I think adjusting to Mary Ellen and me living here has been harder on Raymond than anyone. Not that he's ever said one word but, for sure, he and Molly don't get a minute alone.

I didn't really feel like Molly Lanigan, I felt like Cinderella arriving at the ball when I walked into the Legion Hall on Raymond's arm. I had a fizzy feeling in my chest, as if something really big was going to happen. My dress was the colour of an aqua crystal, a jersey knit that swirled around me like the ripples in a pond when a pebble drops. When Raymond took my coat and went to the cloakroom to hang it up, there wasn't a man in the dancehall who didn't notice me. For a second, as I stood there alone, I wondered if the dress was too much but, when Raymond returned and I saw the approval in his eyes, I knew it was the perfect choice.

The first time Raymond came into Keep-U-Neat Cleaners and Tailors to have a new suit fitted, I'm sure he didn't even notice me. He was busy talking to Mr. Johnson about the chances of a good spring rain. He had a sureness about him, like people do when they're used to having someone else take care of the niggling details of everyday life. But after that first alteration, it seemed that everything he had needed fixing and I soon figured out he'd noticed me as much as I'd noticed him. So I pinned and chalked, took in a seam an infinitesimal amount, or let it out. I could feel him watching me. And that was how we began.

Papa is suspicious of the ease of Raymond's wealth. His belief is that no one should come into money without having to work double-damn hard. And he thinks that if things come too easy, a person will probably never have to develop real character and grit. But as far as I can tell, having money hasn't spoiled Raymond one little bit. It doesn't seem to have made one bit of difference to him that his father bought the Ford dealership just as every cowboy in the country switched from horses to horsepower under a hood. He's as normal as you or me.

Raymond has always treated me like a real lady, as if, by my agreeing to date him, he was the one who'd had the real stroke of luck. He didn't even try to impress me with his car, a brand new Ford Super DeLuxe convertible, and seemed almost embarrassed to be the owner of such a frivolous vehicle. So we walked. We walked an awful lot.

Our first real date was to see *To Each His Own* down at the Lyric Threatre. I'd invited Raymond over for supper a time or two, but the theatre was the only place we could think of to spend some time alone. Mary Ellen and Laura seemed to love living in town, but they had no idea that I'd gotten my own life going and that, sometimes, they might not be welcome to be with me every minute of the day. And I didn't have the heart, yet, to tell them they should make themselves scarce once in a while.

I remember how Raymond stood aside as Jimmy took my arm and led me to an empty seat halfway down the aisle. I noticed that Jimmy's uniform was ill-fitting, and hung on his bony shoulders. Probably a hand-me-down from the last usher who had the job. I could fix that uniform, I thought, fix it in no time at all. But then Raymond stumbled against me in the darkness, and all thoughts of tailoring flew from my head.

The funnies were over and the main attraction had started to roll when Raymond pulled me close and I let myself relax against his arm. Olivia de Havilland swept onto the screen.

"She looks just like you. But nowhere near as pretty."

The Lyric Theatre is darker than the inside of a cow, which was good, because I was blushing so hard I thought Raymond might be able to *feel* the heat. But we've come a long way since that first date and, now, I'm perfectly at home with Raymond, and he with me.

"Shall we dance, or are you going to stand there all night with that far-away look in your eye?" I shake my head, and step into his arms. The music seems muffled, dreamy, our first few steps like we're dancing on a cloud. Four beats in and Sophie's group arrives.

Raymond stops dancing for a moment, and leads me over to Sophie and Chuck. "Come on in, the music's fine." He's trying hard to make Chuck feel at ease but he gets no response. Chuck's face is flushed and he reeks of gin. Sophie does too.

"Sounds bloody slow. Hasn't anyone in this one-horse town heard of the jitterbug?" I imagine Chuck has seen and done things overseas that we could never begin to understand, and he seems to crave action all the time. And Sophie is hanging out with him more and more. I worry about her sometimes, really I do.

The lead singer announces a Bingo dance, and Sophie heads for Raymond like a homing pigeon to roost. I know she's got a sweet spot for Raymond but he's made it very clear to me that, although he and Sophie have a shared history and their families are tight, she's only a friend.

Sometimes I wonder about her motives. She never had the time of day for me before Raymond and I became a steady thing. But there are times Sophie can be a whole lot of fun.

Raymond twirls past with Sophie, but my mind wanders.

Raymond and I saunter arm in arm through the diamond-dusted park. It's a perfect starlit night and, although our breath leaves white puffs in the air, I don't feel one bit cold and don't want to hurry this magical evening.

Raymond stops beside the cenotaph and pulls me down beside him on the steps, which feel as if they've retained years of summer sun. We're already out much later than we usually are and, for one guilty moment, I think of Mary Ellen and Laura. I hope they're not lying awake, listening for my step on the stairs.

When Raymond takes my mittened hands and asks me if I'll be his wife, I can't speak. I can only nod yes. Yes. Yes. He pulls out a purple velvet box and begins to lift the lid.

A crashing drum roll ends the Bingo dance, and my fantasy. Raymond is a careful man, and I'm quite sure nothing will hurry his plans.

~ ~ ~

I am not sure how Mary Ellen is coping. All I know is, when we go to bed at night, she reads for a while, then she mumbles goodnight. I feel like saying, hey, it's me, your sister, Laura

Anne, and I haven't slept for four nights running. In the dusk of our room, I watch her chest rise and fall, rise and fall. But maybe she's faking, lying awake in the semi-darkness like me, afraid to go to sleep, afraid of her dreams.

I dream that night, over and over again, but I change how it starts.

I tell Molly how beautiful she looks.

"Thanks," she says.

"How about you and Raymond stay home?" I ask. "Because you know how Mary Ellen and I just love staying in on Saturday nights." I'm laughing and she doesn't know that I mean every word I've just said. We haven't told her how we have come to love living here, how we look for her neat little notes when we come home from school, how we even like going to church with her on Sunday — well, *most* Sundays at least.

"Mary Ellen and I will entertain," I say.

She nods and says that, just this one time, she doesn't give a darn if she misses a dance. "What do you say we spend a night at home?" she asks Raymond when he arrives, the crease of his dress pants sharper than her paring knife, his striped silk tie perfectly matched to the blue of his shirt.

"Sounds good," he says.

She gets out the cards. We decide to play a winner-take-all tournament of Norwegian whist. Mary Ellen makes popcorn. I turn up the radio.

Raymond deals out our hands.

Mary Ellen and I finally win after the fifth. We're tied up after four and we win only because Mary Ellen has a mind like a steel trap when it comes to cards laid and cards played.

It doesn't hurt that I grand, and between the two of us, Mary Ellen and I have all the aces. Every single one.

Molly and Raymond are the losers but, somehow, Mary Ellen and I end up washing the glasses and the buttery popcorn bowls. When Mary Ellen and I finish cleaning up and come in to kiss Molly goodnight, they are snuggled up on the sofa, and they don't even pretend to move apart.

"Thanks for a swell time," I tell them.

If I can change how it starts, I can change how it ends.

I dream it so often, I start to believe it really happened that way. And then reality hits. Like it did last Saturday down at the Paris Café.

I was treating myself to an Orange Crush float, alone in the booth, me and my science text. My mind was drifting, the boring text was blurred. I was rubbing the palm of my hand across the worn corduroy of the upholstery. The friction caused a pleasant warmth, the repetition was soothing.

"Cold enough?" I glanced at the lunch counter, lined with men, clad mostly in plaid thermal jackets. One of them, a bricklayer or carpenter, I'd guess, by the dust on his shoulders, was speaking to a guy in a suit two stools away.

A suit. Here? Eating lunch at this cafe?

"Anything new come out at the trial?" The man shook his perfectly groomed head.

"Something's fishy. I hear that poor Lanigan girl was blown right out of her shoes. And the car left the scene. Jesus, it must have been going like a bat out of hell."

"Goddamn shame," another guy said. "I hope they put the bastard away. And I hear she was a real looker too."

I stood, stumbled to the till. My stomach twisted and I threw down my quarter. Left without the change.

Tonight, Mary Ellen is restless, all elbows and knees and snorts, so I decide to get up and read for a while. I open the door, slip into Molly's room. Her dressmaker's mannequin, draped with the blue dotted Swiss she'd bought to sew Mary Ellen's graduation dress, stands at the end of her bed. "Molly! Oh my God, Molly, I keep dreaming that you're . . ." I throw my arms wide. Then memory hits like a hammer and I sink, the bite of the maple floorboards harsh against my bony knees.

I feel as if I've stepped into the pages of one of the books that Momma bought for my little brother, where the scene is normal on one page but, on the next, a few things are out of place, like a flower stuck in the milk jug and a cowboy hat for a lampshade. The ordinary pieces of my life have been scattered. Nothing makes sense.

I snap on Molly's bedside lamp and study her empty room. I run the selvage edge of the blue Swiss through my fingers, like I've seen Molly do a million times or more. She used to get a dreamy look in her eyes, as if she could already see the beauty she would create. But the feel of the fabric does nothing for me.

The thought of attending Mary Ellen's graduation has lost its allure. But Momma and Papa won't let us move back home, not quite yet. It's only a few more months until the end of the June, they say. Molly wouldn't like it if you quit now, wasted an entire year.

A film of grey dust covers the walnut of her chiffonier. I lean over, write my initials in the dust with my finger. LAL. Laura Anne Lanigan. Then I write hers, too. MML. Molly Marie Lanigan. I underline them both with a wavy line.

I try MMD. Molly Marie Dunn. If she hadn't died that night, I'm almost certain she'd have been coming home one night real soon, waking us up to show off her ring. She'd have been too excited to think about the hour, to remember that Mary Ellen and I would wake up tired the next day. She would *have* to be really excited to forget her focus on our schooling.

I can see the sparkle in her eyes, the way she tilts her hand in the circle of the lamplight. Look at all those rainbows, I hear her say. Aren't they something?

I've seen him walking past our house. Looking. As if he hopes to see her again. I used to think that, one day, he'd ring the bell and come visit, but I've finally realized he never will. Maybe he can't bear to be around us, with Molly gone.

MMD. My shoulders are heavy, my feet encased in clay, but I plod to the hall closet, find the lemon oil and a soft rag. I polish Molly's dresser until it shines. It really, really shines.

The farm looks the same although, of course, everything has changed, for all of us, since Molly died.

Doilies of dirty snow cling to the shoulders of the lane, but the sun will soon take care of that. I will be so happy when this winter is finally over.

Mary Ellen pushes the back door open and we step inside. The kitchen is spotless, even the corner near Papa's easy chair. No overflowing ashtray, no scatter of newspapers. The little green radio is silent, no muttering or music from the CBC. Hand towels lay carefully over the worn spots on the arms of his chair. For a moment, I wonder if this is really home.

Momma's wooden butter bowl is in the centre of the table, filled with coloured eggs, blue and purple, pink and green. I pick one up, roll its cool smoothness in the palm of my hand.

There are patterns drawn around the circumference of each egg, stickmen, flowers, initials. Dyeing Easter eggs? This year? I wonder, sometimes, where our mother gets her strength.

"Laura, Mary Ellen, is that you?" Her voice trills from the second floor.

I put the egg down, pick up another, bright pink, the colour so deep it's almost red. A row of ragged hearts ring the egg and at the top, someone has drawn a pair of lopsided angel wings.

Carl, I think.

I wonder what they've told him. I wonder, really, if he'll ever understand.

The house is never this quiet unless Carl's asleep. Maybe he's napping and maybe Momma is curled up beside him, comforting him and, somehow, comforting herself.

"Yes, Momma, it's us. We've come home."

I lay my book bag on the sideboard and, as I do, a newspaper clipping slips from my textbook and onto the oiled oak.

Sad File — Item #4

Preliminary Hearing — Fatal Accident Case; Committed for Trial

Female Passenger Testifies — Miss Sophie Conrad, a passenger in the front seat, said she felt a bump as the car crossed the intersection and that she had asked the driver to go back. They then drove around the block and saw an injured girl lying in the road. When asked why she did not accompany the others when they took the injured girl to the hospital, Miss Conrad said that her mother lived close to the scene of the accident and so she decided to stay with her mother.

I've underlined the headline in red, so Female Passenger Testifies jumps right off the page. For the life of me, I cannot figure out why Sophie went to her mother's house that night. Wasn't she supposed to be Molly's friend? And even if she wasn't, why wasn't she compelled to stay and stare, like onlookers at accidents always are?

I fold the clipping quickly and stuff it back into the file. For sure, I don't want Momma to see.

Momma's wicker basket is sitting on the buffet and is overflowing. I touch a bundle of letters and cards, tied with a pink ribbon. Mass cards and condolences. Oh Momma, I think. Why don't you put those away? But while I'm waiting for Momma, I shuffle through the pitiful contents of the basket. A letter from Aunt Florence catches my eye. I unfold it and begin to read.

Boston, Mass.
Feb 20, 1946
Dearest Sister,
We received your letter today. It was an awful shock to hear of Molly's sudden passing. I know how you all must feel. God's ways are hard to understand, but I know he will give you all the grace to bear this cross. I don't know yet if we should tell Pa, he is so frail now we mostly try to keep upsetting news away. But I was wondering if maybe you should write him. He is awful good to pray and that's what you all will need. I had her enrolled in the Purgatorial Society and will send you the certificate. I also went to confession and will receive for her tomorrow and will pray for you all.

My fingers begin to curl, but I stop myself from crumpling the letter. At least Aunt Florence has got it right that God's ways are hard to understand.

If Molly really is in Purgatory, that twilight zone between heaven and hell, and it's up to us to pray her way out, I may lose what little faith I still have. Molly was so good, so kind. Really, what's the point? A test for the rest of us, to see if we'll remember her for more than a year or two? Punishment for Molly, who's only crime that I can see was walking home from a winter dance in her high-heeled shoes? If God's plan truly is for souls to finish their earthly tasks, he should have paid a little more attention. Stopped that speeding car. Or had Molly slip on a patch of ice and fall to the sidewalk, out of harm's way. Even had someone take the wrong coat from the cloakroom after the dance, so she'd have been held up by finding that person and making the exchange. I am sure the One who's supposed to be all-seeing, all-knowing, could have changed the chain of events if He really gave a damn.

Now there's a whole lot of us wandering around with unfinished business. Maybe not Momma but, for sure, Papa. Raymond. Most likely Mary Ellen. And certainly me.

I smooth Momma's letter against my thigh. Take a breath before I continue to read.

I suppose losing her was pretty hard on Lloyd. That man has set his heart on his daughters, that is for sure. I guess Laura and Mary Ellen will miss her too. I hope they will be able to keep up with their schoolwork. Are they staying alone in town until the school year is over? I imagine they are old enough to manage quite well by now.

There is precious little one can do from this distance, but I thought of the graduation dress. I imagine Molly was planning to sew it, but if that work is left undone, I offer my assistance. I am sure you are not up to sewing just now.

Maybe a new dress would be good medicine for Laura
as well. If you could send me the girl's measurements,
I will check the sales downtown. Of course, there are
shortages everywhere, so they may not have a choice of
colour or style.

Let me know what you think. I could ship the dress
early enough to leave time for alterations if need be.

I hope you are all keeping well and we would like to
hear more details of the funeral when you are able to
write. You can rest easy about Molly, as she was a good
girl and always attended church and said her prayers.
She will now be the brightest bead on your rosary of
memories.

Your loving sister, Florence

PS — if you had a notice, I could send it to the Casket, *as*
I am a subscriber. And of course, we are all praying too.

The thought of Molly's name on a list of the recently
deceased, of strangers checking and deciding whether to
choose her name to add to their prayers *really* makes me
want to punch the wall. Molly doesn't need the prayers of
strangers. She probably doesn't even need ours. Molly's name
in the *Casket* might seem a good idea to Auntie Florence, but
it makes me mad as hell.

I tuck the letter into my pocket. Sad File #5. Soon I'll have
a whole Sad Book.

Later, in my swayback bed under the slanted ceilings of the
old house, I reread the letter. All this 'she's in a better place' is
about to make me scream.

I am surprised that someone in this praying-all-the-time,
tithing-even-though-you're-behind-on-your-taxes kind of

family hasn't been granted at least one small vision, like the girl who saw the Virgin Mary on the back of her cornflakes box. Maybe a vision of Molly sitting safely somewhere, beside a flowering lilac bush, maybe even reading a fashion magazine. As happy and healthy as she ever was. And maybe that lucky person could apply to the Pope, get the vision certified as a bona fide miracle. Become famous for a while. And that person could tell me again and again how absolutely real the vision was, how they could smell the soft green of freshly mown grass, the perfume of the lilacs, newly opened and oozing their heavenly scent. How they could feel on their skin the lightness of the breeze and the warmth of Molly's smile.

And then I might believe. Really, truly believe.

Because I am seriously starting to wonder about God and the certainty my family seems to share that He is a good shepherd who always takes care of His flock. Of course, I can't tell anyone. If Momma even imagined I was losing faith, it would break her heart a little more. And she's had enough of that.

I don't study science anymore. I study the File, arrange and rearrange the scanty pieces of that night. I've made a diagram of the scene. I even reread Mr. Woodard's notes. *Vector diagrams can be used to describe the velocity of a moving object during its motion. For example, the velocity of a car moving down the road could be represented by a vector.*

Chuck Harmon is driving. Sophie Conrad is beside him in the front. In the back seat is Harmon's brother, Dan, who, when questioned at the inquest, says he was too drunk to remember anything and is "summarily" excused.

It is established that the car passes through the intersection, grazes Raymond and tosses him aside and then hits Molly full on. Some time later, the car that hit her returns to the scene.

Too many gaps, I think. Too much wasted time.

Papa and I ran into Chief Harris one day, down at the café. "My most sincere sympathy." He stood by our booth, his cap in his hand. My hamburger stalled, midway between the pool of ketchup on my plate and my open lips.

I hate it when people walk by us without saying a word, as if nothing of note has happened in our lives. But I also hate it when they stop to give their sympathy. They don't know what to say, and neither do I. I was glad Papa was with me that day.

Chief Harris had a fresh haircut, shorter than short, and his face was a dangerous red. "If it helps at all, we're still working hard on the case."

"Good," Papa said. "Sympathy's not what we need just now. Answers are."

So Papa and Police Chief Harris are doing it too, arranging and rearranging the scanty pieces of Molly's final night. Do they see the car approach the intersection? Can they tell for sure if it stops or doesn't? Who do they see through the frosted glass?

I feel sorry for Raymond. When we bump into him down at the café, he quickly finishes his coffee and leaves without stopping to talk, just nods his head as he hurries by. One of these days, I might grab his hand, say "Hi, Raymond, how ya' doing? I know you miss her. I've seen you walking by, staring at her window."

Maybe *he* could remember something. Some detail that's missing in the paper. Maybe he's the guy I should be showing the Sad File to.

Sad File: Item #6
     Cold Creek Gazette — *Verdict in Lanigan Trial*
     Chuck Allen Harmon was convicted today of manslaughter
     and was sentenced to two years less a day in the Regina
     Correctional Centre.
     I fold the paper closed, because that's what the case is now.
Closed. But it doesn't feel closed to me.

     We've remembered to turn the lights off in the upstairs hall and in the living room. Yellow light pools in the grain of the kitchen table. I run my fingers across its surface and feel a little ridge. Maybe it's time we oiled the oak.

     Mary Ellen is studying Chaucer for her History of English Literature exam and I have my science notebook open on the table. We have eaten spartanly, tomato soup and salmon buns. Again.

     Mary Ellen's snaps her fingers, loud, like the crack of a whip. "Wherever you are," she tells me "you better come back."

     "Mmm," I say and I pull my textbook closer. As I do, my fingers slide inside the cover and I feel the bulk of my file. "Sorry."

     And I try, I really do. Every time I get my mind almost around the concept that matter can neither be created nor destroyed, my ears start to ring and I get kind of dizzy. And the more I read about vectors, the less I understand.

     "This is hopeless," I tell Mary Ellen, and I close my text. "I'm going to bed."

She frowns slightly, but she's so focused on her studies that she doesn't say a word.

I decide to sleep in Molly's bed tonight. Sleep is sporadic for me and, when Mary Ellen talks in her sleep, as she's been more apt to lately, I give her a jab with my elbow. Sometimes, a little too hard. It's not her fault that I can't sleep. I open the Sad File, sprinkle its contents across Molly's blue chenille. I slide beneath the blankets and, when I pull the bedspread up to my chin, the papers flutter to the floor like snowflakes, the kind that were falling the night Molly died.

I close my eyes and suddenly smell soft lilacs, Molly's evening scent. I am not surprised to feel her hand slip into mine. Somehow, we float up and through the yellow wallpaper roses. I can feel my heartbeat quicken, but I'm not really scared. Not with Molly holding my hand. Maybe *this* is heaven, I think.

But then I know it's not, because I see Molly and Raymond step into the intersection, see the oncoming car hesitate and then pick up speed. When the car hits her, her grip tightens on my hand, but we don't exchange one word. We float above the car as it leaves the scene, watch as it screeches to a stop in the shadows of the maple trees west of the park. Sophie Conrad loosens her grip on the steering wheel and opens the driver's side door. She slides from the driver's seat and trips around the front of the car, the staccato of her heels ricocheting off the red bricks of the nearby library. Lines of horror are etched on her face by the marble of the moonlight.

"*Sophie* was driving?" My words puff out like little cotton balls.

Chuck opens the passenger door and steps outside, whispers in Sophie's ear. She slides into the passenger seat and Chuck gently closes the door.

Dan Harmon, feeling sick from too much booze and the wildness of the ride, sits hunched over in the back seat, his head in his hands, until Chuck opens the door, pulls him to his feet.

Chuck and Dan huddle in the frozen air, which turns white from their rapid breathing.

Eons go by.

Finally, they clasp their hands together and I half expect one of them to pull a knife, make two little cuts and mingle their blood. But they don't really need to, they're already brothers, after all.

I hear again the crack of frozen metal, the slamming of doors. Dan drops onto the freezing leatherette of the back seat with a solid smack and Chuck Harmon settles himself behind the wheel. I see the heave of his chest as he draws a deep breath and then eases the car slowly away from the curb.

Sophie is crying softly.

"Don't," Chuck says. "Too late for crying now." He looks sick, but it's Sophie who asks him to pull over and she stumbles from the car, pukes in the bushes at the edge of the park. The sharp smell of whiskey rises all the way up to Molly and me.

I wrinkle my nose. I have always hated the smell of whiskey, so harsh and so strong. "Chuck swore that *he* was the driver. With his hand on the Bible, he swore."

I turn to my sister. "Why? I have to know why."

Puffs of cotton again and I don't know if Molly has even heard.

And then we float forever. Or so it seems to me. And we are looking into the women's bathroom of the Healy Hotel, on a Tuesday afternoon. I watch as Sophie Conrad quietly miscarries in the second stall. She leans against the partition for a moment before she pushes the handle down and flushes the whole mess clean away.

Somehow, I am right inside her head.

Besides the cramping, Sophie feels a huge weight lift from her shoulders. She has not yet told anyone, other than Chuck Harmon, of her pregnancy. Theirs was a sudden, home-from-the-war romance and, early on, Sophie had begun to have her doubts. But then she missed her December monthly, and January's too.

And then I remember Molly's moss-green cashmere straining across Sophie's breasts as she turned, admiring herself in the mirror above Molly's walnut chiffonier.

"Oh," I softly say. "I would *never* have guessed."

The tough kernel that has lodged in my chest these interminable days softens, begins to open like a velvet crocus in the green of early spring.

Maybe, I think, there are things in this world we can only strive to understand. But if we are very lucky, a perfect intersection of vectors *can* occur and we are able, for a fleeting moment, to really see. I turn to hug Molly, to tell her I love her and that I'll never forget. My arms fold around only darkness. But before she left, she kissed me. I know that she did.

I felt it on my cheek, as soft as the wings of a butterfly.

BONNIE DUNLOP has developed a strong and growing readership in Saskatchewan and beyond. Her stories have appeared in many literary journals, and have been read on CBC radio. Her first book, *The Beauty Box* (Thistledown Press) won the Best First Book Saskatchewan Book Award. She lives in Swift Current, Saskatchewan.